JOURNALSTONE'S

2010

WARPED WORDS

FOR TWISTED MINDS

COMPILED BY

CHRISTOPHER C. PAYNE

JournalStone

San Francisco

This is a work of fiction. All of the characters, names, incidents, organizations, and dialogue in this novel are either the products of the author's imagination or are used fictitiously.

JournalStone books may be ordered through booksellers or by contacting:

JournalStone
199 State Street
San Mateo, CA 94401
www.journalstone.com

ISBN: 978-1-936564-00-2   (sc)
ISBN: 978-1-936564-01-9   (dj)
ISBN: 978-1-936564-02-6   (ebook)

Printed in the United States of America

JournalStone rev. date: October 8, 2010

Cover Design Shannon Stamey and Denise Daniel

Edited by Whitney L.J. Howell

CHECK OUT OTHER JOURNALSTONE PUBLISHED BOOKS

DUNCAN'S DIARY, BIRTH OF A SERIAL KILLER

LEARNING TO CRY

THE GARGOYLE PROPHECIES, PART I

THE SAVIOR RISES

DEDICATION

I would like to dedicate this book to all of us, but sadly I cannot. I fear not a single soul would begin to understand. So instead I will dedicate this book to nobody, so rest assured, everyone will surely be insulted.

CONTENTS

HUDDLED MASSES

BY

COREY R. SCALES

Vaughn and Trish Embers were 10 minutes into watching a porn DVD when the scurrying in the walls first started. Even though they knew the surprisingly affordable colonial was old when they'd first moved in three months before, the thought of a possible rodent problem deflated the mood instantly.

"I told you we should've had an exterminator spray the place before we moved in," Vaughn grumbled, hitting the pause button.

"You did no such thing," Trish said, turning to him.

"Well, I *wish* I had, then."

"Jesus, I hate rodents. Do we have any kind of poison or something to set out?"

"The closest thing would be that Bundt cake in the fridge your Aunt Violet made for Christmas. I'm sure that'll kill **anything**."

After pondering the possibilities of their visitor possibly turning up in their bed later, Vaughn made a late night trip to Walgreen's for several boxes of d-Con™ Mouse Bait and various glue traps.

Placing the items in areas they thought a mouse might frequent, they went to bed and listened in the dark for further scurrying.

* * *

After nearly a week of no noises within the walls, they determined that the poison had done its duty and went about planning their first dinner party since moving in. Although they'd opted not to invite co-workers to their foray in entertaining, Vaughn had asked Neil Germano over from his office at the Department of Health. After all, he was the one who'd seen the house for sale and suggested it to them in the first place. Trish had invited her older sister, Carmen, her brother-in-law, Dale, and her best friend, Keysha.

Considering how badly the gathering would end, the beginning was fun for everyone present. Vaughn had made his mom's recipe for jambalaya, which went over even better than he and his wife anticipated. After playing several games of bowling on their Wii system, they all sat in the living room drinking coffee.

"So, what do your neighbors here rate?" Neil asked Vaughn.

"I'd give 'em about a 33."

"And what kind of 'rating' are you talking about?" Carmen asked curiously, moving the sugar cube-filled cup away from Dale before he could add more to his coffee.

"The Lunacy Scale," Vaughn responded, biting into one of the raspberry coffee cakes Keysha brought over. "Me and Neil came up with it during the last company retreat they forced us to go on."

"Basically," Neil sighed, "it's a way of ranking just how crazy your neighbors or co-workers are. One through 25 are basically normal, 25 through 35 could benefit from occasional therapy and minor anti-depressants, and 40 and up is when you need to hide the sharp objects."

"From what me and Trish have seen, no one around here we've met so far is destined to start running around in their underwear and screaming about the government putting LSD in the drinking water."

"Well, there's Mrs. Bondelli," Trish offered. "Anyone with that many gnomes on their front lawn is clearly batshit."

They all laughed.

"Hey, Vaughn, can I get that jambalaya recipe from you before I leave?" Keysha pleaded. "My boyfriend only knows how to make chili."

"Hey," Neil shrugged. "What's wrong with chili?"

"You need to show Dale a thing or two in the kitchen, Vaughn," Carmen joked. "I don't want him to get his own show on the Food Network. Just something he can make with no fear of the place burning down."

Dale chuckled politely, casually flipping his wife the bird by scratching his chin with his middle finger.

"It's pretty easy, really," Vaughn shrugged, glancing around for something to write on. "You got a notepad or something?"

Keysha grabbed her oversized purse from the floor to retrieve her day-planner, and two of the largest rats Vaughn had ever seen burst from it and landed in her lap.

*   *   *

"I thought you said she was on a diet," Vaughn bemused as they walked up their driveway. "What was she doing with cookies in her pocketbook?"

"They were *Atkins* cookies, Vaughn. Jesus, could you reboot your sensitivity chip or something?" Trish eyeballed him. "Keysha's probably going to relapse with something like that happening. She still hasn't returned any of my messages."

Vaughn and Trish had stayed two days at a nearby Best Western before they decided to brave returning home. After explaining their situation to Vaughn's Aunt Francine, she let them borrow one of her largest tomcats named Azabache.

Once disengaging the alarm system, Vaughn set down the pet caddy he'd been lugging. He released the large black feline, who dashed out and immediately began sharpening his claws on the side of their loveseat.

"Azabache! No!" Trish hurried over to him, shooing him away before any real damage could be done. "Why do I feel like we should've just done a search for exterminators in this area?"

"But, we've already got an exterminator right there," Vaughn pointed toward his aunt's cat, who sat grooming himself on the carpet. "Decon doesn't have shit on that little hairball-coughing sociopath. Cats are natural predators, Trish. It wouldn't surprise me if those rats got one whiff of Azabache and committed mass suicide."

"As long as he doesn't start pissing all over the house," she grimaced. "There's nothing worse than the smell of cat urine. It makes ammonia smell like honeysuckle Febreze®."

After setting up a litter box and food/water dish in the kitchen, they left Azabache to search and destroy.

*   *   *

Vaughn was working on several case files he'd brought home when he heard the cat's hiss from downstairs. He hurried into the guest bedroom, which also doubled as a makeshift gym, and got Trish's attention from the treadmill.

"I think he caught something," he whispered excitedly, as they descended the stairs.

"How can you be sure?"

"They don't just hiss at nothing," Vaughn assured. "I hope he bites its damned head off."

"Y'know what, Vaughn?" Trish protested. "You're really pole-vaulting over the line into being disgusting right about now."

They cautiously crept into the kitchen just in time for a dark shape to dart between them, Azabache right behind it. The chase came to an end in the dining room beneath the china cabinet. Dishes rattled as the cat could be heard attacking the rodent. A moment later, Azabache emerged triumphantly with the limp figure in his jaws.

"Oh my God..." Trish muttered in disgust, wincing and shutting her eyes. "It's like one of those nature shows or something."

"Marlin Perkins would be proud," Vaughn chuckled as he hurried to grab a dust pan and garbage bag. Managing to coax the cat into depositing its kill into the bag, he tied it in a knot and affectionately scratched Azabache between the ears.

*   *   *

They found the eight inch hole in their basement laundry room the next morning, ragged around the edges and staring at them like an orifice. Trish, who refused to go near it, was insistent that they call a pest control company that would come on a Saturday at short notice. Vaughn, having scooped up their feline guest from his perch atop the entertainment center, shook his head.

"Why mess with a good thing?"

Azabache, during the previous evening, had succeeded in slaying two more rats. He'd been rewarded with a can of Albacore tuna Trish picked up from Wegman's, which the cat had devoured in less than two minutes.

"Do you see the size of that thing?" Trish motioned to the hole. "Cat or not, I don't feel at ease doing laundry or anything else in this house while we've got a bottomless pit in our wall."

"Trish, I really think you're-" Vaughn began, but his wife shook her head.

"And don't tell me I'm overreacting, either. You **know** I have a thing about rodents, even the so-called 'cute' ones like squirrels or woodchucks. See, you deal with this kind of crap for a living. Of course, it's not gonna freak **you** out."

"I go to restaurants and see if the kitchen staff's digging in their asses. And, as for that hole-"

"You mean that *abyss*?" Trish smirked.

"Do you really wanna cough up a couple hundred dollars to some old smelly guy in coveralls, when we've got a rodent's mortal enemy itching to mow down every squeakin' last one of 'em?"

13

Reluctantly, Trish agreed, and Vaughn set down Azabache in front of the opening. The cat sniffed a few times curiously, his furry head cocked attentively. A moment later, his body went poised low and a long growl escaped from his throat. He scurried with lightning quickness into the hole, loudly ascending the wall with vigor.

"When he's done we're going to Home Depot and spackling over that hole," Trish announced, looking tense.

Despite his amusement at his wife's uneasiness, he knew Trish had valid cause to despise anything even remotely rodent-like. When they'd first met at Morgan State, she'd been staying in an apartment building that'd been overrun with them. With a roommate that frequently left half-eaten pizza and take-out scattered around their living-quarters, she had to start sleeping with traps surrounding her bed.

Azabache's wail from within the walls was so sudden that it made them both jump a step back, glancing in surprise at each other. There was a commotion they couldn't quite make out, as if the cat were struggling past something.

Was he driving the rats toward the hole?

When Vaughn cautiously leaned toward the wall, a black blur shot out of the opening and collided with him. He and a very terrified Azabache tumbled to the floor. The feline was in such a hurry to get away that he ended up scratching Vaughn's forearm in the process. Before they could collect themselves, the animal was already halfway up the basement stairs.

*   *   *

Malik Houston, the technician that Pied Piper Exterminators sent out, was neither old nor smelly. He bore more than a passing resemblance to a very young James Earl Jones in rimless glasses as he observed the hole with a penlight.

Azabache, after his exodus back upstairs had fled into his pet caddy and refused to step out until Vaughn had returned him to his aunt's house. The scratches he'd inflicted in his hasty escape, although cleaned up and bandaged, still were sore to the touch.

"Exactly how many rats are we talking here?" Vaughn asked, trying not to envision a horde of black furry bodies bursting from out of the plaster.

"Couldn't tell you exactly," Malik shrugged, putting away his light. "If I had to guess, based on what you described earlier, I'd say at least 20."

"Well, I feel better now," Trish smirked. "We might as well go back to the Best Western."

"I wouldn't go packing my stuff up just yet," he offered, opening the large duffle bag he'd laid atop their washing machine when first arriving. "Not until I do a sonogram on your walls."

"Are they pregnant?" Trish laughed weakly.

Malik smiled, removing a device that reminded Vaughn of a large polygraph machine. It was accompanied by a palm-sized PDA screen, various wires, and several suction cups. Applying KY Jelly to the cups, Malik carefully began attaching them to the wall.

"Well, it's not exactly the same kind you'll find at an obstetrician's," he informed them as he worked. "But both machines more or less do the same thing. Most exterminating companies make an educated guess as to how many rodents a home is infested with, and then base their course of action on that."

"And charge an arm, leg, and one kidney in the process," Vaughn added.

"Basically," the technician nodded. "But, this method is gonna give us a visual of exactly what we're dealing with."

"That thing's gonna take pictures of the insides of our walls?"

"Well, nothing Herb Ritz-worthy you'll want framed above the mantel. But we'll get an image of where the rats are nesting and how many. Once that's done we can either fog them out, or I can cut into the wall and-"

"'Cut into the wall'?" Vaughn protested, his square jaw going slack. "As in plaster and all other kinds of stuff everywhere?"

"Relax, Mr. Embers," Malik turned to him casually. "It's doubtful it'll even come to that. And, even if it does, I'm also a licensed contractor and can redo your wall the same way – if not better than – it was."

"How long is the sonogram supposed to take?"

"Well," Malik responded, listening to the wall with a stethoscope. "The scan is going to cover your walls from top to bottom. So, we're looking at two or three hours. If you guys wanna go watch a movie on DVD or something, I should have some results by the time you're done."

*   *   *

Vaughn and Trish were near the end of *V for Vendetta* when Malik appeared in the living-room doorway. He stood there looking slightly perplexed, cleaning his glasses with a handkerchief. Trish got him a soda from the fridge, which he thanked her for and downed half of in mere moments.

"Okay," he exhaled. "The good and bad. How do you want it?"

They opted for good.

"The remaining rats in your wall seem to be fleeing your home."

"How?" asked Trish. "We didn't see any come out of the hole downstairs."

"Rats are experts at finding entrances and exits we wouldn't normally think about. Hell, they can squeeze through an opening the size of a silver dollar. Most likely it's one of the air ducts that lead to your yard."

"Well, don't let the backdoor hit 'em in the ass on the way out. What's the bad news? They chewed through the phone lines or something?"

"Not exactly. The rats seem to be hurrying to get out because of the *other* object I picked up inside your basement wall."

"What 'other object'?" Vaughn frowned.

Once back in the basement, the X-ray imagery Malik showed them reminded Vaughn of the science films his class would have to watch periodically in grade school. Small figures that were obviously rats occasionally scurried past, sometimes running into each other. But, as Malik scrolled toward the right, a significantly larger object manifested.

"I have no idea what it is, but the rats either avoid going near it or are leaving the house altogether to get away from it."

*   *   *

Malik had been hesitant about fogging the walls on such short notice until they offered to pay him an additional hundred if he could start immediately. Neither Vaughn nor Trish were ecstatic about what this was going to cost, but they didn't want to continue staying in a house with a festering animal carcass (what Malik estimated it might be) only a wall's distance between them.

Even though he seemed like a fairly decent guy Vaughn had asked Neil from work to stop by the house while they left Malik to his task. The couple spent most of the day running errands: garden supplies from Home Depot, an oil change at a center kind enough to be open on Sundays, and a trip to Target to replace their vacuum that had seen its last carpet. After having heard nothing by two o'clock that afternoon, Vaughn was just about to reach for his cell when Neil called.

"Did he call you yet?" his co-worker answered.

"Anyone ever tell you not to answer the phone with a question?"

"What're you? My mom?" Neil shot back casually. "So, did your exterminator contact you?"

"No, Trish and I have been running errands all day and thought he must've spoken with you or something."

"Hell, I never even got to **see** him – let alone talk with the guy," Neil replied. "I'm outside your place right now, and his van is still parked at the curb. I rang your bell, banged on the door, and even called the number on the side of his vehicle to see if his bosses know where the hell he is."

After seeing the look of concern on his face, Trish urged him to put Neil on speaker for them both to hear.

"Neil," she spoke, "Can you peep through the kitchen window and tell us if you see anything? Maybe he was just in the bathroom or something."

"Trish, I've been around for about two hours and he's not here. I already checked the window back there after I tried the bell and knocked. So, unless he's taking the mother of all dumps, no one's in your house."

After thanking Neil for his patience and sending him on his way, they began the drive back.

"He is so getting fired when we call Pied Piper," Vaughn growled through gritted teeth. "There's probably fumigation crap all over the house."

"But, there's too much of this that doesn't add up," Trish mused as rain began spattering the windshield. "Who just up and leaves both their equipment and van?"

"Folks have done weirder stuff for no reason. Maybe he got a really good look at just how much of a job he'd have ahead of him and took off. What kind of contractor moonlights at a pest control company, as much as they make? I thought something didn't sound right with that."

"What if he had an accident?" Trish turned to him. "A piece of timber could've knocked him in the head when he tore into the wall."

"For all of the money we're giving up to get this done, that dude better have a knot on his head the size of a grapefruit."

*   *   *

Checking through the rear window of the van only revealed a copy of *Penthouse* resting atop several pieces of equipment. They cautiously ventured into the house, Vaughn grabbing an aluminum baseball bat from the foyer closet.

"Malik!" he called as they edged through the ground floor. The stillness in response only added to their unease. Grabbing her cell, Trish began dialing.

"Who're you calling?" Vaughn frowned in confusion.

A moment later the chorus to Zapp & Roger's "Computer Love" could faintly be heard from the basement.

"That's his phone, I guess," Trish shrugged as they went for the basement stairs.

"Nice ringtone."

They found Malik's cell at the base of the hole in the wall, which was now nearly six feet tall and about four feet wide. It reminded Vaughn of a large mythic beast opening its maw to yawn –or snarl. He couldn't imagine venturing into such a space even with a hundred tungsten lamps. Malik had covered everything in sheets of thick clear plastic, his cutting tools resting atop the dryer. The fumigation canisters lay unopened beside a circular saw.

The smell hit them right about then, their noses wrinkling in disgust. It wasn't the odor of decomposing animal flesh, for which they were grateful. But, rather, it just smelled *pungent,* like overly fermented vegetables that you wouldn't dare eat no matter how attractive the plate appeared. In addition to its overwhelming ripeness, the odor made them strangely lightheaded.

"Do I even wanna know what that is?" Trish spoke through her sweater.

*   *   *

After getting Pied Piper's answering services several times, Vaughn and Trish reluctantly accepted that they'd have to wait until the following morning to have Malik's departure explained. His wife had refused to return to the basement until Vaughn had carefully tacked up one of the plastic sheets over the gaping hole, which failed to make it less menacing.

When their doorbell rang around 7 p.m., Trish hurried to open it, expecting a heavily-bandaged and crutches-addled Malik with a story about dragging himself to the nearest emergency room. Opening the door, she was surprised to discover their gnome-loving neighbor, Mrs. Bondelli, eyeing her with concern.

"Uh- hi, Mrs. Bondelli."

"Good evening, Trish," the elderly woman nodded. "I really hate to bother you when you're probably about to start on dinner."

"Oh no, ma'am," Trish shook her head and stepped aside. "C'mon in."

Vaughn, who'd been looking through the yellow pages for law firms, got to his feet as they entered the living-room. "How're you and the gnomes doing?"

Trish, standing behind their neighbor, shot him a seething look.

"Just lovely, dear," she smiled. "I was coming back from the senior center and noticed that pest control truck still sitting outside. I didn't know they worked this late."

"We just wanted to do some last minute maintenance," Vaughn lied casually. "You never can be too careful. The van's having electrical problems, so it might be the battery."

"Your exterminator might want to get a jump or something," she offered. "They clean our side of the street tomorrow morning and I'm sure he'd hate to end up getting a ticket. I heard they've gone up to $75 dollars!"

"We'll definitely give him the heads up when he gets back," Trish assured her.

"I'd love to stay, but I'm expecting a call from my daughter in a bit," she sighed, walking with Trish toward the foyer. "I must say that I love what you've done with the place. It's a wonderful home, and it would've been a shame to let it go to ruin after that tragedy eight years ago."

Trish gently touched the woman's shoulder, keeping her voice calm. "What tragedy?"

"The Pimbleton Case? It was all over the news for months. I'm surprised you haven't heard about it. They really should've given you the story when showing the place, not that it would have any effect on the home itself. I mean, a house is still a house. But, people have a right to know when they're investing a great deal of money."

"What happened?" Vaughn inquired, clearly worried.

"They lived here for several years, and one day the father up and murders his wife and daughter without a second thought. The police made the newspapers keep the details scarce, but he supposedly did something so terrible to the bodies that the coroner wasn't certain how they even were killed."

Vaughn glanced at Trish, who looked noticeably pale. The reason for them finding this house at the more-than-reasonable rate was now sickeningly apparent.

"Did they catch the husband?"

"Oh yes," Mrs. Bondelli nodded. "Someone like that, they can't just let stay at large. He ended up in a hospital out in Carroll County for people that aren't right in the head. I'm sure his aunt that came to visit the family for awhile must've been especially hurt by what happened. I can't recall her name, but I think she was from Europe or someplace."

Unfortunately, she couldn't provide any more information that was helpful. They both walked her to the door and watched her disappear down the sidewalk.

* * *

Pied Piper, who informed them the next morning that they'd heard no word from Malik, sent a second technician with a tow truck to retrieve the van and equipment. He assured them that the proper repairs would be made within 48 hours, as well as the fee cut in half for the inconvenience they'd experienced.

They might've missed the impromptu home invasion that night had Vaughn opted to take the beltway home, the 45-minute traffic deadlock having spared them the whole ordeal. But, Vaughn, being compelled to take the scenic route home after having dinner at Chevy's, got him and Trish home mere minutes after the intruder arrived.

Malik's handiwork had temporarily silenced their alarm system, so they'd made it a point to leave the living-room light on. Having entered the foyer they were in the process of removing their coats when the man in the dirty scrubs jumped Vaughn.

"You moved her!" His breath reeked of cigarettes and halitosis.

"Moved *who*?!" Vaughn struggled to throw the wild-eyed man off him until he pressed the paring knife to his throat.

"Get off him!" Trish was now brandishing the aluminum bat, ready to bash their intruder's skull in.

"You moved her!"

"We heard you the first time!" Vaughn protested, starting to realize what that larger object they'd seen on Malik's PDA might have been.

"Why'd you have to go and cut into the wall?" the guy cried like some frustrated child. *"It would've been just fine if you'd left it alone!"*

"**We** didn't cut into the damned wall!" Trish corrected, still holding her weapon. "That was the guy from the pest control company! Maybe you oughta be pressing a damned knife to **his** throat!"

"You swing that, and he's dead!" the man threatened, his eyes frantic.

21

"If you even nick him I will beat your ass with this thing like you've got some candy in you!"

"Trish," Vaughn spoke calmly, "put down the bat."

"Like hell!" his wife declined.

"Baby, this is Mr. Pimbleton." Vaughn was breathing shallowly through his nose.

"I don't give a shit who this crazed hobo ass is!" Trish's cheeks were flushed now.

"*The former owner of this house.* Please, Trish, just put the bat down and everything's going to be okay." His eyes went to their unwelcome visitor. "You got a first name?"

The intruder wasn't quite sure what to make of this. "Ted."

"Okay, then, Ted," Vaughn replied evenly, "I'm Vaughn and this is my wife, Trish. What is it that you seem to think we moved?"

"Not 'what'! *Who!* I put her in the wall before the police came for me, and she's not there anymore!"

"Who did you place in the wall?"

"My Aunt."

*   *   *

Not only was Vaughn able to persuade Trish to lower her weapon, but managed to get Ted to release him, as well. The nervous man still held on to the knife, but, at least, it was no longer pressed against Vaughn's jugular.

"Aren't you supposed to be in a hospital somewhere staring at ink blots right now?" Trish wasn't the least bit interested in being civil.

"I found out a week ago the place had been sold when my cousin came to visit," Ted revealed, scratching his unruly beard stubble. "They send the soiled linens out to be cleaned, so I was able to hide in the laundry. The hospital has so-so security."

"We noticed." She glared at Vaughn when he lightly nudged her. "So, you wanna tell us why you murdered a helpless old woman and stuffed her in our basement wall?"

"'Helpless'?" A hoarse hiccup escaped his throat that could almost be a laugh. "Yeah, that's a good one. She was about as helpless as a hungry water moccasin."

"Is it true you killed your wife and daughter?" Vaughn asked, weighing out just how far gone this man was.

"It's my fault they're dead, but I'm not the one who murdered them."

"Look, Ted," Trish studied him, "it's not a good time to be vague right now."

"Did you know 'Ring around the Rosie' was really about the Black Plague?" he suddenly asked.

"They talked about it on the History Channel once," Vaughn offered.

"I didn't know until six years ago when I was looking through an encyclopedia on Europe at the hospital library. We used to sing that all the time as kids, none of us having a clue as to how screwed up it actually was. It's amazing all the terrible stuff's that's hidden as something sweet and innocent. For Christ sake, even "Rock-a-bye Baby" is about abusing kids."

"Your aunt..." Trish probed, her free hand absently playing with the keys in her jeans pocket.

"All the family told me about Edina was that she was our rich great aunt from somewhere in Europe, but that could've been anywhere. I mean, Europe's huge. My aunt came to stay with my cousin in Delaware for a while. I met her only once when I was 9 after my cousin's mom died two months after she got there. She paid visits from time to time with members of our family, often lavishing her fortune on them as she did. Other than pinching my cheeks and talking like one of those people off Masterpiece Theater, I guessed she was all right."

Ted related that he'd thought nothing about his aunt until the mortgage became a burden, getting laid off from his job as a brick layer at Tiber Construction. They'd been living there for a few years and, faced with the possibility of having to move, he figured they could tolerate sharing their home for a while with an elderly relative if it meant salvaging it.

"I honestly thought she was rather sweet at first," Ted shook his head in disbelief. "Her accent and how she loved making tea for all of us. I knew she had to be up there in years, especially since she wasn't exactly 35 when I met her as a kid. But, to be elderly, she was spry as hell and took good care of herself."

"How long did she stay with you?" Vaughn asked.

"She had to have been here about three months," Ted replied, wiping perspiration from his brow. "I know that because Justine Iverson, who babysat for the Yardly family across the street, went missing a month after she'd been with us. She'd come by once selling chocolate bars for her school, and Aunt Edina had insisted that she wanted to order five whole boxes. There was talk that she'd run off with some guy from school, but it never really panned out. Cheryl, my wife, began having these episodes where she'd get fatigued in the middle of making dinner or heading off to work."

Ted told them that his daughter, Pattie, started displaying similar symptoms of fatigue a week after her mom was able to return to work. Her kindergarten teacher had confided that the child would often fall asleep during story time, needing to be gently nudged awake. It began to get so frequent that Ted and his wife ended up taking her to a pediatrician, who informed them that the child was suffering from some sort of anemia.

"I came home early from a job interview to find my aunt in my daughter's room, softly singing to her in what I guess was Welsh or something. Pattie was lying on her stomach deeply asleep, and I probably would've left them alone until I heard the *sucking sound*. It reminded me of the noise that tube makes when they place it in your mouth at the dentist. I called Edina but she wouldn't answer for some reason, so I walked over to them-"

Ted looked green, as if he could feel an earlier meal slowly working its way back up.

"What'd you see?" Trish found herself asking, having been pulled into the man's tale.

"Her hand was resting on Pattie's arm, but it... *wasn't*. It looked like Edina's fingers had fused into her skin, and I could see these veins pulsing from my daughter into my aunt. I started shaking her to make her stop, and she quit singing, turning to look at me. And that's when I almost fainted because she looked to be in her mid-fifties, like God had turned the clock back on her himself. She smiled at me and said it had to be done, that it was *'part of the agreement'*."

"An 'agreement' between who?" Vaughn wondered.

"Do you know what a Plague Crone is? In that book I read on the Black Death, they were supposed to be creatures that rescued people from the disease as it spread throughout Europe. They'd keep an entire family safe from harm, but they demanded something in return. One – and sometimes two members – of the family would be given to the Plague Crone, who slowly sucked their life energy out of them. They were ancient old hags, but they started to look less like that the more they ingested human energy. Before they left, the Crone would also reward the surviving family members with gold.

"I don't believe it," Trish muttered, visibly uncomfortable. "So, you're trying to tell me that you broke into our house and held my husband at knifepoint because of an old woman that pays families to let her suck up their relatives?"

"Lady, I don't really give a shit what you believe at this point," Ted sighed. "I just know what I saw that day was real. When she looked at me, it was like an invisible pair of arms grabbed me, forcing me down next to her on the bed. *I couldn't move, and I knew she was doing it!* Pattie had just enough strength to turn toward me, and I could see her face looked like...*something was caving it in from the inside*! AND I COULDN'T DO ANYTHING TO STOP HER!"

Ted suddenly broke into ragged sobs, wiping his nose with one of his grimy sleeves. Vaughn, although knowing that this man had held a blade to his skin minutes ago, felt a pang of pity for this disoriented person.

"She said that a crone would attach itself to a family," he continued, "often following them and their descendants for generations. Edina told me she came to America for the first time during the big Influenza Pandemic in 1918, holing up in a massive compound with my great granddad and his extended family as the flu wiped out millions. They renewed their pact with her once it was over, calling on her over the generations to come. There weren't any more real pandemics as time went on, but members of my family sent for her when their money was scarce or times got really desperate. She became a *member of the family*, basically; the kind you hope never pays you a visit. After a while, my relatives stopped telling their kids what Aunt Edina really was, just mentioning that she was a generous person in times of a crisis."

"Where was your wife during all of this?" Trish suddenly asked, standing close to Vaughn.

"She'd already taken Cheryl while I was out, placing what was left of her in the shed where I kept the firewood. My pager, which I kept on my belt, went off right then. For some reason, that seemed to have distracted her where whatever hold she had on me broke. Before she could start in again, I grabbed Pattie's princess phone and smashed Edina in the head with it. She fell over, and I kept hitting her in the head until my arm got tired, noticing that what was running out of her wasn't blood. It looked like...black *pus* or some sort of congealed fluid that couldn't possibly come from a human being.

"Pattie was nothing more than a skeleton with skin stretched across it, my wife looking much the same when I worked up the courage to look in the shed. I knew that I didn't have much time so I got my work tools from the basement, taking down a portion of the wall, and wrapping up my *aunt's* body in garbage bags. It was tight in there, but I shoved her in as far as I could and then poured quick lyme over the body. Redoing the wall took awhile, but I got it where no one would notice it'd been disturbed."

"Who called the police?" Vaughn asked. "Someone obviously did."

"I did," Ted shrugged. "I'd placed Cheryl and Pattie's bodies in our bed, and then I downed a bottle of pills. The police were supposed to have gotten there after it was too late to revive me, but that didn't exactly work out right. Naturally, they saw the condition of their bodies and just knew I'd done something terrible they couldn't explain. Even if I hadn't stopped talking by that point, there was no way I was gonna say anything about that awful thing I'd buried in the wall. They put me in that hospital, and I'd hoped that the history of what happened could keep anyone from buying this place. I guess that didn't pan out too well, huh?"

"We didn't know anything about it until Mrs. Bondelli told us." Trish corrected. "And, whatever happened to Justine? The girl that was selling chocolate?"

Ted stared tiredly at her. "What do *you* think happened to her?"

Suddenly, he set the paring knife down on the ground. "I guess it just doesn't matter anymore, really. She's gone, and there isn't shit any of us can do about it now. Can I use your bathroom? I've been needing to take a leak for about forever."

Ted staggered on shaky legs up the stairs to the main bathroom, the door shutting softly. They stood there awkwardly for a moment, Trish turning to Vaughn.

"They'll be here any moment now," she whispered.

"Who?"

"The police," Trish withdrawing her cell from her jeans pocket. "When you asked him a question earlier I managed to dial 911 and started tapping S-O-S in Morse code. They've probably been listening to most of our conversation."

"Will you marry me?" Vaughn whispered, his eyes wide in amazement.

"We're already married, honey," Trish squeezed his hand briefly. "But, sure, why not."

"How did you-"

"Girl Scouts."

*   *   *

The police banged on the bathroom door twice, announcing themselves and ordering Ted to exit with his arms raised. When they finally burst in to find him dead, it wasn't that much of a shock. The most horrid thing was that he'd ingested every last pill in their medicine cabinet, deeply slashing both his throat and wrists with one of Vaughn's razors.

Pied Piper finally arrived the following day to repair their basement wall, informing them they'd be receiving a lifetime warranty against issues with the wall and pests in general. Vaughn and Trish figured that the company wanted to stay in their good graces at any costs. They chose not to ask them if Malik had ever shown up.

A week after Trish learned she was pregnant, Vaughn began his project of converting their gym room into a nursery. The treadmill had been the only item that'd required additional help, and he'd snagged Dale to cart it with him into the spacious attic where the new exercise room had been relocated.

"Make sure you keep using all of this shit. After the first kid is right about when this starts forming," Dale joked and patted his own Buddha-like belly.

They spotted the crack in the ceiling above their bed shortly after making love late one Saturday morning.

"I told you that treadmill was too heavy to put up there," Trish commented, laying her head on his chest.

"You did no such thing," he snickered.

Reluctantly, he got up and threw on his boxers and sandals. "What kind of cheap-ass floor can't even support a second-hand piece of exercise equipment?"

"Second-hand?" Trish protested. "Carmen said she brought that brand new."

"Remind me later to talk about your sister and her mixed messages in sending out gifts."

He retrieved his cell from the nightstand on his way out.

From the high attic window Vaughn could plainly see the small pile of bricks that lay atop the treadmill, the metal bent in around them. He hadn't liked the idea of Trish using it while she was pregnant, but was sure that she'd be thoroughly upset when she saw the damage. The hole in the triangular ceiling above wasn't anything like the former eyesore that Malik had left a month before in the basement. He wasn't looking forward to making the call to initiate the repairs, but dialed Pied Piper in the hopes that their warranty included *all* of their walls. Being told by a recording that, due to the voicemail being full, he'd have to try his call again later Vaughn clicked off. He noticed the flashing icon of new messages, and he put the phone to his ear.

"You have one message," the sexless voice informed him, and he hit '1' to hear the call.

An icy jolt of pain suddenly seized his limbs, reminding him of the millisecond he'd touched a frayed wire on the family Christmas tree growing up. He could only move his head a few fractions.

Please, God, not a heart attack, he pleaded. *Not with the kid on the way!*

In his paralysis, he watched a short rain of still more bricks toppled on to the treadmill with a cloud of dust. When the body fell out atop everything else, it looked less like a corpse than it did a haphazardly-made scarecrow dressed in Malik's dark jumpsuit. Somehow, he'd hit the speaker option before his motions froze.

"*Hey, Vaughn,*" Malik called him from the grave. "*I told you I'd give you guys a ring if I ran into any problems. Well, remember that object I showed you on the sonogram's screen? I need to go a little further into your wall than I estimated. Don't worry, I'm not charging you any extra for this, and I'll have everything patched up.*"

Vaughn had no idea how Malik's message had managed to still be in his phone, and he'd never spotted it. But, it hadn't been the first time that a voicemail for him went into the wrong inbox.

"*It's probably nothing but me needing to get this equipment checked,*" said the dead technician that now lay emaciated before him. "*But that mass of whatever the hell it is...I could almost swear that it's* moving.*"

Something that might've been a hand once appeared from the hole above just as Malik clicked off, the sexless voice stating that there were no further messages. The fingers were mummified, but Vaughn could make out the smudged diamond bracelet on its wrist as yet another brick fell away. There was a piece of black plastic, which could only be from the garbage bag Ted had used, caught in it.

When he saw the tendrils of gray hair emerging from the dark hole, Vaughn summoned everything within him to scream. The most he could manage was a wet mumble, his vocal cords like knotted cables. Edina, prying loose a cluster of plaster, finally had enough space to turn her dirt-encrusted face toward him. He wasn't sure if the rodents had been responsible for gnawing away most of her face (before learning what she really was). So very little of her feature remained. The empty black sockets of her eyes, which had seen nearly every form of pestilence known to man, gazed down at him ravenously.

If she had any lips left, she'd probably start licking them right about now, Vaughn thought as the famished crone began lowering herself from out of the hole.

DEATH BY DARKNESS

BY

JASMINE JUNE

Emily Young peered out of her bedroom window into the darkness that lay just beyond the border of her back yard. Her body trembled with uncontrollable fear as she caught glimpses of the shadowy figures lurking in the thick air, creatures that were darker than the night itself. Their eyes were blacker than anything she had seen; two spots of emptiness nestled within more darkness.

Emily hated the night. She knew other girls that were afraid of the dark, as well, but not like she was. Her friends made her feel silly when they came over for slumber parties. Ten years old and still sleeping with a night-light? At least she wasn't one of those kids who wet the bed.

The hair on the back of Emily's neck suddenly stood up, as if lightening were in the air. She could feel something watching her as she slowly turned her head. The hallway light had been turned off while she was looking out the window, and she hadn't noticed. Those dark eyes, like tiny black holes that threatened to suck everything into their existence, peered out at her from the vast emptiness beyond her door. The creatures hissed at her, just a few feet from her bed. She quickly turned back to the window, shaken and terrified, but knowing they couldn't enter her room so long as the light was on.

Emily's father Rob came into the bedroom. The sight of his daughter shaking as she stared out her window was still something to which he had yet to grow accustomed.

"Emily," he said gently. "Come away from the window, sweetie."

He watched with a breaking heart as his daughter turned to face him with her blue eyes misted with tears.

"It's okay, darling. You can sleep with the light on, and everything will be fine."

"I want to light the candle, too," She said, glancing around him into the hallway. "And, can we leave the hallway light on?"

Rob felt his patience wane.

"I've already explained to you that the candles are a fire hazard."

"Please, Daddy. It's fine. Nothing is going to catch fire. I'm always very careful."

Rob frowned. He knew that if he pushed this, a tantrum would ensue.

"Fine," he stammered. "Light the damn candle." He turned around and stomped out of the room, calling good night over his shoulder as he walked down the hall. How did parents deal with things like this? How did they keep it together? He knew it was common for kids to be afraid of the dark, but this was starting to get ridiculous.

He went into the kitchen and poured himself a shot of scotch. His wife Karen was at the sink, finishing up the dishes from dinner.

"How was Emily tonight?" she asked.

"The same as always," he answered. "Actually, maybe even worse."

He took a swallow and enjoyed the burn as it went down his throat. It was a moment of distraction from his agitation.

Karen sighed and wearily wiped her forehead with the back of her hand. Blonde wisps of hair had fallen out of her ponytail to dangle in tiny curls around her face. Her blue eyes were tired, full of worry. Rob found the physical similarities between his wife and his daughter striking; pictures of Karen as a child were often confused for photos of Emily. They had the same creamy skin, the same spattering of freckles across the nose. Only the contrast in clothing gave the photos away.

"I think we need to send her to a psychologist, Rob. I can't stand watching her struggle all the time. Do you know she won't sleep over at her friends' houses anymore because they don't sleep with night-lights? This phobia of hers is going to ruin her social life. She only has three years left until she's in high school. Can you imagine how the kids are going to respond if she freaks out in class? The last time the power went out during school, she was in hysterics."

Rob nodded. "Alright. I'll look into it tomorrow. I hate the thought of sending my kid to a psychologist, though. You know they're going to point fingers at us. They always do that. It's always the parents' fault somehow. And, I'm a good father. I wish she'd just grow up and snap out of it already."

Karen walked over and put her arms around Rob. His Old Spice cologne smelled good, and she breathed it in deeply. So comforting, the familiar scents of her family. Sometimes when she was out shopping, she'd spray a bit of the cologne on her wrist if she came across a bottle. The smell would instantly conjure up feelings of being loved, of feeling safe.

"It's okay," she whispered. "Everything is going to be okay. We'll get it figured out."

For Emily, things were not okay. Ever since she was a little girl, she had seen creatures in the darkness, and she knew what those creatures were. She could hear their thoughts, like scratchy whispers inside her head. They were soul snatchers. Like vultures, they could kill their prey if they wanted to, but they preferred to lurk on the perimeter, hovering close by as death slowly presented itself.

The unsuspecting soul was simple to snatch as it emerged from a dead body, but the soul snatchers were lazy creatures; they didn't want to work very hard to steal the souls. Old people who died peacefully in their sleep were the easiest; their souls were at such peace that they were completely unaware of the evil crouching in the darkness, like a cat waiting to pounce on its prey. A soul that was emerging from a violent death was trickier, as its defenses were already up and bracing against an attack. The soul snatchers rarely went after these. Better to steal the souls of old people and of children. A child's soul was so innocent, so easy to entice and lure away.

Emily knew this, and it terrified her. She knew that the soul snatchers needed nourishment in order to survive, and they could only exist within the dark. Light would snuff out their essence as quickly as blowing out a candle flame.

During her younger years, Emily's natural instincts kicked in whenever she saw the soul snatchers, and she would look away, diverting her eyes quickly so that they didn't know she had seen them. This was when she believed in things like Santa Claus and unicorns and fairies; she was too innocent to know what was real and what was make believe.

However, as the years passed and the lie of Santa Claus was revealed, her belief in mystical creatures turned to disappointment. When discovering that these things only existed in storybooks, Emily became more and more alarmed that the soul snatchers didn't die away with all the other imaginary beings. She began to wonder about them, to stare at them rather than divert her eyes. And she began to notice that they were everywhere; they existed *with* the darkness, so that something as simple as turning off the light meant instantly being surrounded by them.

The soul snatchers at first didn't realize Emily could see them, as it was so rare to be seen by a human. But as Emily started to pay more attention to them, the soul snatchers noticed. They hated that she could see them. Her eyes were pinpoints of light that bore into their bodies like a burning knife. They began to stalk her, to torment her with their thoughts whenever she was close enough to listen. They sent her images of soul snatchers ripping apart her soul and sucking it piece by piece into their gaping mouths.

The hands on the clock slowly ticked towards the end of the school day. Just a few minutes left. Emily sat at her desk with her head resting on her arms. She was exhausted from so many sleepless nights. For a while, leaving the light on had been enough. Lately, though, she drifted off to sleep only to be confronted by vivid nightmares, and would wake up screaming several times throughout the night. A foggy memory of a whispered threat lingered in her ears each morning: "We'll get you in the darkness. We're waiting for you."

The last time the electricity went out was a close call. She had been sitting in class, trying to figure out the math equation the teacher had written on the board. When everything went black, all the students screamed in startled excitement. Emily screamed, too, but her voice died away as an icy grip tightened on her throat. A static sound, like white noise, filled her head. She could barely breathe. And she could see the soul snatchers suddenly beside her. She stood up, knocking over her chair, and ran out of the classroom, down the hall, and out the front doors, all the while hearing the ragged breathing of the soul snatchers as they pursued and taunted her.

Out in the sunlight, Emily felt the icy grip vanish, and she began to scream with her recovered voice. Her teachers and classmates, along with the principal, had rushed outside to see what was happening. All they found was Emily, screaming unintelligibly about the darkness. Her parents were finally called to come pick her up. The whole thing horribly embarrassed Emily, but at least she had learned her lesson: from then on, she had a flashlight with her at all times and spare batteries, too.

A shrill ringing erupted over the loud speakers, and the students rose in practical unison, thrilled that another school day had come to an end. Emily grabbed her bag and was packing up her homework when her best friend, Sherrie, approached.

"Hey Em! My mom said it was okay to have a sleep over this weekend. Want to come over? I have Justin Bieber DVDs!" Sherrie squealed and clapped her hands together. "Ooh! And I can do your hair!"

Emily opened her mouth to reply, but Alicia, the queen bee of the 5th grade social scene, cut in. "Do you own a night-light, Sherrie?"

Sherrie shook her head no and looked down at the floor.

"Then, I believe Emily's answer is 'no'. Unless you don't mind sleeping with the light on. Hmm, but then you still have the monsters that live under the bed. And, the boogieman in the closet. You should really spend more time in the kindergarten class, Sherrie, since you like to hang out with kids who act like 5 year olds."

Alicia tossed her long, auburn hair over her shoulder and walked away with a smug grin.

Emily fought back the tears that threatened to emerge from behind her eyes. She wished she could be normal like everyone else, so she wouldn't feel so alone.

Sherrie put her arm around Emily's shoulders. "It's okay, Em. We've been friends since kindergarten, and nothing is going to change that."

Still stinging from Alicia's words, Emily simply nodded.

"I'll ask my parents about this weekend."

She grabbed her bag and rushed out the door and into the hall, head down, cheeks burning with embarrassment.

Emily didn't see Alicia and the other girls waiting by the janitor's room, she was so engulfed in her thoughts, her eyes fixed on the floor. Suddenly, she felt a hand grab her arm and she was yanked inside the room. The sudden plunge into darkness was so unexpected that she didn't react at first. Then she started to scream as the soul snatchers emerged all around her, whispering their scratchy threats in her ear. Her scream died as an icy, unseen hand tightened around her throat.

Someone next to Emily stifled a giggle. Emily kicked out hard with her foot and connected with soft flesh.

"Ouch!" a girl wailed.

Emily reached around and caught a handful of hair. She pulled as hard as she could.

The girl screamed.

"You're going to rip out my hair!" Emily pulled harder. "Okay! I'll turn on the light!"

The room flooded with light and Emily collapsed, sucking in huge gulps of air, tears streaming down her face, her body shaking uncontrollably.

Victoria, Alicia's right-hand girl, stood glowering above Emily.

"You little psycho," she spat. "It's just the janitor's closet. What are you afraid of? You really are crazy, aren't you?"

She walked out of the room, rubbing her shin where Emily had kicked it.

After a few minutes, Emily slowly got up. She was still shaking and a little disoriented. That had been much, much too close. She touched her throat where the icy hands had squeezed. Her skin still felt cold.

Rob noticed that Emily was unusually quiet at dinner. His parent radar went up as he observed his daughter pushing her food around her plate, not really eating anything. Any questions he asked received short, one-word responses, and she kept her eyes lowered on her plate.

He had planned on telling her about the meeting he booked with the child psychologist, but now he couldn't find the courage to bring it up. His little girl just seemed so fragile. She seemed like one of those porcelain dolls, beautiful and delicate, so easily breakable.

Karen spoke up for him. "Emily, honey?"

Emily remained silent, but gave a small nod.

Karen looked nervously at Rob and cleared her throat.

"Your father and I love you very much, and we are concerned about your fear of the dark."

She saw her daughter wince, but she went on.

37

"We set up a meeting for you with someone we think might be able to help. Her name is Caroline Greenfield, and she works with children who have phobias. Your dad is going to pick you up from school on Friday and bring you to your first appointment. I think you'll like her. She's very nice."

Emily sighed. "I don't have a phobia," she muttered. "You never listen to me."

"Being afraid of the dark to the point where it affects your life is a phobia, Emily," Rob said matter-of-factly. "It even has a name: nyctophobia."

"Can I be excused?" Emily asked.

"No," said Rob. "Eat your supper."

"But I'm not hungry."

"If I tell you to eat your supper, then you eat your supper. Do as I say," Rob's face flushed red as he felt his anger rising. "Do you always have to be so difficult?"

"Fine," Emily said through clenched teeth.

Karen sat back in her chair, her heart aching as she watched the scene unfold between her husband and daughter. They used to be so close. For years, Emily was the perfect cliché of "daddy's little girl." She could climb onto his lap, bat her little eyelashes, and get anything she wanted. Rob had never even raised his voice at her, but Emily's growing fear of the dark and erratic behavior had changed all of that.

Karen just wanted things to go back to the way they used to be. She really hoped that Caroline Greenfield could work some magic.

The car ride to Caroline's office was excruciatingly quiet. Rob had tried to engage Emily in conversation, but she only stared out the window and sulked.

The office was in one of those buildings that housed all sorts of different companies and services. The sign by the elevator had a list for each of its five floors. Services included dental, chiropractic, massage, homeopathy, and so forth. It made Rob feel a little uncomfortable to know that behind each door, there was someone naked on a table or in a chair with their mouth open or having their back cracked. It all seemed a little too intimate and the walls a little too thin.

At least Caroline's office was bright and comfortable. It made the experience feel less clinical and more personal. Although, Rob was unsure whether that made him feel more or less at ease.

Emily seemed to perk up at the sight of the place, though. She almost sighed as she looked around at the bright yellow walls, the comfy-looking orange sofa, and the colorful lamps that were in every corner.

After shaking Rob's hand and going over the initial paperwork, Caroline instructed him to sit in the waiting room while she had a one-on-one session with Emily. Rob felt relieved to have the burden lifted out of his hands for once and, after giving Emily a hug, gladly left the room.

Emily quickly knew she would easily like Caroline. The friendly demeanor of the 50-something woman seemed grandmotherly, even though Caroline was several years younger than her own grandmother. Caroline wore a black skirt with a red blouse, and red heels that made Emily think of the ruby slippers Dorothy wore in "The Wizard of Oz."

The brightness of the room also pleased Emily. There were no darkened corners or looming shadows to be found. The oranges, reds, and yellows that colored the room and its various objects were like sunshine.

"Have a seat, please," Caroline said and motioned her to the orange couch.

Emily happily sunk down into the plush cushions. She wished her own bedroom looked like Caroline's office. Instead, her room was drab with grey walls that were supposed to have been purple. Rather than repaint, her parents had simply color-coordinated everything to match the grey. That meant her bedspread was a boring white, and her area rug was a dull blue. Maybe Dad and Mom would change the colors for her if she asked. She made a mental note to pose the question when she got home.

Caroline sat in a plush, red chair across from the couch. She crossed her legs and opened a notebook that was in her lap.

"So, Emily, do you understand why you are visiting with me?"

Emily nodded.

"Yes, Mrs. Greenfield."

Caroline waved her hand. "Oh, please call me Caroline. The word 'Mrs.' makes me sound so old," she said, as she winked at Emily. "Can you tell me about yourself? What is your favorite color, your favorite subject at school?"

Emily thought for a moment. "My favorite color is yellow, and I like art."

"Oh, yes," Caroline nodded. "Your parents showed me some of your artwork. You draw beautiful pictures of flowers, and I love the big suns that you draw. All of your pictures are very cheerful."

"Thanks."

"You seem like a good kid. Cheerful pictures, good grades, and nice friends. At least, according to your parents, of course." Caroline leaned forward. "Can you tell me about your friends?"

Emily had received so many insults from classmates and frustration from her parents that Caroline's kind words made her instantly like the woman. Maybe this was someone who would understand? Emily kept so much bottled up inside her, and she desperately wanted to let it all out.

"Well, my best friend is Sherrie. We've been friends since kindergarten. We both love ice-cream, and Justin Bieber," Emily said, and she lowered her eyes and grew quiet. "And, she doesn't mind if I leave the light on when I sleep over."

Emily watched for Caroline's reaction, but the expression on her face remained warm and kind.

"Can you tell me why you want the light left on?"

After some hesitation, Emily explained, "I can't be in the darkness."

Caroline thought for a moment before responding.

"Now, you say can't, and that seems interesting to me. Did you mean to use that word, or do you mean that you don't like the dark or are afraid of it?"

"I'm not afraid of the dark," Emily said, somewhat defiantly. "No one listens to me."

Caroline suddenly looked very serious. "Emily," she said with sincerity, "I promise you that I will listen to you and that I will believe what you tell me. Grownups often have a hard time trusting kids, but I've been working with children for a long time, and I understand what you have to say is important."

Emily didn't say anything for a little while. Could she really trust this woman? Caroline was awfully nice, and the chance to confide in someone was tempting. In fact, Emily yearned to have someone believe her, to protect her from the soul snatchers. The experience in the janitor's room flashed through her mind. What if next time the soul snatchers succeeded?

In a bit of a panic, Emily began to spill out her fears. "There are creatures that live in the darkness. They are evil, horrible creatures. Most people can't see them, but I can. And they hate me for it! They hate that I can see them! My eyes hurt them, but I can't stop myself from looking at them. When I turn my back, I know they are still there. I can feel them watching me."

Emily shuddered and sank further back in the couch. Her hands were starting to shake a bit, and she tucked them under her legs.

Caroline wrote a few things in her notebook.

"Do these creatures have a name?"

"Yes. They are called 'soul snatchers.' They eat people's souls! But, only after they die. But not with me. They want to kill me and get my soul so that I can't look at them ever again."

By now, Emily was shaking all over. She wanted Caroline to believe her, to protect her. She didn't want to die.

"How do you know these things about the soul snatchers? Have you seen them do any of the things you described?"

"I can hear them. Their voices get into my head. They tell me how they are going to kill me. They send me pictures of how they are going to eat my soul!"

Emily covered her face with her hands and began sobbing.

"You're safe here, Emily," Caroline said soothingly. "Nothing can harm you. It's okay."

She wrote a few things down in her notebook and tried another tactic.

"Emily, have you lost anyone close to you? A family member, or even a pet?"

"No," Emily sobbed.

"Has anything bad ever happened to you while you were in a dark place? Did you ever read a story or see a movie that had something scary to do with the dark?"

Emily shook her head and continued crying.

"Okay, sweetie. We don't have to talk about this anymore. Would you like a teddy bear to hold? I have some really great ones. I always liked teddy bears when I was a kid and found they made me feel better."

Caroline got up and pulled a large, plush, brown teddy bear from a toy box and handed it to Emily.

The bear felt so soft and comforting. Emily hugged it to her chest. After a little while, her sobs subsided, and she looked up.

"Do you believe me?" she whispered.

"Yes, Emily, I believe you," Caroline paused. "Do you have any ideas of how to get rid of the soul snatchers, or how to protect yourself from them?"

"They can only exist in darkness. As long as there is light, they can't get me."

Caroline frowned.

"Emily," she said tenderly, "I'm not sure if you can avoid being in the dark for the rest of your life. I'm sure it must make it hard for you to do things and be places if you are always avoiding the dark. Don't you want to lie under the stars or watch a movie in the theatre?"

"Yes, but I can't. I don't have any choice."

"Well, I hope you know that you can talk to me about anything, and hopefully we can come up with some ideas that will help you. Thank you for talking with me today."

After years of feeling isolated and hopeless, a slight feeling of relief came over Emily. She finally had someone who believed her.

Rob and Karen sat at the kitchen table after Emily had gone to sleep. Karen was anxious to hear what the therapist had said. Rob avoided Karen's gaze and sipped on a glass of bourbon. A lump was in his throat, and no matter how many sips he took of the burning alcohol, he just couldn't seem to find the words. He was still getting over the shock of what Caroline had told him.

Finally, Rob managed to muster up his courage.

"Do you know if anyone in your family has a history of schizophrenia?"

Both color and expression instantly drained from Karen's face, giving her the appearance of a corpse. Her mouth hung open slightly, and she stared blankly at her husband.

"Sweetheart?" Rob asked, his eyebrows knitting together with concern. "I'm sorry. I didn't know how to tell you."

He sighed, exasperated, and ran a hand through his hair. "Caroline said she'll need several more sessions with Emily before she's sure and a write up of our families' medical history."

"My grandfather was schizophrenic," Karen whispered.

"How do you know for sure? He passed away when you were a child."

"I actually heard my parents talking about it a few times. I think maybe they worried about my brother and me. Also, my cousin, Lorraine, had problems, but she committed suicide before she was diagnosed with anything."

Tears welled up in Karen's eyes.

Rob reached across the table and held her hand.

"Hey, we'll get through this. Caroline said that there are medications that Emily can take, and she should be able to lead a normal life."

"I don't want my 10 year old daughter to be on medication," Karen said firmly. "Do we have another option?"

"I don't know. We're not even sure if she has schizophrenia. Let's give it a few more sessions with Caroline, and then we can see what our options are."

Karen nodded, numb from the feeling of being so powerless.

Several weeks of hour-long sessions with Caroline Greenfield led to little improvement in Emily's behavior. She still slept with the light on and a lit candle, as well. She refused to talk to her parents about what she said to Caroline during their sessions. When asked, she simply retorted, "I've already told you everything, and you didn't believe me."

However, Karen and Rob knew from Caroline what was being discussed between her and their daughter. It didn't seem like Emily was making any progress in getting over her phobia, and both parents were dreading that schizophrenia was a viable diagnosis.

The one thing that had changed, though, was Emily's mood. A new spark was in her eye. She seemed like someone who had stumbled upon a newfound faith. The dark cloud that had hung above her head for years was now interspersed with rays of sunlight.

Rob asked Caroline about the improvement in Emily's mood.

"She smiles now. She eats her dinner without complaining. She even had Sherrie sleep over last weekend, and the two of them spent the whole time giggling and laughing. She still left the light on when they went to bed, but she didn't seem as embarrassed about it as she usually is."

"Well," Caroline said, "I think it may be because Emily thinks that I believe her stories about the soul snatchers. I think she has found an ally in me, and that gives her courage and a sense of empowerment. I don't doubt that Emily believes these creatures to be real, and that is what concerns me."

"So, she's not starting to come around? Has she said anything that indicates she's becoming less afraid of the dark?"

Caroline sighed.

"You have a very sweet little girl. She is bright and intelligent and kind. But she is very troubled. Mr. Young, I've worked with many children who have had severe phobias – it's part of my expertise – and it saddens me to say this, but I think we are dealing with a much bigger problem here. I'd like to try putting her on a medication. Not a very strong one, just something mild to see if that helps her."

"No," Rob said. "Not yet. There must be something else we can try."

"Well, there is a tactic that has been used for curing phobias, but if Emily doesn't have a phobia, then I am afraid it could have a very negative result."

"What is it?" Rob's heart beat a bit faster in anticipation.

"In many cases, a phobia can be overcome if a person faces the thing they are afraid of. It usually takes repeated exposure to the phobia, but eventually the person gains power over their fear as they receive concrete evidence that they are safe and in control. Now, this doesn't always work, depending on the reason behind the phobia, but in many cases it does."

"And do you think it could work with Emily?"

"I don't know. If she does have a phobia of the dark, then exposing her to darkness and showing her that nothing bad will actually happen – proving to her that she will be okay – might make her realize that she doesn't have to be afraid."

"Really? That seems like a great idea! Why didn't you bring this up earlier?"

"Because I don't believe that Emily has a phobia. I think that she has a psychological condition, and that she truly believes the creatures called soul snatchers exist. If you expose her to her fear, her mind may conjure up any number of conclusions as to why she remains physically okay, and the problem will not go away."

Rob could barely contain his excitement as he explained to Karen what Caroline had said. He felt like an explorer who had stumbled upon buried treasure. He just had to keep digging, and soon he'd reach his goal.

Karen was less than enthusiastic.

"I don't know, Rob. Every time she's accidentally been in the dark in the past, she's gone into hysterics. She's already been exposed to her fear, and it has never helped."

"But she was only exposed for a short period of time. What if she had to be in the dark and couldn't leave? Eventually she'd realize that nothing was hurting her and that she was fine."

"I just can't picture doing that to her. Can you imagine how terrified she would be? My poor girl. I can't do it."

"It's either we try this as a last resort or we put her on medication."

Karen frowned. She felt like a torture victim who was being pulled apart in one of those medieval contraptions that tugged from both ends of the body until it was ripped in half.

"You can try it, if you think it will work, but I'll have no part in it. You're on your own with this, and if it doesn't work then, I guess, we'll have to start medication."

Karen's voice cracked and tears streamed down her cheeks. She had never felt more defeated.

Emily stared out the window of the car. Dinner with her father had been an unexpected treat. Just the two of them, eating hamburgers and French fries and even a banana split for desert! Emily had felt happy sitting in the brightly lit restaurant with her dad. For so long he had been angry with her, and now he was suddenly nice again. Maybe Caroline had talked to him. Caroline believed she wasn't crazy, that she didn't have some silly fear of the dark. Maybe her dad was starting to realize that, too.

However, Emily's happiness soon turned to sickening dread during the car ride home. The sun had set hours ago, and darkness was everywhere. The road snaked through the dark forest, only illuminating the first fringe of trees with its headlights. The soul snatchers lurked just behind the trees, where the shadow of darkness swallowed all shapes and forms to make what looked like a black void of nothingness. Only the soul snatchers were visible in that darkness beyond, their eyes fixed on Emily's as she stared out the window.

"Emily," Rob said gently, "I'm going to turn off the car light."

Her eyes widened, and she whipped her head around.

"No, Dad! Don't do it! Please, don't do it!"

"But it won't be that dark inside the car, there will still be some light from the dashboard."

He hated driving with the inside light on.

Emily went into hysterics.

"No! It's not enough. Please, Daddy, please!"

Tears were already falling from her eyes and she looked as panicked as a deer caught in the headlights.

Rob felt his patience break.

"You know what? This is ridiculous. There is nothing to be afraid of, and I'm going to prove it to you."

He suddenly swerved off to the side of the road, slammed the car into park, cut the engine, and practically ripped Emily from the car.

"Dad! What are you doing?" Emily screamed and clawed at his face. "Put me down! Daddy, please, put me down!"

But Rob had had enough. He carried his daughter kicking and screaming into the woods. He stopped as soon as the thick canopy of leaves blotted out the streetlights so that they found themselves in total darkness.

Emily struggled as hard as she could against her father. She even bit him. She screamed and pleaded, but her cries were soon strangled as icy hands clamped around her throat. The soul snatchers were clinging to every part of her body like leeches, sinking their shadowy fangs into her skin, slithering into her pores, creeping through her open mouth, entering through her eyes. Emily could feel them inside her, feel them traveling through her blood stream up to her brain.

"We've got you Emily," they whispered, as they squeezed out her soul and devoured it with their hungry, snapping jaws.

Rob felt Emily stiffen in his arms.

"There you go," he said, taking it as a good sign that she had stopped struggling. "Nothing can hurt you. I'm here, and you are safe with me. See, Emily? You don't have to be afraid of the dark. There are no soul snatchers. They don't exist."

He hugged Emily tighter when she didn't answer.

"I'm sorry. I know you're going to be mad at me, but I had to show you that there was nothing to be afraid of. It's for your own good."

Suddenly, Emily's body started to convulse in his arms.

"Emily?" Rob cried out in alarm. He quickly laid his daughter down on the ground. "Oh my God, Emily!"

He watched her eyes roll into her head. Panic seized him like a vice. What was happening?

"Emily, I'm so sorry! Emily!"

He pulled out his cell phone and called an ambulance.

"My daughter is having a seizure. We're at the side of the road on Route 65, just before Old Danforth Road."

He shut his eyes and prayed, knowing he would never forgive himself.

Michael Crocket pulled back the stiff white sheet from the small corpse on the table. Rarely did he choke up during his work, but there was something about the innocence of this one that broke his heart. He had a daughter the same age at home himself and couldn't picture ever losing her.

"What's the prognosis?"

Robert, the finest mortician Crockett Funeral Home had, said as he entered the room.

Michael sighed. "The autopsy papers said it was a panic attack-induced seizure."

Robert looked over Emily's lifeless body.

"What an awful way to go, especially for a little girl."

"Be sure to do an extra good job with her, okay?" Michael asked.

Rob nodded. "I'll make her look like a little angel."

"Good, because she *was* somebody's little angel, and the service is going to be open casket."

"Don't worry boss, I've got it covered."

Robert shook his head sadly.

"I really hope that when I go, I'm one of the lucky ones that dies peacefully in my sleep."

SAYA

BY

CHANDRU BHOJWANI

Ashok looked at his watch before he turned the page and continued to read the file of his next patient. It was almost 9 p.m., and he hoped his new client would arrive soon.

"Dr. Virani, your son is on line two," the secretary informed him via the intercom.
"Thank you, Monica. You know you can leave. There is no need for you to stay."
"I'll wait for you to finish up, Dr. Thank you."
"Are you sure? I can close up myself, you know?"
"That's alright, Dr., I don't mind."

Ashok switched lines to speak to his 6-year-old son, Jai.

"Hello?"
"Papa, when are you coming home?" Jai squeaked.

"Soon beta, I just have to finish up some work. Aren't you supposed to be in bed?"

"Papa, there is a monster in my room! It's not letting me sleep again," he sulked.

"Oh, is that right? It's back, is it? Alright, I'll come home soon and take care of that monster, ok?"

"Promise?"

"Yes, beta, I promise," Ashok said, reassuringly. "Let me speak to mummy."

Ashok looked at his watch again and then the door, anxiously waiting.

"Ashok, why aren't you home yet?" Sonia asked sternly.

"I'm still waiting for my client."

"At this hour? You normally finish up by 6," she nagged.

"Yes, but I told you I'd be late today."

"This late? Ashok! What kind of psychiatrist stays open at this hour?"

"Sonia, I have to go, I can't have this discussion now."

His frustration began to take over.

"Ashok, I'm worried about Jai. He hasn't been sleeping. His teacher called and said he falls asleep in class. His school work is suffering, and he just looks haggard. I think we need to see a pediatrician."

"Sonia, please, can we talk about this when I get home?"

"Ashok, this is your son, for God's sake!" she shrieked.

"Fine!" Ashok screamed back, "I'll set up an appointment. Ok?"

"Fine! Your dinner is in the fridge."

She slammed the phone down.

Ashok replaced the receiver and began to pace around his office, trying to get his wife's irritatingly nagging voice out of his head. Eight years ago, it was the sweetest sound he ever heard uttered. Today, when he hears her call his name, he can feel his blood pressure rising.

He once again began to wonder why the property billionaire and philanthropist, Rakesh Mehta, sought out his services. And, why would he have requested such a peculiar hour? Ashok was aware of his capabilities, and knew he wasn't considered a renowned psychiatrist. Yet, this pillar of society wanted to speak with him and only him. This was too good of an opportunity to pass up!

"Dr. Virani, your client has arrived," buzzed Monica.

Reaching over the desk, he pushed the button on the phone and instructed his secretary to let in the most prominent client he'd ever had (and possibly ever would have). Standing upright, he began to straighten his tie. For the first time since he had opened his practice, his hands were clammy, and he did his best to hide his anxiety.

Rakesh Mehta walked in and immediately, his presence could be felt. A tall, broad man, with thick hair, his aura and charismatic smile could capture a room. Ashok noticed that Mehta was much bigger in person than the papers and magazines suggested.

"Dr. Virani, thank you for seeing me at this hour," Mehta strode forward with his hand outstretched.

"Oh, it's my pleasure, Mr. Mehta," responded Ashok, as he tried not to wince when his hand became engulfed in Mehta's vice-like grip.

"Please, call me Rakesh."

Rakesh released the doctor's hand, noticing the pained expression sweeping across the doctor's face. "Unfortunately, my schedule is rather hectic. I apologize for the late hours, but this was the earliest we could meet."

They continued the exchange of formalities as they sat down and shared their opinions about the sudden heat wave. Ashok was curious, and while he wanted nothing more than to move onward with the session, he was seasoned enough not to let it show.

"I'm sure you're wondering why I wanted to see you, Dr. Virani," Rakesh asked while unbuttoning his impeccably tailored pinstripe suit.

"It certainly did cross my mind."

"Well, why does anyone want to see a psychiatrist? To hear themselves talk of course!" Rakesh smiled, easing Ashok somewhat.

The irony wasn't lost on Ashok. In this situation, it was he that was supposed to calm the patient. However, Mehta stature was so immense, Ashok couldn't help but feel out of his element.

"Dr. Virani, I am sure you are aware of my public image and standing in society?"

"I am," Ashok nodded, maintaining his poise.

"Then you understand that anything discussed in this session cannot leave this office, no matter what the circumstance might be?"

"I'm surprised you're asking, Mr. Mehta"

"Please, call me Rakesh," he interrupted.

"Rakesh, you must be well aware of the doctor-patient privilege by which we are bound."

"Indeed, I am Dr., but I do need to protect my interests. Certainly, you understand?"

"Of course."

"Then you wouldn't mind signing this confidentiality agreement?" he asked, as he pulled out an envelope.

"Mr. Mehta, I mean Rakesh, I assure you this is not necessary."

"I hate to put you in this position, but this is a necessity for me," his tone quickly became stern.

"Rakesh, I can't sign any documents without my lawyer having a look first."

"Then, I'm sorry, but I cannot continue this session without a signature on these papers."

Mehta stood up and began to place the envelope in his pocket. Ashok twitched and was uncertain about what to do. This was highly irregular. He justified the situation to himself – why would a man of Mehta's prominence want to swindle a mediocre psychiatrist like him?

"Please, Mr. Mehta," he stood, "we're here to help and heal, and if this is what we need to do to guarantee you peace of mind, then so be it."

He reached out for the papers.

"Thank you, Dr. I understand I've put you in an awkward position, but, like I mentioned earlier, it is a necessity for me."

He handed over the envelope.

"I assure you, it's nothing more than regular boilerplate information. To put it bluntly, if any of our session is disclosed to anyone, I can sue you for anything and everything you own."

Ashok's hand paused an inch above the paper, and he looked up, disturbed.

"I'm sure that won't happen…it's not as if you intend to leak any details to the tabloids, do you?" he smiled

Ashok smiled back nervously. He signed and handed the documents to Rakesh, who promptly returned it to the inside pocket of his suit jacket. Ashok sat down, feeling a little rattled but was ready to push forth.

"Shall we begin?"

"Yes, let's. Do you mind if I walk around, Dr.?"

"Well, usually patients find it easier to sit or perhaps lie down."

"Well I prefer to walk while I speak, it helps me communicate more effectively. I hope that's alright?"

"Whatever you're comfortable with, Rakesh."

"Thank you."

Rakesh paced around the small room, absorbing the vast amount of information that surrounded him. He inspected Ashok's degrees on the wall, his books, even the family photographs.

"You have a beautiful family, Dr. Virani. Is that your son?"

"Yes, his name is Jai, he just turned six."

"Adorable."

"Thank you, but you haven't come here to talk about my family, have you?"

"Of course not," he laughed, "I've come to talk to you about mine."

He turned towards Ashok and smiled.

"Do you know anything about my family, Dr.?"

"Well, I know what I've read. You lost your parents at a young age and were raised by your uncle and aunt who dealt in garments. That's pretty much all I know, just what I have picked up here and there in the papers."

Rakesh once again faced the walls, ignoring the fact that Ashok was scribbling away on his note pad.

"Well, allow me to fill in the missing details. Lata, my older sister, was my parents' pride and joy. She was also the closest thing I had to a parent. We weren't from a wealthy home, Dr. Virani, so both my parents worked hard to provide us with a decent life. My mother was a nurse, and my father managed a factory floor. They both worked long hours, well into the night. They left me home alone with my sister on most occasions"

"Dr., it's your son on line one," the intercom buzzed.

"Monica, you know not to disturb me when I'm with a patient."

53

"Yes sir, but your son said it's important."

"Monica, he's six for God's sake! You should……."

"Sir, he's bawling on the phone," she interrupted.

"Dr., please take the call, I'm sure it's important to your son."

"I'm sorry, Rakesh, I won't be a moment."

"Of course."

"Hello? Jai? What's the matter?"

"Papa, it's in my room again and won't leave me alone. It's troubling me," he sobbed.

"What is, beta?"

"The monster, Papa. Papa, please, please come home. Please Papa, please!"

Ashok could barely understand what his son was saying through all the wailing.

"Jai, let me speak to mummy."

"Papa, please! The monster's here! It said it won't leave me! It's sitting on the bed now, Papa! It's coming closer and closer!"

"Jai, beta, calm down. Stop crying. Let me speak with your mummy. Jai? Hello? Jai?"

Realizing his son had hung up, he called his wife's mobile phone.

"Hello?"

"Sonia, can you please check on Jai, he's in hysterics! Please, handle this! I'm in the middle of a session."

"What happened?" Sonia was alarmed.

"Nothing, he's just talking about the monsters again. Please just go upstairs, and get a handle on this!" he hung up, frustrated.

"I'm terribly sorry about that, Rakesh," he said, regaining his composure.

"It's quite alright. Is everything ok?" Mehta asked, sounding genuinely concerned.

"Yes, yes. You know children and their wild imaginations. My son insists there is a monster in his room that has been bothering him for the past few days."

"I think every child has a healthy fear of the monster in their room," he smiled.

Ashok was confused with that response, but paid it no heed. Instead, he picked up his note pad and asked Rakesh to continue.

"As I was saying, my parents worked late into the night, and it was Lata who raised me. I was always asleep by the time my parents got home and only saw them briefly at the breakfast table. Close to my 7th birthday, my father passed away in a fire at the factory. It was a tragic scene, numerous employees died that night. I'm sure you're aware that India isn't well known for its safety standards."

Ashok instinctively wanted to say something but knew better, and allowed Rakesh to continue expressing himself.

"We received some compensation, but it wasn't enough. My mother began working double shifts at the hospital and began to run herself into the ground. I saw her even less. Lata became my mother."

Rakesh stopped walking around and sat down across from Ashok. He took a sip from his water cup and smiled at the doctor.

"I understand you live near the Rajni Estates in Parelle."
"Yes," Ashok was surprised, "Yes I do, but how did you…how did you know?" he stammered.
"It's my business to know, Dr. Virani. Information and knowledge are important commodities. Acquiring it and containing it is what controls the business world."

Ashok sat silently, unsure about how to respond.

"Don't be alarmed Dr. Virani, I own a great deal of property in that area, so I'm bound to know," Rakesh smiled.
"Oh I see, ok," Ashok said, reassured once again.
"Are you aware of how my property empire came to be?"
"Well, I understand you have purchased land and some of your assets are construction companies."
"Yes, well, before all that happened, it was more primitive, if you will. My mother passed away when I was 14. Being aware of our situation and the impact her long hours had taken on her health, my mother had prepared a decent insurance policy in case of her demise. Being the entrepreneur that I am, I took a portion of it and invested. You see, the area

near Rajni Estates, where you live, was very dilapidated during my youth. I hated coming home to such a morose and depressing surrounding. Hiring some of my friends, we began to refurbish homes. It began first with painting and repair, and then turned into brick and mortar work. Some children used to play, I used to work in order to make a living. It helped me deal with the loss of my mother. It also allowed me to stay away from home."

Ashok quickly wrote down in his notepad. *Mehta had a desire to stay away from home*. It wasn't surprising since he had lost both his parents and lived in semi-poverty but still, something about it sounded ominous. Suddenly, he felt his mobile phone vibrate against his waist. Picking it up, he noticed it was a call from home.

"Rakesh, I do apologize, it's my wife."
"Please, by all means," Rakesh insisted.

"Hello?"
"PAPA!" Jai screamed. Ashok wrenched the phone away from his ear, grimacing in pain. The loud blood curdling scream startled Rakesh. "PAPA!!!" he screamed louder and longer.
"Jai? What happened?"
"PAPA, HELP ME!!!" he screamed again, "I'm begging you, HELP ME!"
"Jai, what's the matter? JAI?"

It was no use, the line had gone dead. Immediately, he called the house, and Sonia answered.

"What happened? Jai just called me screaming!"
"I know, I just heard. I'm heading upstairs. Let me see, and I'll call you."

Ashok replaced the phone on to his belt and looked at Rakesh who had a concerned expression on his face.

"Is everything ok? Perhaps we should end the session?"
"No, I'm sure my wife will take care of it. It's ok. Please continue."
"Are you sure?"

"Yes, I'm sure it's nothing. My wife will call momentarily telling me it's ok. Please continue."

Ashok ruffled through his notes and began.

"You mentioned your work allowed you to stay out of your home and gave you an opportunity for a brighter future. What were you running from?"
"It wasn't what I was running from but rather, whom?"
"Excuse me?" Ashok asked
"You see Dr., there is something I haven't mentioned to you about my childhood. It is, in fact, the reason I am here today. It all started near the time my father passed away.
"When I was seven, Lata used to creep into my bed with me."

Pausing briefly, Rakesh unbuttoned his top button and loosened his designer tie. Taking a deep breath, he cleared his throat and continued.

"She threatened that if I told anyone what she was doing, she would kill me. Then again, who could I tell? Even if I wanted to, she was the only parent I had. I both loved and hated her. At first, she convinced me this was how a sister loves her brother, but I knew it was wrong.
"There were times I cried through the whole experience, begging her to stop, but it didn't matter. She used to take me to school and back, made my meals for me, just as a loving parent would. Then at night she had her way with me, in ways I can't even bring myself to remember without becoming nauseated."

Mehta reached for the tumbler of water and took a sip to moisten his parched throat.

"The abuse continued for years. When our mother died, I hoped it would end, but it didn't. Since Lata was my guardian, I couldn't leave her. I had no place to go. So, I began to spend as much time away from home as possible, hoping it would stop. It didn't.
When Lata started having boyfriends, I hoped it would stop. It didn't.
Every night, I feared entering my bedroom. I wanted to sleep, hoping that she wouldn't wake me, but I couldn't even close my eyes

because of the fear, the anticipation. I was haunted every night until my nightmares became my reality, a reality that took place almost every night."

Mehta paused once more and ran his fingers through his thick, grey-stained hair as he leaned back in the chair.

"She said she'd never leave me. That she loved me. That we were meant to be together forever."

They sat silently. Ashok waited for him to continue. Mehta, stone-faced stared into Ashok's eyes.

"When I turned 15, Lata was still abusing me. I knew then it was true, she was honestly never going to stop creeping into my bed. For as long as I could remember, I had lived in fear and cried myself to sleep. She tortured me and found pleasure in doing so.
"I realize if I wanted it to stop, and I had to be the one to stop it."

Sitting back in his chair, Ashok tilted his head ever so slightly and gazed at the ceiling trying to digest everything he was hearing.

"She had a party in our house for her 21st birthday. It was a Saturday. I was put in charge of the bar, so I made sure the alcohol kept flowing throughout the night. More importantly, I made sure Lata's glass was never empty.
"Finally, in the early hours of the morning, the last of her drunken friends left. Lata had passed out on the sofa. I picked her up over my shoulder and brought her into my room and lay her on my bed."

Rakesh leaned forward, placing his elbows on his knees and intertwined his fingers. His voice softened.

"I opened up my cupboard and removed all the clothes. There was a large hole in the back I had dug over the past few days, as I had prepared for my freedom.
I bound and gagged Lata before placing her into the cavity. I lit a large candle, carefully placing it next to her. I wanted her to watch the light die with every second that passed, until she was immersed in absolute darkness. I wanted her to suffer the torment of waiting for the inevitable.

I watched her for a moment in her unconscious state. She seemed so peaceful. After the moment passed, I sealed her in, alive."

Ashok's phone vibrated once more, and he picked it up without hesitating or asking for permission.

"WHAT!?"
"Ashok you need to come home now!"
"Why?"
"It's Jai! Ashok, he won't stop crying. He's so cold. He keeps rocking back and forth shivering and murmuring. He keeps saying, 'help me, help me.' He won't even look at me. He just looks straight ahead and rocks. I slapped him but I can't snap him out of it. I'm really scared. Please come home we need to take him to a doctor. Ashok, please, hurry!"
"I'm coming. Give him half a valium and put him to bed. That should calm him down."

Ashok looked up to find Rakesh standing by the door.

"I'm sorry, Rakesh, it's an emergency. My son needs me."
"I understand, Dr., don't worry about it."
"Perhaps we can reschedule, I'd like to help you."
"Help me?" Rakesh smiled, "I've made peace with my demons Dr., I am here to help you."
"Help me? What do you mean?"

The statement didn't make any sense.

Rakesh was half way out the door, then he paused and turned.

"Dr. Virani," he sighed as his grip on the handle tightened. "You're living in my house." Rakesh turned towards him, "Your son, Jai, he sleeps in my room." He paused, "I'm sorry, Ashok," whispered Rakesh before he gently pulled the door closed behind him.

Overcome by a numbing sensation, Ashok tried desperately to process all that had just transpired. Like a man running against a typhoon, his mind fought to understand and confirm what his gut already knew. Seconds that felt like hours passed, and when he looked back at the door, Rakesh was long gone.

Lunging towards the phone, Ashok's fingers, now trembling with adrenaline, dialed his home. Frustrated by the busy tone, he threw the receiver on to the desk and ran out the door.

"Dr. Virani, what's the...." The secretary tried to ask, only to be ignored by the sprinting psychiatrist.

Jamming the accelerator to the floor, Ashok snaked through the cars that littered the road on this dark night. His mind struggled to remain focused as he replayed the events of the night. The client that was his meal ticket, the savior of his practice, turned out to be anything but. His screaming little boy just needed his father to protect him from his nightmares - they had to be nightmares.

"It's not possible....," he whispered as he ran another red light.

Throwing the car door open before he even came to a complete stop, Ashok left the car running as he ran up the driveway to his house. Beating on the door with his one hand, he furiously rang the doorbell with the other.

"Open the bloody door!" he screamed.

Frustrated, Ashok leaned back and kicked the door open, causing it to swing forward with such force that it rebounded off the inside wall and flew back towards him. In that split second, he saw his wife standing in front of him with tear-stained mascara streaming down the front of her face. Catching the door, he pushed it back and grabbed his wife by her shoulders and asked.

"What happened? Where is Jai?"

Sonia stood still, unresponsive.

"Sonia?" Ashok raised his voice. "SONIA? Where is JAI?"

He shook his wife vigorously, trying to snap her out of her catatonic state to no avail.

"Crap!" he snapped, before side-stepping her and running up the stairs to his son's room. "Jai? JAI?" he yelled as he threw open the bedroom door.

His son's room lay in utter disarray. The blanket, chair and lamp were all on the floor, and the single bed had been moved to an odd angle.

"Jai?" Ashok yearned for a response, a clue, anything as to where his son was hiding.

He flipped the light switch but remained bathed in darkness when it failed. Using the glow from the hallway, Ashok frantically turned the room upside down while screaming for his son. Unsuccessful, he searched the rest of the house, the bathrooms and even searched the kitchen where he noticed his wife, standing silently still, like a broken, vacant, lifeless shell. She just stood there, staring at the front door, immobile and unresponsive.

"Sonia. I need you to tell me where our son is? Please. Snap out of it, and tell me where Jai is?" he pleaded.

The black, salt-stained mascara had turned hard and crusty on her skin. Her pupils, now dilated, stared into nothingness. Ashok noticed she wasn't even blinking. Raising his hand he brought it thundering down and slapped her across the face. The noise echoed through the silence in the house as Ashok waited for a reaction. Moments passed, but Sonia gave no indication she was even alive as her hair fell in tangled clumps, strewn about her face.

"Sonia, WHERE IS OUR SON!" he screamed, sending globules of spit flying in all directions.

Nothing but silence fell upon both of them, and all he could hear was his heavy breathing. His heart pounded viciously, and his body throbbed with each beat. His gut told him where he needed to look but his mind struggled to accept it. Pushing Sonia to the side, Ashok grabbed a flashlight from the chest of drawers at the bottom of the stairs and ran up once more to his son's room.

Pulling open the doors to the cupboard he was greeted by a row of neatly hung clothes, perfectly aligned as always. Grabbing them with both hands, Ashok pulled them off the rail, sending hangers flying into the air.

He shined the light on the back wall and noticed the amateur workmanship. Ashok's chest heaved heavily as unfathomable fears began to creep into his soul. His scientific mind was bending to the illogical will of the paranormal.

"It's not possible!" he whispered.

Placing the flashlight on the bedside table, he aimed the beam towards the back wall before picking up the standing lamp. As he gauged the weight of the heavy-based fixture, his eyes remained fixed on the bricks in front of him. Amidst the dark stillness, Mehta's last words echoed in his mind.

"Your son…sleeps in my room."

Letting out a scream, Ashok lifted the lamp over his shoulder and ran to the wall. Chips of brick and mortar ricocheted off the sides of the cupboard as the psychiatrist violently bashed the base into the back of the structure. Cracks began to form on the bleak, grey surface and with each blow, his scientific mind came to terms with what he once perceived as illogical.

"JAI!" He screamed, praying to hear his son's angelic voice respond. "JAI!!!"

Painful tears streaked down his dirt-stained cheeks. Finally, a solitary brick flew back and after a momentary pause, he jumped forward and tried to look through.
Darkness was all he could see.

"Jai? Beta? Can you hear me? Speak to Papa, beta? Don't worry," he gulped, "Papa will get you out."

Fueled by fear and adrenaline, his swings got mightier as the wall started to give way to his will and might.

"Don't worry, beta, Papa's coming!" Ashok repeated reassuringly. "Papa's here. Almost there, Jai, almost there."

Knocking through a few more bricks, Ashok dropped the lamp and started to pull at the remaining structure with his torn, bloodied hands.

Finally, he stuck his head through the void into the darkness on the other side.

"Jai?' Are you there, beta?"

Stepping back, he grabbed the flashlight and leapt back through the cavity, into the darkness, and shone the light around. The circular beam travelled along the walls of the long, narrow channel as Ashok continued to walk forward, detecting a blinding stench. Covering his nose with his dirt-covered shirt, he moved on.

"Jai? Jai? It's Papa. Jai?" Ashok called out.

The secret passageway ran the length of the house and even with the flashlight, Ashok struggled to see clearly. Suddenly, catching his foot on a protrusion in the floor, Ashok tripped and fell forward onto the ground. Moaning in agony, he reached out to the flicking beam of light and brought the flashlight to himself. As he got up on one knee, he slapped the base of the light until the beam remained steady. Covering his nose again, he turned the flashlight to the floor and noticed a large black clump that had caused him to lose his footing.

Lifting his head, he turned the beam, and his gaze followed. As he gasped, the air escaped his lungs, and his body suddenly turned cold. There she lay, balled up in a semi-fetal position, nothing but bones and rags covering her. Realizing he was no longer breathing, Ashok inhaled deeply, only to cough brutally as the dust contaminated his lungs. Returning the light to the corpse, he followed the torso and uncovered the rag around her mouth, firmly attached, just as Rakesh had described. The beam continued down the limbs and Ashok noticed the worn ropes hanging off her hands. As he inspected the body, the light began to flicker once again. Ashok caught a glimpse of another shape in her arms, and anxiously turned the light before it went out completely. Recognizing the vibrant colored garment, Ashok jumped forward.

"Jai? Jai?" He shook his son by the shoulder before picking him up and pulling him to his chest. "Jai, it's Papa. I'm here, Jai. Wake up."

Ashok patted his son on the back as Jai's limp head rested on his father shoulder. Concerned by the lack of response by his son, Ashok felt for the light on the gritty ground. Struggling, he laid his son on the floor and crawled on all fours in search of the comforting luminous glow. Finding it had rolled behind him, Ashok picked it up and smacked it to life.

"Jai," he called out as he turned and shone the light on his son.

Lata's dead arms were once again draped over his son as she held him close to her bosom. Scrambling towards his son the flashlight fell out of his hands, and the beam landed on Jai's face.

"JAI!!!!"Ashok shrieked as he fell backwards and continued to kick away from this thing that used to be his flesh and blood.

Jai's face had withered and aged as though he had been there for decades. His once innocent eyes were now wide open and fear-stricken. Sunken cheeks revealed his cheek bones, and his skin was pale and rotting. The light from the torch flickered on Jai's lifeless face before dying out again.

*   *   *

The ambulance ushered the catatonic Sonia away while the police tried to question Ashok with little success. The burly cop looked at his partner before calling out to the paramedics waiting in the second ambulance.

"Take him to the hospital, we'll have to question him there. We aren't going to get anything from him here."

Wrapping him in a blanket, the paramedics helped Ashok up and guided him to the white van with the flashing lights at the end of the drive. Turning his head ever so slightly, Ashok peered over his shoulder and saw the yellow tape that had barricaded his house. He noticed the front door was still ajar but couldn't muster the strength to say anything.

The two men in bright yellow jackets helped Ashok up the steps and placed him on the stretcher before shutting the van doors. As they strapped him in, Ashok sat up and looked through the glass panes at his home once more. The van wobbled gently as it maneuvered its way over the gravel path and around the remainder of the driveway out of the gates. Overhanging trees and unkempt bushes started to obstruct Ashok's view as the distance between him and the house grew. A sudden gust of wind caused the van to sway and startled everyone in the vehicle except Ashok.

"PAPA!!!!! PAPA!!!!!" The wind carried his son's loud cries.

Suddenly, the partly open door slammed ferociously shut, from the inside. Ashok watched and remained silent as the van left the premises.

In the Hindi language, "Saya" means both "Shadow" or "Spirit."

THE BOYFRIEND

BY

ANNASTAYSIA SAVAGE

"Mom, thanks again for letting me move back in with you. I promise I won't be a burden. It's only until I find a job and get my feet on the ground … and then I'm outta here, promise," Nadia said to me as she held her hand up like she was taking an oath. Her smile beaming, she turned to go upstairs to her room.

I smiled to myself and picked at the hangnail I just couldn't stop messing with. Of course, I'd help her out. She's my daughter, all I had left from my wrecked marriage. And she had just graduated from college and really, had nowhere to go – yet. She was at the top of her class, so the job offers were bound to come rolling in sooner or later. I was hoping it was later, rather than sooner, as I could really use her company right now. I wouldn't dare tell her that though. I didn't want her to think I was needy or trying to smother her. I looked up at Nadia again, as the hangnail began to bleed and put my finger in my mouth.

Even though she's my daughter, and I'm very biased, she really is one of the most beautiful girls I have ever seen. At 23, she has her whole life ahead of her, and I admire that. I watched her as she jogged up the stairs, her ponytail swishing back and forth, and I secretly hoped she would stay forever. With the noises I had heard last night still fresh in my mind, I didn't want to be alone in this big, old house anymore. Especially now, since the sounds have become a sort of macabre soundtrack, like eerie backdrop music, for daily life in this aged Victorian farmhouse.

Nadia stopped in the middle of the staircase and turned to look at me, a questioning expression on her face. Fear washed over my body like a prickly shower. *Oh God, did she hear them, too? What do I say to her?* The scraping noises coming from the attic moved to the forefront of my consciousness. Since all of these strange sounds had become normal background noise I no longer really heard, like when the furnace kicks on or when the refrigerator hums. I panicked, remembering how scared I was when I first heard them, and felt for my little girl now that she might experience them as well.

"What honey? Did you hear that too?" I asked quickly, almost too abruptly, and I knew my eyes were as wide saucers.

With her expression turning even more enigmatic, Nadia wrinkled up her face and answered, "No, I didn't hear anything Mom." She smiled at me and shook her head. "I was just going to say that J.P. is coming over for a while, after he gets off work. We're just gonna watch a movie and order some pizza, his treat, you can join us if you like...or...I could tell him some other time if you don't feel up for having anyone over. It's your house. "

She shrugged and looked down with her lips in a pout, as if in defeat. My daughter always did know how to work me. Pulling on my heartstrings, she could play me like a fine-tuned violin.

Sighing long and bittersweet I answered her, "Sure sweetie that sounds good, I could use the company. Just because you live with *Mom* again doesn't mean you can't have a life."

I guess I'd have to get used to her not being a child anymore, though, I didn't have to like it.

"Thanks Mom, I love you."

She turned and ran the rest of the way up the steps to her room. As she disappeared around the corner, I got a glimpse of a dark shape going the opposite direction. Must be her shadow I told myself, but I had a feeling that wasn't it. Forgetting all about my stupid hangnail, I went into the parlor to regroup for a minute. I literally hadn't slept in days, and I was beginning to feel the repercussions. I had been telling myself the noises I was hearing, and now the shadows I was seeing, were the end result from lack of sleep. But I was still unconvinced. With unsteady legs I sat down on the overstuffed ottoman to try and rationalize what was happening to me.

Was I going crazy? I know I heard those noises. I've been hearing them all week. Now, I'm seeing things? Obviously Nadia didn't hear or see anything, but what does that mean? It's more than just this old house settling. It's more than just a lack of sleep. I wouldn't have thought so before, but after last night, I know something's going on.

Looking at my arm, I saw that the scratches were still there, fresh, red, and swollen. Little dots of blood had hardened sporadically along the cut-marks. It resembled a Marquis de Sade connect-the-dots game. Shivering, I tried to clear my mind of the bad feeling I was suddenly getting. Maybe with Nadia here, things would be different, things would hopefully settle down.

Shutting my eyes to the world around me I took a long, measured, deep breath until I thought my lungs would burst. I exhaled and felt a little of the stress and tension leaving my body. I rolled my head on my neck and shrugged my shoulders. *I could really use a vacation.* I decided to try the ohm technique I had learned when I took that meditation and yoga class at the Y. At the time, I thought it silly and pointless. But now, I was willing to try anything. Clearing my head and relaxing all my muscles, I began.

"Ooooohhhhhhmmmmmmmmmm."

"Oooooooohhhhhhhhmmmmmmmmm."

"Oooooooohhhhhhmmmm."

Low, slow and even, I continued with the universal buzz. I let my hands rest, palm up, on my thighs and kept going. Ridiculous as it may seem, it appeared to be working. *Boy, those Yogis really know their stuff.*

I was getting lost in the practice when I felt Nadia's tender touch on my shoulders. She began massaging them, and I sighed. Having her here with me made the future seem brighter. She rubbed gently along the top of my shoulders and up to my lower neck. I felt her thumbs working circles at my occipital base and let my head tilt back into the pressure she was exerting. *I'm really gonna like having her around.*

Her loving hands slid back down, skimming my collarbone, as she began working out the kinks in my upper arms. I allowed myself to be lost in the moment. I felt myself drifting. I was moving further and further away from all my present troubles and enjoying the thought of time spent with my little girl. I let her rub my worries away, and I was so relaxed when she stopped that I could have fallen asleep right then and there. Who knows, I may have.

"Thanks, sweetie," I said as I turned to look at her. But she was gone. Just like that – gone. Almost as soon as I realized how quickly she could disappear, I heard her upstairs giggling, apparently on the phone. Cold prickles of fear washed over me. *How could she have been down here, massaging me, and then made it back upstairs so quickly? And made a phone call. Or did the phone ring and she answered it? Did I fall asleep sitting up? It is possible; I have never felt so tired in all my life. And I was so relaxed…*

I could hear the distant approach of the garbage collection truck. The birds were singing outside. Nadia was upstairs in her bedroom, talking on the phone and all seemed so … normal. But I knew better. Something was going on. I found it really hard to believe everything that had been occurring was from lack of sleep. Either I was losing my mind or … I couldn't yet face the other possibilities.

I tried, once again, to relax and found some consolation in focusing on the more pleasant sounds of life around me.

A low, slow scratching sound began to come from the dining room, shattering my moment's peace and silence from the clamor my house had become. *It's never left the attic before.* Every hair on my body rose to attention as I stood, hesitantly, to go investigate. I had to do this, if only for my own sanity.

As I walked down the hallway, I tried to convince myself it was just the cat playing around in the paint trays left from today's latest project. Knowing the week's events, I had a sinking feeling it was more than that. The floor boards creaked, and I almost laughed. I remembered when I was a child and that used to be the most frightening sound to me as I lay awake in my bed at night.

Things certainly change when you're an adult. The things that scare you when you're supposedly grown up are more sinister and … real.

I approached the room with trepidation, my stomach began to feel nauseated, and a shiver ran down my rigid spine. Cold sweat broke out all over my body, seemingly drenching my clothes, as I held the wall to steady myself. A smell of rotten, putrid, decaying flesh permeated the area, knocking me to the floor. My head felt dizzy, and I put my hand over my mouth to quell the sudden urge to heave my guts up.

I felt a heavy hand, a man's hand, on my shoulder. Paralyzed with fear, this hand slowly slid down my arm and came to rest on my thigh. I felt the fingers caress my skin and saw goose bumps form where the invisible touch passed. Shivering violently, I began to wonder how long it took to suffocate as I realized I had stopped breathing.

With now measured, but heavy breaths, I watched the events unfold. My skirt began to slide up my leg, exposing more flesh, and I could see finger rakes appearing where the unseen hand had just been. As this indiscernible "thing" moved further up my thigh, I felt my heart pounding, threatening to release itself from my chest. I grabbed at my skirt and yanked it back down. The scraping noises grew louder.

I could still feel whatever it was sliding eerily up and over my hips, to my waist, on its way to my stomach. The scraping sounds became faster, more persistent. My invisible molester had reached my chest and as the buttons to my blouse came undone, the scream I had been stifling burst out of my clenched mouth. The scratching reached a crescendo and then the pocket doors to the dining room slid shut with such force - it made my heart feel like it was going to explode out of my heaving chest. All went silent.

"Mom, are you okay, what happened?" Nadia asked as she ran down the hallway to my side with concern in her eyes. I hadn't even heard her coming. And the house, it seemed so … silent.

"Yes, I, uh…" I looked around. The smell was gone, the scratching had stopped, and everything seemed, well, normal. "Yes, I'm okay, I'm just so tired."

I tried to sound convincing, but I wasn't sure that Nadia believed me. From the look on her face, she seemed not only worried, but seriously afraid. I smoothed my skirt down and straightened my sweaty hair. Then, as I gazed into my daughter's eyes, I saw her fear.

"What is it, Nadia?" I had maybe a little too much aggravation in my voice as I said this, but I was teetering on the brink.

"I'm just worried about you. I thought I heard you scream, and then you slammed those old doors so loud it made me jump. I thought something happened. You've been working so hard on fixing up the house that you haven't really been taking care of yourself. I mean, for Pete's sake, you tore down an entire wall by yourself. Not to mention, I know you, you probably haven't slept in days."

"Seriously, its okay, I'm okay. I'm just so tired from all this remodeling, and I couldn't sleep last night so I kept working. You're right though; I've been pushing myself too hard, but without your father around…" I couldn't finish the sentence.

I was still so angry at Jake for leaving. And he had the nerve to leave before we had finished the restorations. Now, if there were any chance of my selling this money pit, I had to go it alone. Nadia looked at me with pity in her eyes. She was just as angry at her father, but I think she understood the divorce had been long coming.

"Why don't you go watch TV and wait for, what's his name, J.P.? I'm gonna wash the dishes from last night and then go to bed. Tell J.P. that I said thanks for the offer, but I'll have to take a rain check. I really am so tired."

I smiled the best I could muster under the circumstances and patted her hand.

Nadia helped me up, gave me a hug and looked at me with curious eyes.

"I just don't feel like you're telling me the whole truth," she said, eyeing me suspiciously. "I don't know what I would do if anything happened to you."

"I'm fine, just very, very tired," I replied. She seemed somewhat more convinced as I forced a smile. Nadia sighed, appearing to accept my answer and then smiled back.

I hugged her again, assuring her I was okay.

She went to the living room while I, somewhat shakily, made my way to the kitchen. I stood at the sink, lost in my thoughts and wondered if I should call a shrink. He could at least give me some valium or something to calm my nerves. Screw the shrink, I should call a priest. I know what I heard. And that smell, I have never smelled anything so awful. It smelled worse than the time, at our former house, when our dog Briar had dug up Nadia's dead cat, about two weeks after it died.

I have got to get a grip on myself. I looked once again at the scratches on my arm then I felt an odd burning sensation on my stomach. Lifting up my shirt to find the source, I was instantly sick. The contents of my stomach emptied into the sink.

My head swam with possibilities. Was I somehow doing this to myself? I wiped my mouth with the back of my hand and looked again. Four bloody scratches traveled across my stomach and then up, diagonally, disappearing under my bra. They burned, like a cat scratch, and cold fear raced through my veins as I tried to imagine who, or more aptly, what had made them.

It must have happened when I slid down the wall, I must have scratched myself on the exposed brick. I was pretty faint. I told myself these things, though somehow, I knew I was lying to appease my troubled mind.

I had felt a hand caressing me, touching me, like my husband used to do. *I know what I felt, I know what I saw, I know what I heard, and I know what I smelled.* A sudden realization came to me that I didn't quite want to face. I had a dream last night. I dreamt of my husband, again, and we were in love, like when we were young.

He made love to me with such rough passion I had woken with a start. Was it really a dream? Is that how the scratches on my arm got there? With my breathing coming in short gasps, I needed to calm down or I was going to have a massive coronary. I reached for the bottle of prescription sleeping pills my friend Dana had given me and then thought against it. As much as I'd like to, I couldn't go doping myself up when all of this is going on. I needed my head as clear as it could be, under the circumstances.

I decided to lose myself in last night's dinner mess while trying to think of my options. Rinsing out my vomit and then filling the sink with hot soapy water, I began some serious reasoning.

A: I was experiencing something paranormal, something otherworldly, and it was not a nice entity.

B: I was imagining things (I quickly checked the scratches, nope, still there, I was not imagining things.)

Or C: I was just plain losing my mind.

Option C was the most logical thought. If it were option A, option C would soon follow anyway, so let's just skip the middleman.

As Nadia sat on the couch waiting for J.P. to get here, I semi-watched her through the archway and from across two rooms from my vantage point washing dishes. Opening up the floor plan really made this place feel better, at first. Nadia thought so, too. It was good to have her back. It was a nice distraction from my current emotional train wreck, and we could spend time together.

We have a chance now to become the kind of friends that mothers and daughters usually are. We'll get out tomorrow, go shopping and have lunch. I smiled to myself and went to get some S.O.S pads out of the pantry.

As I searched the cabinet door, once again the icy fingers of fear gripped me. The S.O.S pads weren't where I put them. I always set them on the third shelf with the rest of the cleaning supplies. *I know I put them there, I just purchased them this morning, and they were right there.*

As I rummaged around, I felt that familiar panic of possible dementia set in as I searched frantically to find them. Suddenly, there they were, practically right in front of my eyes. I laughed to myself. *Here I am, becoming irrationally upset over misplaced S.O.S. pads; I really gotta get some sleep.*

As I went to reach for them, I felt something wet and hot, sliding down my neck. With a loud SLAP, I smacked my hand on my neck like I was swatting a mosquito the size of Texas. There was nothing there. I checked my hand, just in case. Nothing. Then I felt it again. This time it was slow and deliberate, it and traveled across my collarbone.

I ripped open my shirt to find the nasty little culprit. I saw nothing but a glistening trail that whatever it was left in its wake. *I am losing my mind.* I wiped the snail-like goo from my body and looked at it on my shaking hand. Slowly, it began to dissipate until there was nothing left but the horrible feeling of being violated yet again, as well as the feeling of insanity setting in. I took a deep breath, forgetting about the S.O.S. pads. My only thoughts were that I needed to get out of there as fast as I could.

Suddenly, the hot, wet feeling was on my ankle. Looking down, of course I saw nothing, which made me laugh. *Going insane can make you find humor in the strangest things.* It began to move up my calf, little by little, until it came to rest on the back of my knee. Then, I recognized the feeling. It was the same as when my husband used to run his tongue along my ear.

I shuddered. The movement began again. I was paralyzed with fear and perhaps, maybe this time, a little curious. It ran up my thigh and then jumped to my neck. It paused, as did my breathing, and I know I felt breath. Hot, heavy breath on the pulse of my jugular. Then the tongue began to move again, up to my earlobe.

THUMP!

I nearly jumped out of my skin as I threw myself against the pantry wall. The sweat that had beaded on my brow and upper lip trickled down and hit my blouse leaving dark, tiny little circles where it soaked into the fabric. I looked down and saw the S.O.S. pads lying on the floor next to the clothes soap. Then I glanced up to the shelf where they had just been.

Fester, our calico, was peeking his head out from behind an extra large box of dryer sheets to peer at me with his green oval eyes. Damn cat!

He must have knocked them to the ground.   Then an ill, sickening feeling washed through me. Was it the cat that was licking me? No, couldn't be, that doesn't make sense. Did I enjoy it? NO! Definitely NOT! *I really am losing my mind.*

Pulling them from behind the box of laundry soap, I shook my head, rubbed my tired eyes and took them back to the sink with me. It must be because I'm so tired, coupled with the stress of rehabbing this house ... and my divorce. I'm lonely. And miss the companionship of my husband; Lord knows I don't miss his constant arguing, though. And when was the last time I got laid? Yeah, that must be it. I'm just so freakin' tired I'm having waking sexual dreams.   Who says paint fumes can't get you high?

I laughed at myself, to myself, for a second time.   I shook my head as if the action would rid me of terrible thoughts. Out of the corner of my eye, once again, I saw a dark shape or form cross into the dining room. Not wanting another episode so soon, I let this event go. I had to.   It was probably the cat again, plus, I didn't think my heart could handle another run in with whatever was disturbing the peace here.

My mind is playing tricks on me because of all that's happened tonight. Lack of sleep can do strange things to a person.   A loud meow from the cat snapped me back to reality, even though it caused me to jump yet again.

I reached to shut the water off. *How long had I been standing there*? The bubbles were almost to the point of overflowing, and it seemed to me that only a mere second ago, I had begun filling the sink. *I've got to get a grip.* I grabbed a pan from the water and set to work, determined to pull it together.

"SHIT!"

My hangnail burned when it hit the water, and I could have cried on the spot. Exhaustion was taking its toll on me. To get emotional over a little hangnail was not a part of my demeanor. It was finally becoming apparent – the effects of fatigue were taking their toll. All of these things, all of the noises and odd occurrences were because I was so bloody tired. I promised myself a long, hot bath and bed as soon as the dishes were finished. *Things will be better in the morning after a good night's sleep.*

Scrubbing last night's lasagna from its dish, I looked up to see Nadia sitting on the couch with a very cute young man. I smiled. J.P. must have gotten here while I was having another "occurrence" in the pantry or while I had zoned out in front of the sink.   He looked just her type.

He seemed tall and lanky, most likely close to six foot five. He was a good looking kid with shoulder length dark hair, almost black. He was dressed in a black suit (probably his work clothes) and didn't seem to be able to take his eyes off of her, as if he were hypnotized. I always said my daughter had exceptional beauty.

I smiled to myself remembering young love and the rush of feelings it brought. I looked up again from the soapy water, and this time his arm was draped around her. He still was looking at her, though Nadia seemed much more interested in the television show. That's just like her, I thought, playing hard to get. *Yeah girl, make him work*! I smiled to myself, glad for the distraction, rinsed the spatula, and put it in the drainer.

Still holding on to the brief moment of happiness that watching my daughter and her boyfriend brought, I glanced up again to witness once more, the endearing scene. J.P. was closer now, and I saw him kiss her cheek. I wondered how long she had been with him. I didn't think it could be very long, she had only told me of him tonight.

A small amount of sadness crept over me realizing that she wasn't my baby girl anymore. She didn't have to *report* to me. And for all I know, she could have told me, but I've been so wrapped up in the remodeling and strange events that have been unfolding here, maybe I just didn't hear her.

I stopped what I was doing at the realization that for the first time in what seemed like ages, the house was quiet. All I could hear was the distant sound of the television. My eyelids felt so heavy, and my body was following suit. *Stay focused, finish the dishes and then bed...*

I looked up at Nadia and J.P. again. I watched motionless as his tongue was in her ear and his hand was sliding up inside her blouse. My first reaction was *not my little girl*! Then, as I gripped the sink's edge I reminded myself that she was a grown woman, even if a young one. I had to handle this with diplomacy, especially if I wanted our relationship to grow and have her stick around for a while. I have to remember she's grown up now with...

RAP! RAP! RAP!

I jumped; the dish towel dropped from my shoulder, and I had to stifle a scream. My God, one loud knock from the pizza delivery guy and I'm about ready to jump out of my skin. Or was it the house? No, it had to be the door. As soon as the remodeling is over, I'm going to take a little vacation. All this madness going on here is really getting to me.

"I got it Mom!" Nadia yelled, and I heard her padding across the floor to the front entryway. I sighed with relief that this noise was real. I also felt better knowing that it had caused enough of a disruption that the boy's hand was not traveling up my daughter's blouse anymore.

I looked at my own shaking hands, felt my breath coming in quick gasps and realized I was coming unglued. Never again will I let myself go so long without proper sleep. Or let myself paint without a mask on and the windows open. I laughed. *I could be a case study in sleep deprivation or the effects of paint fumes. I should call the local university and see if they're doing any studies.*

Stooping down to retrieve my dish towel, I hit my head on the corner of the sink. I instantly became so angry that I punched the bottom cabinet in front of me, causing little blood droplets to appear on my knuckles. *This will never do.*

Trying to calm myself so I didn't have an aneurysm, I smoothed my hair and stood up. I put my bloodied knuckles into my mouth and then adjusted my flustered self for the millionth time today. *This is getting old real fast.* I heard Nadia coming towards the kitchen and tried to get a hold on my breathing. I picked up a glass and pretended to be busy at work, concentrating on invisible stains instead of invisible hands. All I needed was for her to think I've totally lost it. *Can your daughter have you committed?*

"Mom, this is J.P."

Putting on my widest smile, trying not to think of this boy groping my daughter's chest, I rinsed the glass, began to dry it and turned around. I was nonchalant and casual. I was the cool mom who didn't embarrass her kids. *Yeah, that's who I was, I mean am.* Plus, I had changed my mind. It would be good to have some pizza, spend time with my daughter and just forget about all the crap that's been going on around here. Even if things aren't ordinary in my home, I can go through the actions of normalcy and hope that life follows suit. And I can make sure he's not groping my daughter all night.

"Hello, I've been…" and the glass fell from my hand and shattered into a million pieces, just like my sanity, as I completed my turn.

"Jesus, Mom, what's wrong with you today," asked Nadia as she stooped to clean up the mess I had just made.

"I'm sorry, it, it just slipped," I stammered while staring at J.P. I must have looked like the insane person I felt like because the poor kid cleared his throat and backed up a little.

"Hi, Mrs. Thompson, I didn't mean to startle you. I know I knocked pretty loudly, I'm sorry. Didn't Nadia tell you I was coming over?" said the five foot nine blond-haired boy wearing jeans and T-shirt.

The last thing I remember is being put into the ambulance as they injected me with something that made me feel all warm and fuzzy. All the neighbors had started to gather on the sidewalk around my house like people do when there are police cars, ambulances, and rescue workers in their vicinity.

I tried to get one of them to listen to me, but I couldn't speak. I knew I had to tell Nadia something...but what was it? I can't remember. Why did I feel afraid for her to stay alone in that house? Does it even matter? My world faded to black, all I could hear was muffled voices in the darkness.

"This is the second time someone has gone crazy in that house..."

"Nah, man, more like seventh..."

"Remember that lady that clawed her own eyes out..."

"It all started with that family who ran a funeral parlor outta here..."

"Yeah, didn't that kid of theirs rape and cut up all four of his sisters..."

"Yeah, he did, but he also raped and cut up about 20 other women before they caught onto him. They say he used to drag them around the house, positioning them in different places, before he cut them up and disposed of them under the floor boards and in the walls..."

"But nobody knew what was going on, some say the parents covered for him..."

"Yeah, 'til the police got a call about the smell..."

"That's what they say... I heard he disemboweled himself and bled to death upstairs while the detectives spoke with his parents downstairs ..."

"They still ain't found his body..."

"Ain't nobody left alive that really knows what went on in that house…"

PERFECTION

BY

AVERY K. TINGLE

It's another beautiful, rainy day in the city. The skies are gray, and the rolling clouds silently battle each other for territory overhead. There is no thunder to disrupt my thoughts, no lightning to threaten power outages, just gentle oncoming rain, doing its job perfectly: giving life to what deserves it, washing away what does not deserve to exist.

Everything is perfect.

I leave work, as I always do, at exactly five in the evening. I have a mundane position, and I like it that way. The less attention I draw to myself, the better. I've held the same generic occupation for most of my professional life, since I was just out of college. The world had no need of my expertise, as no one really used computers anymore, even back then. It is just as well. Had I gone into my profession of choice, I may very well have been incarcerated – or worse. My job keeps me below everyone's attention, and I that is how I like it. It is perfect.

I observe my co-workers as they scurry about, covering their heads with their briefcases or papers or whatever they have handy in a vain attempt to avoid the rain. They laugh at each other as they scatter from the building and awkwardly race to their cars, trying to escape the so-called "miserable weather."

I've always welcomed these months and detested summer. Blistering heat serves no purpose except to force one to remain indoors. Rain keeps everything comfortably cool and allows the planet to do its work without our interference. Let what grows grow. Let everything else die out. This has always been the way of things.

With my head unshielded and held high, I make my way down the stairs of the towering building and into the parking lot. Some of my colleagues glance at me uncomfortably and look away the second I make eye contact. We've worked in the same office these past 20 years, yet we have never known each other's names. I have no need to know them, nor they any need to know me. My job as human resources assistant allows me access to the more intimate details of their lives, and I wonder how some of them are still breathing, much less gainfully employed. Times like this, I wish it would rain harder, hard enough to take these people away from this world.

I make my way to my vehicle which looks like virtually every other automobile in the parking lot, save for the pristine white exterior. It never gets dirty no matter what it endures. The vehicle is 13 years old and runs like new, thanks to some modifications I've made. Other than my family, no one has ever seen the inside of my car. No one will *ever* see the inside of my car, for if they did, I'm sure they would either try to steal or destroy it. Luckily, I have prepared for both possibilities.

I open the car door and step into the roomy interior. There is no front seat, no backseat, no steering column, no brake, and no gas. There's nothing that indicates my car is even a vehicle. Rather, the interior is lined with jet black leather that forms a perfect square once I am inside and the doors are closed. From the ceiling, a flat screen TV drops, ready to broadcast the top news stories on demand. A surround sound system broadcasts the latest analysis from the world's financial markets. Tinted windows with holographic projections give the impression that one is driving the car as normal, but in truth, no one is driving at all.

I stretch out where the passenger seat should be and command the vehicle's on-board computer to take me home. The vehicle does the rest. A pleasant, automated female voice, programmed to sound like my wife, asks if I wish to view any panorama during the drive home. No. Now, I wish only for silence.

For some reason, my employer saw fit to strap me with an assistant – he gave an assistant to an assistant. The boy means well, fresh out of college and eager to please, but he's sloppy in his endeavors. Believing me to be a coffee drinker, he brought me a cup first thing this morning, and it wound up on my lap after I had told him coffee was not required. I wonder if the boy needs improvement.

The drive home does not take as long as usual. I arrive in 32 minutes instead of 40. I wonder if the new fuel cells I've installed have done something for its performance. Not that I care about such things. I need to keep the vehicle away from mechanics, so I do all of the work myself.

My house is nondescript, just like my job, and my neighborhood, and for that matter, my neighbors themselves. I live in a pleasant, modest little suburb. It doesn't allow much for privacy from the pesky busybodies, but it keeps the degenerates away. Each house looks like the next, and they are built practically atop one another, rounding about the cul-de-sac.

I've made no aesthetic modifications to my home, and it resembles every other home on the block. It is perfect.

The ride, as always, has been refreshing. I step out of my car and arm its automated defenses. Not that I need worry about such things here, but chance favors the prepared mind. If my family is following their schedule, my children should be either assisting my wife with dinner or performing their own duties. I see no need to disturb them, and I'm still enjoying the rain.

I move around the left side of my house to the garden that would surely win awards, if I bothered to enter a contest. The ground is remarkably lush and fertile here — my little secret. It is beautiful to see, with multi-colored azaleas lining the small garden, framing my hydrangeas and camellia bushes.

I left just enough room to walk and tend to the ground, along with a spare patch of fertile dirt behind the arrangement, just in case. Colors range in an orderly fashion from green to bright red to sky blue. I stand in the midst of what I have created and draw in a long, slow breath. The air is never fresher than it is right here. The rain will do these plants some good. It is perfect.

It is 5:45. I must tend to my family.

Victoria, my wife of two decades, is the envy of every other wife on the block. She looks as though she graduated college yesterday, with bright, idealistic blue eyes and curly blond hair that falls to just above her perfectly-shaped butt. Long, supple legs support her athletic frame, and she sports high, plump breasts. The sight of her is arousing to me, even after all these years.

She's hard at work making dinner when I enter our home through the back door. I smell steak, perfectly seasoned with pepper and garlic. A large Caesar salad sits in a bowl at Victoria's left, green beans are slowly boiling on the stove to her right, and she rinses her hands in the sink. I watch her slowly, meticulously wring her hands, gently running her fingers over her arms, her bright red mouth parting as she exhales.

I walk over to her, placing my arms around her, and she purrs, reaching up behind my head to welcome me home.

"I suppose dinner can wait a bit," she whispers. She keeps most of her attention focused on me as she reaches over to the stove, reducing the heat on the green beans.

She leads me to the bedroom. With just enough aggression to make it interesting, she begins removing my clothes. With a hungry look in her eyes, she pulls me on top of her, and we make love as we did in our youth. It is passionate, torrid, and exhilarating. I am not as young as I once was, so my energy quickly expires.

My wife is an understanding woman. She doesn't mind in the least. She gives me a pleasant smile as I change into a sweater and slacks. These are comfortable clothes worn only around the house. She gingerly replaces her outfit and winks at me knowingly before exiting the bedroom. I smile. Everything is perfect.

Minutes later, Victoria calls us for dinner. I am the first to arrive, as always. She sets the table perfectly, placing the platter with evenly sliced strips of steak in the center, surrounding it with the bowls of Caesar salad and green beans.

Our children enter in an orderly fashion. Alexander, our oldest, is a tall, muscular boy of 17 with well-kept brown hair and intelligent eyes. His sister, Julie, is 10 minutes younger than he and is gifted with her mother's beauty. Bright yellow hair that is neatly kept at her shoulders and bright green eyes are her best features.

Christopher is only 10 years old, and he, while precocious and headstrong, is still a handsome boy with a perfect round head, freckles he has yet to outgrow, and inquisitive, dark brown eyes. They all sit. I begin to dish up first, passing the steak to Alexander, who always begins the dinner conversation.

"Alexander," I begin, "How was your day today?"

"It went quite well, thank you for asking," the young man replies. "Coach Myers was so impressed with my tryout that he made me a starter."

"Alexander, that is excellent," Victoria beams. I'm not as impressed, but I let mother and son have their moment. "What position?"

"Quarterback, Mommy," Alexander answers. "Apparently, Coach Myers hadn't encountered anyone who could accurately throw a football while running before." My son turns to me. "Now, Daddy, I don't want you to worry. I'm not going to become so engrossed in athletics that my studies will be neglected."

I smile involuntarily. Alexander is such a good boy.

"In that case, I hope you have a marvelous…season, is it called?"

I regret that I'm not more informed on my children's interests. I was never an athletic child, and as I grew into adulthood, I never had a use for sports. Alexander was born with his mother's drive and passion for physical competition.

"Thank you, Daddy," Alexander acknowledges me with a smile. "And, I understand if you don't want to attend any of my games. I know football was never of any interest to you."

"Thank you, Alexander. You're always so considerate."

It dawns on me that my son might be injured playing this barbaric, pointless sport, and that could never be allowed to happen. I would have to keep an eye on him. But now that Alexander had had his turn, it was time to move onto my other children.

"Julie?" I turn my attention to my middle child and only daughter. "Share your day with us, please?"

Julie nods her head at me, and her bright, beautiful, hazel eyes sparkle as she neatly chews and swallows her green beans. She is careful to be sure no food remains in her mouth as she begins to speak, and that causes me to smile. She is so well behaved.

"Daddy, I auditioned for the play just like you suggested…" Her voice saddens as it trails off, and she begins to move her food around aimlessly with her fork. I sit — we all sit — with bated breath.

"And…?" I finally ask, trying not to show how much I am anticipating an answer.

She looks up, smiling and laughing, "Mrs. Cavanaugh cast me as Juliet! She gave me the lead role!"

All at once, we chuckle and exhale. Victoria laughs, a light, flighty, innocent laugh, and I find myself falling in love with her all over again.

"That's *excellent*, Julie!" I exclaim. "How about you and I go to the library after dinner and pick up the original play? This way, you can study it and truly grasp Juliet's tragedy."

"Oh, thank you, Daddy!" Julie beams, "I was afraid to ask because I thought you'd be too busy! Thank you!"

"I'm never too busy for my children," I reply, feeling paternal pride at their successes.

There is still one more, and he seems withdrawn.

"Chris?"

My youngest son jumps when I say his name. I only now realize that he hasn't touched his food, and he seems pale. His eyes are wide as he looks at me.

"Y-yes, Dad?"

"Chris," I remind him gently, "How many times do I have to say it? Call me *Daddy,* son."

Chris quickly nods.

"O-okay, *Daddy.*" He emphasizes the word.

"There, that's better. Now, would you like to share your day with us?"

Chris' eyes dart to his waiting siblings and mother, who patiently sit, staring.

"Um, nothing special happened," he says quickly.

I wait, but he says nothing further. Strange, he never stuttered before. Almost like… No. I mustn't think back.

"Nothing?" I finally inquire. "Nothing at all?"

"Nope. It was just another day at school, Daddy. But I am really, *really* looking forward to going tomorrow, okay?"

Julie laughs and pats her little brother on the back.

"You are such an ambitious boy, Chris."

"I was the same way when I was his age, wasn't I, Daddy?"

Alexander looks at me as he asks his question.

I nod, smiling broadly.

"Absolutely, Alexander, and look where it's taken you. Chris, you're a good boy for wanting to become educated. You'll go far in life, I promise."

I can't tell if Chris is breathing. He hasn't blinked in forty-five seconds. I believe he's sweating. Is he coming down with something? The stammer is new; he may need improvement. He nods quickly, *too* quickly, recoiling under his sister's touch.

"T-thank you, Daddy."

I motion to my beautiful family, "Now, let's enjoy this meal your mother was kind enough to cook."

"Aren't you forgetting someone, Daddy?" Julie asks me.

"Oh! Victoria!" I exclaim, "I'm so sorry! How was your day, sweetheart?"

Victoria looks at me as though she's surprised I called her name. She holds up a finger, laughing as she swallows her food.

"Oh, you needn't worry about me. I love hearing how our children are progressing. Especially little Chris."

She reaches over to rub his head. He flinches at her touch. I wonder about Chris.

"Well, my day was…" She trails off, playing with her salad as she ponders the right words. "…eventful, I guess you could say. I was out doing the shopping when a very strange man approached me."

"Strange? How so?" I inquire.

"Well, he was certain that he knew me, although I was more than certain I had never heard of him."

That's not terribly unusual.

"Everyone makes mistakes, honey. Pay it no mind."

"Oh, I didn't, dear. It's just that he was so certain! He was even mentioning things that, um…" She uncomfortably glances at the children and giggles nervously. "Well, things I can't repeat in front of our children."

That is *very* unusual.

"Please, dear, keep going."

"Well, his name was Thomas, and he approached me as though we were old friends. He seemed like a nice enough gentleman, but I am a happily married woman, and there are just certain ways men are not to speak to or touch married women."

I make a mental note of the name Thomas. Victoria continues.

"When I put him in his place, he seemed apologetic, but he began to recall times when he and I, apparently, used to do very interesting things! Honey, I know my memory is a little spotty at times, but please tell me, were we ever separated?"

"No."

"Wow, then he was making up some very lurid stories about him and me sneaking off together and even making plans to be together! He said it all stopped after I came home two years ago, but what an imagination the man had!"

I have a hard time looking at my food, my children, anything. I have a hard time controlling this rage that came from nowhere, having known so little of Victoria's private life. I had known there were problems, but this…this was beyond redemption.

"This man…Thomas…" I mask the anger in my voice, "Did he say where he lived? Where he was staying?"

"You know," Victoria went on as if just then remembering some detail of the conversation with Thomas, "He did, in fact, leave me a business card. He told me to call him if I ever needed anything. You know, it was very odd, but towards the end of the conversation, it was almost as though he were afraid for me!" She laughs out loud, "As if I could be in any danger!"

My family joins in her laughter and look for me to join in. I smile, which reassures them. Inside, I'm seething. How could I have known so little of what went on in my own house?

I am calmed down by a flashing reminder as to why I began my work two years ago. Since then, my household had been running perfectly. That was all that mattered. Still, there was this to attend to.

"Victoria, your honesty is a shining example for our children. Would you please pass me that business card?"

"Dad, what're you gonna do?" Chris blurts out the question.

It takes me a second to compose myself before replying, and I try not to let my glower burn into Chris.

"*Daddy* is going to call the man and talk to him, that's all. Mommy is right. Men should never speak to married women in a certain way, and Daddy is just going to remind him of that."

Chris says nothing. Alexander and Julie nod in admiration of me, as they should.

I look back to Victoria, who has gone back to her meal. "Victoria?"

I extend my hand, "The card, please?"

"Oh!" Victoria says with a start, giggling and rising. She fishes the small business card out of her pocket and passes it to Julie, who passes it to Alexander, who passes it to me. I notice for the first time that Chris has not stopped staring at me, and his eyes are accusing.

I don't address him. Instead, I look at the business card. It belongs to one Thomas Moyer, who, regrettably, lives in the city. The card states his business as a private investigator, and he works out of his home, which is in one of the more run-down areas in the city. I wonder what Victoria may have ever seen in this filth, but it's in the past now, no need to dwell on it.

I look around the table to my children, smiling. Only Chris does not return the gesture. I extend my hands to all of them, maintaining the façade of perfection.

"Come now. Let's not let all of this wonderful food your mother made go to waste! Your mother had a brief episode at the grocery store by what was clearly a lonely, desperate man hoping for some attention from a beautiful woman. We will not dwell on it any longer. Let's eat!"

"Especially," Victoria finishes, "because it was a G-rated episode."

We all chuckle briefly, and I cut into my steak. One bite reveals a fatal error; the meat is too tender, too chewy, and I feel blood ooze between my teeth.

I retch, spitting the rare meat back onto my plate.

"Oh, dear!" Victoria exclaims, rising suddenly. "I'm so sorry! I thought you said you wanted your meat medium rare!"

"Medium *well*, Victoria," I correct her, trying to keep my anger from erupting. No matter how many times we go through this, she just can't seem to get it right. "Sit down. We'll address it later."

"Dad, it's not that big a deal."

I do not like the rebellious tone Chris uses toward me. I look sharply at him.

"I have told you not to meddle in the affairs of adults, young man."

I do not like the look he gives me. The boy clearly must be dealt with.

"Would you like my steak, Daddy?" Julie asks.

She's so sweet.

I shake my head, moving to the Caesar salad in the separate bowl that Victoria has prepared.

"No, Julie. You go ahead and eat your food. But thank you for offering."

We eat the rest of our meal in silence. I curse myself, and the work that lies ahead. Where did I go wrong with Victoria? Why is this never exactly as it should be?

When the meal is complete, Julie, Alexander, and Chris clear the table without saying anything. Chris nearly drops my plate. Something is wrong with him, but Victoria must be addressed first. The children excuse themselves to their homework, leaving Victoria and me alone.

She looks up at me with reddened eyes. She knows.

"Come, Victoria," I say gently. I try to make this as easy on her as possible. "To the bedroom."

"I...I really thought you said..."

"I know." I almost feel sorry for her. "But I didn't. If you search your memory, you'll recall the truth. And...mistakes...can only be tolerated for so long. Now come."

Victoria takes her time in dabbing the corners of her mouth before slowly pushing away from the table. She keeps her eyes down. She folds her hands in front of her and exits through the kitchen behind her, and from there, she heads up the stairs to the bedroom. No sounds can be heard from the rooms in the hall. The children are doing homework as they should. I follow her into the bedroom and close the door. She whirls on me suddenly.

"Will...will it hurt?" she asks, afraid.

I smile.

"No, dear. You won't feel a thing. I promise."

"O...okay." She begins crying. "I'm—I'm sorry."

I nod. The time for apologies has passed.

"On your knees, please."

She obeys dutifully, turning around, and kneeling. She lowers her head.

I reach over to the dresser to a bronze lockbox that can only be opened by my fingerprint. I touch my index finger to the reader on the front of the box, and the lock gives, allowing the box to open. Within is a .45 automatic handgun, unregistered, of course, and a silencer. I affix the silencer to the handgun and turn back to Victoria, who has not moved. I lower the muzzle of the gun to her head and with no hesitation, squeeze the trigger.

Her body flops forward, thrown to the ground by the terrible force of the bullet I just fired through her brain. Her head explodes in a beautiful, visual symphonic delight as gray brain matter, combined with my own rainbow of colored wiring and green circuitry are suddenly and violently revealed for my perusal.

Were I a surgeon, this process would be much less enjoyable. But I confess it is this part I love the most, seeing what I have created splayed about, the first impressions of what was right and what must be perfected.

Victoria's head is more pieces than I can count; no one would ever be able to identify her. The shredded stub of her neck spits blood and oil onto the floor. I'll need to have one of the children clean it up while I rebuild.

I replace the gun in the bronze lockbox and quickly slip on a pair of latex gloves. I squat, quickly rifling through the remnants of my wife's cybernetic mind and — there.

Reinforcing the Black Box in titanium proved a wise idea; it survived the bullet. With the first two models, rebuilding had taken weeks. People had begun getting suspicious, but I had alluded that Victoria was enjoying her time in Italy and I, being the good husband, had no problem with my wife wanting to better herself. To make the story complete, I had programmed Victoria 2.0 with the ability to speak Italian like a native. No one had been the wiser.

Unfortunately, Victoria 2.0 had the audacity to question me *in front of my children*. Clearly, more work was needed. I originally had such high hopes for Victoria 3.0.

Fools say a soul cannot be replicated. I say there is no soul, only man's vain hope that their actions in this world may be justified in another that couldn't possibly exist. I wonder how anyone could possibly believe in things they cannot see, hear, have no definite proof of, but it's not my concern. Their beliefs are for my exploitation, in this case. I am building their better world, right before their eyes. And they are none the wiser.

This Black Box, with the pulsing green light in its center to indicate it is still functional, contains what one would call a soul: virtually every quirk, mannerism, and personality trait, recorded during lengthy periods of observation. It is all programmed into routines and then inserted into the bodies I create. Bodies which are perfect replicas of the originals; as they wear down over time, they even appear to be *aging*.

Having been at this for more than two years, I understand why my genius went unappreciated by the masses. Had the world been aware I had the knowledge to do such things, I would never have come this far. It would've been so simple to check my background, which I listed plainly on my resume…but the world was so desperate to fill slots left vacant by plague victims, no one looked twice at anyone looking for work.

As always, I allow myself a moment of reflection, sitting at the foot of the bed I share with my wife, who will unexpectedly lose another member of her family, forcing her absence for seven days, which is more than enough time to ensure that Victoria 4.0 is ready to fulfill her duties.

Perhaps it had been a mistake to marry a woman clearly not ready to settle down, and step into the role of wife and mother as every woman should. The first decade of our marriage had been difficult, at best. Victoria was willful, arrogant, and flirtatious with other men, with no sense of duty. Oh, but how the children loved her.

Of course they did, as she indulged their every whim. Imagine: consumption of large quantities of *sugar* after dinner? Dessert is just child abuse veiled in tradition, if you ask me. Saturday mornings spent before the television watching poorly animated and equally crafted stories that were neither funny nor relevant? It was a recipe for madness.

Yet, I could tolerate all of this. My wife was beautiful, and she was mine. That was all that mattered. It was her threatening the status quo that forced me to take drastic steps.

I think we need time apart; her words will stay with me forever. *You're always angry, and you're always yelling at the children, so I will take them with me, and you can find a better job – something that makes you happy. Your children are frightened of you, Robert, so it's best I take them and go…*

It was the second time in my life I gave into the impulse, but I could no longer bear it. Wasting away as a glorified file clerk to support a rebellious wife and three children, only to have her tell me she was *leaving me?!*

She never had a chance. Rage amplifies strength a thousand fold. I throttled the life from that wench, wrestled her to the ground even as she silently pleaded with her eyes, striking vainly at my arms as I forced the breath from her body.

Then, of course, I realized I had a problem. Just as quickly, I happened across a desperate solution, one even *I* didn't think would work.

But it had. Amazingly, it *had*. Victoria 1.0 had not been a resounding success, not by any stretch, but she was as alive as alive got without breathing.

If anything was salvaged from that debacle, her voice emulator was perfect. She had shorted out within a week, while driving Alexander home from school. There had been a car crash, and far worse than Alexander being injured, he had discovered the truth about his mother.

In his prime, I may not have been a match for him. Lying prone and helpless in a hospital bed, dispatching him was easy. Alexander 1.0 had yet to require improvement.

But twins know. Somehow, they always know. And seizing upon that supposedly-intangible bond between brother and sister made programming Julie 1.0 remarkably easy. Julie was originally shy and stuttered when she spoke. *Disgusting.* Yet it was so easy to fix with a language and speech modifier! But I couldn't throttle poor Julie, no. So having Victoria slip something into her dinner was her way of passing. I had her perfect replacement waiting, and no one was the wiser.

I toss the Black Box to myself as though it's a coin, and I feel my spirit renewed with the challenge of a new Victoria. This one would be programmed with better cooking subroutines, and then I would turn my attention to Chris—

A door slams hard downstairs. Panic grips me.
I don't bother to lock the bedroom door – I know Julie and Alexander wouldn't betray me – and race to the front door, which is swinging open from the force with which it was slammed. I step out onto the front porch and look around.

Chris is gone.

As is the business card. I could've sworn I…

Damn that boy.

This is inexcusable, but easily rectified, I tell myself. First, I must get Julie and Alexander to bury Victoria 3.0 in the azalea graveyard. She'll join the bodies of every other failed creations and their original models, who've been buried and feeding the garden all these years.

Then, I must send them for Chris, and they must bring him back alive. No one will question a brother and sister seeking to retrieve their runaway brother, the one who makes up crazy stories about Daddy killing their family and turning them into robots.

Unfortunately, Chris will need improving too, but all of this can be wrapped up within a matter of days.

Soon, everything will be perfect.

INEVITABLE DEATH

BY

CHRISTOPHER C. PAYNE

I live in a small, two-bedroom house in the beautiful sunny state of California. My house might be smaller than some, but it is cozy. It's adorned with beautiful hardwood floors and detailed molding that signifies a house of its age. I try to overlook the draftiness. On most days, there is a slight breeze that whisks through the cracks in the creaking, old windows and doors. It has character, my old house, and it's this character that is underappreciated in my generation of demanding, non-stop activities that push us to constantly overachieve.

I have only lived here a short time, but I am happy to share my house with several brothers and sisters of my own, as well as, three beautiful young girls to whom I am not related. One is 7, one is 12 (she just had a birthday), and one is 14 but will be turning 15 in just a few weeks. The three girls are all lovely young ladies who are not always as respectful as one might hope. But they have good hearts and a softness about them that only youth possesses.

In addition to our full and lively household, there are two dogs of vastly differing stature. One is a Labrador Retriever, and the other one is a Chihuahua mix of some kind. The little one can't weigh more than 14 pounds. He is cute compared to his lumbering, overly exuberant playmate, with her whiplash tail that can only be described as a weapon. While she does not wield it intentionally, the effects are the same as I have now been beaten with this flailing appendage on several different occasions. It is not very convenient to be forcefully reminded that all objects must be kept at a strict minimum height level in order to avoid the inevitable smacking the vicious tail can dish out.

The last of our group is the father of the three girls. He is middle-aged, having just turned 42. With the exception of occasionally raising his voice, he seems to be a good soul and easily expresses his genuine love for his three lovely, little girls. I love cozying up in the back in a corner as he snuggles the little one in his reclining chair. The two of them look so enamored, sitting close together as we all watch an episode of *Amazing Race* or *American Idol* on the flat panel TV above the white painted brick fireplace. He professes not to like *American Idol*, but on the occasions where the three girls are at their mother's house, it is easy to see the contradiction. He watches the show with nary a child present.

We have only recently moved into our little three-bedroom sanctuary. The father split with his soon to be ex-wife about a year ago. The divorce was not well received from the oldest daughter, and her adjustment has been extremely difficult. The two younger girls are taking things as well as can be expected, but as with all fractures of a family, it is not the easiest thing to transcend. Families are made up of all shapes and sizes in today's society, so we have to be ready to openly accept the myriad of structures that are thrown our way.

We have our ups and downs, but as families go we are happily making our way through life, dealing with the odds and ends and keeping our routines spiced up just enough not to get bored. The father tends to work a little too much, but on the days where his daughters are present, he comes home on time and cooks a nice meal with vegetables. The rule on entertainment is no TV until after 9 p.m. He often makes exceptions starting around 8:30, but in general, evenings begin with meal preparation, a nice family dinner and, on most nights, end with some form of reading.

We are somewhat well read as far as families go. There is always a supply of new books on the modern square coffee table sitting in the middle of the family room. The two little ones, as the father likes to call them, enjoy reading, while the oldest has to be pushed most of the time. She doesn't take very well to sitting down long enough and focusing her attention on words. She, as most high school-aged kids, prefers her entertainment in the form of cell phones or her MySpace page (which was recently taken away). I hope she soon discovers the joys of reading and the places one's mind can take you if nudged by a few well chosen words cobbled together to form a magical place.

The only thing I can actually admit to finding truly sad is when the father takes the three kids and the two dogs away for the weekend to their lovely house in Twain Harte. For some reason he continues to leave my brothers and sisters, as well as me, behind.

He does speak to me on occasion, but through today we have avoided that one glaring issue which I can't seem to understand. Admittedly, it does break my frail heart. The only reason I can fathom this oversight is he must be waiting for me to get stronger. Once my siblings and I have matured to a state of readiness, he will then include us in this activity. We continually discuss the stories of this vacation home, and I can't wait to one day be included and feel like I am finally accepted as an equal.

The only other people that periodically visit our house are a friend of the father's who comes over every few days. She is nice enough but doesn't really speak to me directly. I see them holding each other on the couch, and I get jealous because I do appreciate the few times where he and I can be alone. We will always have the two dogs with us, but I would never count them as competition for affection. And, the girls and I will always get along splendidly, bar the minor altercations that sporadically occur between kids our ages.

It is now approaching the end of May, and we have lately been keeping the blinds raised. At times we have been opening the windows, as well. It is a wonderful time of year when it starts getting warm, and the sun shines almost every single day as a soft breeze blows through the house. I feel my skin getting that soft, silky, smooth texture that accompanies the springtime weather as you bask in its glowing feel. I have to be careful as I see my skin beginning to turn red, and the last thing I want to do is burn. The 12 year old just recently returned from the latest family trip to Twain

Harte, and she had that unhealthy burnt-red tint. I am sure the next time I see her; she will be peeling back several layers of lost covering.

There is nothing more refreshing than sitting in the sun as you gulp down a nice full drink of water, letting the cool liquid nourish you as it flows through your limbs, replenishing your essence. I remember hearing somewhere that the human body is made up of 98 percent water. That seems like it is too high of a percentage, but we are all vastly made up of liquid. None of us can afford to get overheated without the replenishment of the much-needed source of energy.

We have modest furnishings in our little home with only a couple of couches, one chair, and enough beds to get us through the chilly nights. We have a dining table, a couple of end tables, and a minimal amount of dressers. The father is always proudly mentioning that everything was bought used on Craig's List, keeping the costs to a minimum. He is a frugal one, that father, as he turns the heat off or way down at night, and during the first month I was here I must admit to getting shivering cold at times. While he watches what he spends on everything possible, he contradictorily spends a fortune at times on frivolous items, surprising me with his lack of judgment.

Happily, that is my biggest complaint. Listening to the stories of others as they come and go, I have it better than most and count my blessings that I have a family as good as the one that I lucked into. As I now sit in the family room, waiting for the father to come home and realizing that tonight is a night we will spend with the kids, I excitedly look forward to the evening. The clock seems to be taking its time as it clicks by each second in slow, painstaking motion with the minutes tick-tocking back and forth in steady rhythmic fashion. How can time move so slowly yet not actually slow down? Perception plays tricks on my mind at times as I sit impatiently looking out the window on the sunny day just slightly beyond my reach.

Finally, the father has made it home, walking through the front door somewhat out of breath. He has ridden his bike to work again today which is about eight miles away. It is not a long ride, but I have noticed he's starting to look trim from the cardiovascular exercise. I have also observed him spending a renewed effort in the mornings with his pushups and sit-up routine. He attempts to do 250 pushups and 300 sit-ups every morning. He falls short of this on most occasions, but even his feeble attempts are showing some results in his physique.

As he puts away his bike, he walks in my direction and, for the first time in several days, addresses my brother directly, stating today was his lucky day. "Lucky Day." I never imagined those two words would change my life forever. That was the moment when my world changed, and everything I thought I had known was taken from me.

The father ripped my brother up with one hand, plucking him from his resting place where he had been fast asleep. I heard him scream, a sound that will never be erased from my memory. As he was crying for help, the father took him in the other room. It would be the last time I would ever see my brother alive.

I heard the slicing noises. My brother cried out for me to aid him for a few minutes, and then his voice went silent. I was so confused. This was the man who had cared for us, fed us, given us water. He was the one protecting us, providing us shelter. How could he brutally torture my brother? Was I now to assume my brother was dead?

It was at that moment the father returned. He casually walked around the corner back into the living room. Red liquid oozed down one of his hands, and I saw the crimson-sheathed layer of skin clinging to his shirt. I could see his mouth still moving, and remnants of my brother's body were stuck to one side of his mouth.

I tried to warn the rest of my family, for now I knew this man was not our friend. He was nothing but a killer, a murderer of the innocent. He placed little-to-no value on the very life we all hold so preciously in our frail hands.

We were all screaming at this point, crying out for anyone, anything to come to our rescue. But alas, we were all too small, too weak to protect ourselves. The inevitable was bound to take place, I guess, as he grabbed one of my sisters, discharging her in much the same way my brother had only recently found his demise.

Right there in front of all of us, he placed her body in his mouth and took a bite. The liquid from her guts squirted out as his teeth met skin, and he chomped down all the harder. He callously bit a large chunk out of her with all of us sitting there, unable to do anything to save her.

I tried not to think of all the things in life she would miss – growing up, watching TV, reading books. There would be people she should have met but, at this point, never would. Her life was cut short. There was nothing any of us could do. She was now dead. My brother was dead. Most likely the rest of us would be dead, as well.

My only hope was his daughters. They would be back soon, and if I found a way to tell them what was going on, maybe they would be able to help us. They were small, as well, but they were good and kind. All of my hope rested on them finding us and saving us from this demonically possessed beast whom I had trusted just a short time ago.

The father spent the rest of the evening sitting in his chair, watching TV as if nothing had occurred. He laughed at Seinfeld, jumped a couple of times while watching a movie, pretending nothing had changed.

I heard somebody speak about psychopaths a couple of weeks ago and how there was one in every random 25 people who had no conscious. One person out of every 25 is a powder keg waiting to explode. If push came to shove, that one person was capable of doing anything without remorse.

Sadly, I now knew this was the case, and even more disturbingly, he was sitting in my living room.

The girls came bounding in the front door, their usual smiles on their faces. The little one talked about a pancake breakfast occurring at her school the next day. The father smiled and expressed his interest in taking her, conversing with his kids like he was a normal human being versus the stone-cold killer of reality.

I reached for her when she passed by, screaming at her to run and please help us. "Take us with you. Help us escape," I blurted out as loudly as I could.

I didn't understand it, but she ignored me, pretending I wasn't even there.

We had never spent a ton of time together – she and I. It wasn't like we were best friends, but she didn't even look at me. It didn't matter how loudly I cried.

"PLEASE, DEAR GOD, HELP US!" my remaining brothers and sisters screamed together, but none of the daughters gave us even a glancing nod.

I wanted to plead with them, beg them, ask them why they no longer cared until it happened again. I can't begin to tell you why or what they were thinking. They were only girls for Christ's sake – little children. How could they have been taught this was ok?

I don't have any of the answers, and it happened so quickly I had no time to even react.

The father reached down, grabbing my only remaining sister and dropped her on the coffee table. She lay there with part of her body on a plate, and that was when I saw the knife in his right hand.

He placed the point inside her midsection, and with the precision of a doctor, effortlessly pushed it all the way in. He carved it to the side, slicing a section away from her as she wailed in pain. Again, he acted like he couldn't even hear her.

The girls just sat watching. The middle child curled her lips in an awkward position while raising her hand.

"Disgusting," she uttered. "I am not eating any of that. There is no way you can make me."

"I want some," the littlest girl yelled.

I felt a tear slipping down; I couldn't believe what I was seeing. He was slicing pieces of my sister off, handing them to this little girl, and she was eating them like candy. You have never witnessed insanity unless you have been subjected to seeing your relative butchered and consumed raw right in front of your eyes.

"Don't wipe your mouth with your sleeve, please," the father said. "Do you know how hard it is to get the red stain out of your white tops?"

He continued like his only concern was cleaning up the blood of my beautiful sibling from their clothes. We were nothing more than a meal for this sick jerk, and he was only worrying about cleaning up.

This was the point in time where I lost all hope. I no longer felt there was anyone to help us, nobody cared what happened. We were all sitting here with nothing left to do but await our death.

It might sound impossibly difficult to lose all hope, but how many family members can you see die, eaten right before your very eyes, before you have to face the reality of your end? *My life is over, let these monsters do with me what the will*, I thought to myself.

I spent the next several days watching more of the same until finally I was the only one left. They were not all my brothers and sisters. I am not even sure where some of them came from, but I noticed a few times when the father and girls came home, they had others with them.

They talked about purchasing some, but somehow the ones they bought didn't taste as good as my family did. Apparently my family was delectable, and even the little girl chimed in how much better a flavor we had.

It is sick beyond belief to murder and torture somebody. It is even more detestable to talk about killing them and how much you enjoyed it. It is beyond anything I could ever imagine to hear a 7-year-old girl talk about the taste in her mouth as she swallowed somebody with whom I had grown up.

I wondered how they would feel. What would they think if I casually sliced them into little pieces, eating them while they were forced to sit and watch?

What would this father go through if he had to stare straight ahead as his daughter was chopped up and eaten while we all sat around and talked about how good she tasted. I knew I had no chance of escaping, but in my mind I still left a small bit of hope that somehow, someway, I might be saved.

Sadly, it is not meant to be, and today, I now face what I have feared and been forced to observe. Today it is to be my turn. Today, my life is going to end.

The father announces that today he will make some cheeseburgers for the girls. He coldly states that, with me in attendance, he is sure the meal will have a delicious flare that has been lacking for the past several months. I have no real understanding of what is making tonight special, but I begin to fathom the possibilities of a surprise that he is so thoughtfully instigating.

After he spends a few minutes admiring my skin and complementing my complexion, he moves to the bathroom where he quickly freshens up, changing out of his sweaty T-shirt. But, he leaves his shorts on for what appears the remainder of the evening. He is always in a little bit of a hurry on nights when the girls are here, getting the meal prepared so he can spend as much time with them as possible.

I hear him in the kitchen as he turns on the oven, mashing the hamburger into patties. I feel myself getting caught up in his exuberant energy as he is now quickly banging pots and pans. It is with surprise when he approaches me directly for the second time this evening. I now admire the strength that he possesses as he picks me up rather easily with one hand, carrying me with him, carefully setting me way up high on the countertop.

I feel very little as he detaches me from my slumbering state of comfortableness, and I contemplate all the possibilities that the evening might hold. I don't understand the large slab of wood he places me on, and the large knife sitting next to the block has me somewhat unsettled. I have now known this man for several months, and it is with a little trepidation that I watch him fluidly navigate on his continued course. Why would he insist on my staying put, and why can't he simply take my life quickly?

He, again, compliments me on my beautiful skin tone and how my perfectly proportioned figure sits stoically, entrusting him with my life as I have done with no other. He hovers over me, staring into me like he owns me. I feel my nerves beginning to perk, detecting a hint of something in his voice. That should have been enough to warn me of the impending dilemma quickly approaching. I feel I know what is going to happen, and the scream that wells up inside my physical being is stifled by his hand as it holds me firmly in place.

With his fingers wrapped completely around me, keeping me from moving in any direction, he laughingly states how delicious I look and what an honor it will be for him to have me for dinner. Not have me to dinner, but have me for dinner. The subtle dynamics of this difference vastly underscore the meaning of what is about to occur. I remember the times I spent in his family room with his children keeping him company and holding my breath, waiting patiently for their arrival. I am a part of this family, a member of this group who loves and needs love as much as any other living thing would.

As he raises the knife slowly arching it downward, I realize how little the father really cares. He has pretended to like me, spent time talking to me, nurturing me to a healthy full complete existence. But in the end, it is all for his own personal, carnal pleasure.

The knife enters me, slicing downward, cutting through me as if I am soft as butter. It doesn't feel as I had imagined as the life fluids begin draining from my insides onto the slab of wood that had only recently been placed like a coffin awaiting my arrival. He does this again and again as I no longer struggle but fall into sliced pieces like dominos on a playing board.

Once this is complete, he throws both the top and bottoms of my physical remains in the left drain of the sink where the hot water runs slowly over me, cascading down what is left of my ripped body. I now lay in pieces, a mere semblance of what I had once been, and I realize I am only going to remain conscious for a few more short seconds. Through the fog, I hear a knock on the door and realize the kids must be here, as they too are apparently going to partake in the carnage of my frail, soft being.

The last words that I hear uttered come from the father in his excited, happy tone. I had grown so accustomed to his voice through the many stories I had heard him reading out loud to the two little ones.

He uttered almost under his breath, "Kids, we are finally going to eat one of the freshest, most scrumptious tomatoes I have ever grown. I just finished slicing it for the cheeseburgers, and dinner will be ready in just under five minutes."

DINNER WITH CRISTY

BY

RHONDA E. KACHUR

10 cups balsamic vinegar
8 cups olive oil
1 1/2 cups brown sugar
2 large minced onions
6 Tablespoons oregano
8 teaspoons black pepper
8 teaspoons salt

It took more marinade than I thought it would to cover all of her. Though, of course, she was the biggest piece of meat I'd ever had the pleasure of preparing. She had to be at least 250 to 300 pounds, which was all the better for my tastes.

Most food connoisseurs hate the excess fat on their meat, but then again they've never had the pleasure of tasting another human. Our fat doesn't get tough when you cook it like pork fat does. In fact, it almost melts in your mouth as you savor the flavor.

I've been a killer for quite some time now, although I hate the term "killer" or "murderer." I find myself to be better than that. I am a hunter. It started when I was around 6 years old. Small animals like squirrels and mice were my first prey, of course. Then I moved up to dogs, cats, and the occasional legal hunting trip. Finally, I began hunting the ultimate game – humans.

My first was when I was 18. He was a tall, handsome, blond jock I knew from high school. He was also mean, conceited, and got what was coming to him.

Men are fun to kill, but hunting another woman is a real treat. Men are easy to get alone. Offer them sex, and they're yours. A woman on the other hand requires much more cunning and skill to separate her from the herd. It makes them so much more fun to hunt!

And while hunting is exhilarating, the actual act of killing my prey is where the real reward is found. Killing them without being caught forces you to be in total control of everything around you – your planning, timing, and execution has to be done just right in order to get away with your deeds successfully. There is no better feeling in the world than being in complete control.

I only started eating human meat about 6 months ago. I'd never had the desire to consume my victims until I had bear cub for the first time. An old friend of mine had been hunting in the woods and had brought his catch back for dinner. I didn't know what I was eating in the beginning. I had assumed it was beef or deer, but it was much leaner and tasted absolutely gorgeous.

When he told me it was a little bear cub he had killed himself, the question of what human meat tasted like first entered my mind. I mean, in a way it would be no different than us eating any form of meat. People have been hunting wild game for centuries in order to provide food for their families. I simply hunted a different kind of game.

The initial introduction was quite a pleasurable experience. I had gone out hunting, as I usually do on Fridays, and met up with a man named Jeffery. He was tall, lean, and a bit hairy for my tastes, but when you hunt the prey I do, there won't always be a 14 point buck standing right in front of you. Sometimes, you have to settle for a doe.

That experience began what was soon to be a normal routine for me. It's a simple one, really, for males. I lure a prospect to my house with the promise of sexual activity, chloroform him, then I usually take my time in disposing of my prize.

But that first time, I was trying something new and wanted to dive right into it. I killed him quickly and proceeded to carefully cut into the muscles of his chest and legs, filleting him if you will. Usually, the screams of agony from my victims make me shiver with joy, but that night it was the anticipation of tasting him that excited me.

Even with him being lean and fit, he did still have some soft spots. We all have a little fat on us. I was a little surprised to see how yellow human fat is. It was almost as golden as corn! I was also delighted to learn his meat was odorless, like a fresh swordfish steak.

I, of course, had cut into a human flesh before, but I had never taken the time to notice these little things. Usually, I would focus on the kill and the screams, but tonight I got into my element and really savored my prey with an exciting new purpose. It was extremely liberating.

I usually like my meat medium rare, but I wasn't sure exactly how to prepare human flesh for consumption. I have since learned from experience that it can be prepared and seasoned the way you would a steak.

Since it was my first time orchestrating a feast of human steak, the filet came out a little dry but had a lovely natural flavor, almost like a mixture of pork and beef with a little more elasticity to it. I found it went really well with a nice glass of Cabernet.

Being that I was raised in the country, I thought it would be a fun idea to make some pork rinds for an after dinner snack, only with Jeffery's skin instead of a pig.

It tasted quite delectable, but unfortunately, the exorbitant amount of body hair became a slight problem. I kept getting little pieces of the black curly fibers stuck in my teeth. After that debacle, I decided to shave a couple sections of his skin and freeze it with the rest of the leftovers. I could always try again another day.

A normal sized human has enough meat to feed me for a good few weeks if I cut it off the bone correctly. The meat lasts longer if the person is a bit larger seeing as I don't mind the excess lard. I actually find it most appealing. And, that brings us back to whom we have on tonight's menu.

Cristy was the name on her driver's license. She is a 29-year-old woman whom I met online a few months back. As soon as I saw her deliciously plump frame, I knew I had to have her. It actually took longer than I thought it would to convince her to meet me.

Usually, I hunted young, thin, attractive women who would meet up with you for drinks the same day you added them as a Facebook friend. Most of them were "models" looking for attention or simply party girls looking for a good time, but Cristy was different.

She wasn't particularly attractive nor was she thin. She was round in both the gut and the face with short, dyed red hair. Her natural brown or dirty blonde color was only visible at her roots. I think what I had found most appealing was her rosy red cheeks. They were so plump and juicy looking. I figured I could make a lovely roast out of them with some fresh potatoes and baby carrots.

From the first moment I started talking to her, I realized she was self-centered and egotistical, despite her obesity. She talked about her new projects and endeavors in the film industry. All she had really done was make poor quality, low budget films that wouldn't even go viral on YouTube.

Of course, her success, or lack thereof, didn't matter to me one bit. My sole concern was an angle – using anything I could to get her where I wanted her – on my kitchen table.

I started talking about a "story" I had written and convinced her she would be perfect in it. She claimed to work in all genres, but said horror was her favorite.

I sent her a quick typed up summary of my first killing, portraying it as fiction of course, and she ate it up. She said she would love to work with me on making it into a "high quality, indie production."

We talked back and forth on the details of where she wanted to shoot and how she thought it should look. I let her drive all of the suggestions, since I knew it would never actually be made. Plus, I wanted her to feel like she was in control of the situation. It was a very frustrating process. All I really wanted to do was taste her, to filet her juicy, plump cheeks. I had this deep, uncontrollable desire to have her as quickly as possible.

After three months of discussing production details of what she said would be her "breakthrough film," she finally agreed to meet with me. Of course, she wanted it to be in a public setting to be on the safe side. Luckily for me, she didn't live that far away from the bar where I usually did my hunting.

I suggested it to her, and she agreed to meet me there at 8 p.m. My mouth started watering at the thought of finally seeing my dinner face-to-face. Just imagining being able to glide my knife through her tender calves and her plump middle section made the wait that much more difficult and exciting.

She said she would be wearing a red headband with black skulls on it just to be sure I recognized her, but I had been studying the structure of her face for so long that I could never forget it. We both logged offline, and I readied what I would need to get her home. She told me she wasn't a big drinker so I knew that simply getting her intoxicated wouldn't do the trick. I packed a small bottle of crushed sleeping pills into my purse and headed out the door.

When I got to the bar, she was sitting at a little table in the back wearing her red headband. I waved hi to her, and she jumped up to greet me, almost knocking the table over with her massive gut. She gave me a strong embrace, and we casually sat down to talk.

I knew I would have to endure a conversation with her just long enough to catch her off guard. But I found it more difficult to hear her banter on about herself face-to-face than online.

It was the fact that she was right in front of me, ready for the taking, but I couldn't attack just yet. We discussed her previous work, her experience as a "film maker," and her thoughts about our wonderful project together, along with other mindless chatter. It was all about "her."

Finally, after an hour of agreeing with all her idiotic ideas, I proposed a toast. Again she reminded me how she didn't like to drink, but I said she had to have at least one quick shot to celebrate her upcoming success. She caved in and I headed to the bar, equipped with my bottle of crushed sleeping pills concealed in the palm of my hand.

I ordered two Lemon Drop shots and ever so slyly emptied the contents of my bottle into one of them. I then went back to the table and sat the spiked shot glass in front of Cristy. We raised both of our drinks in the air and made a quick toast to success and good fortune. As soon as she gulped the whole shot in one mouthful, I knew my fortune was about to change for the better. I, then, patiently waited for the pills to kick in.

When she started to become quite groggy, I asked one of the men in the bar to help me carry my friend to the car. Of course, they all thought she simply had one too many drinks. Only I knew better. My mouth was salivating with the sweet reward of a successful hunt.

As the men and I got her into the front seat of my car, I couldn't help but giggle in delight. The idiots could never grasp the thoughts racing through my mind and the joy I was about to experience.

The drive home seemed like it took forever. So many red lights impeded my destiny with this succulent morsel.

Cristy had completely passed out and had even begun to snore very loudly. Her head lay in a crooked angle, dangling in an uncomfortably odd way.

I finally pulled into my driveway and entered the garage. I closed the garage door and stopped in my tracks. Remember when I said planning was important? Well in all of my excitement, I forgot to plan how to get my dinner, who weighs a substantial amount more than I can carry, into my kitchen.

I looked around to see if there was anything I could use to move her. Luckily the stars must have been aligned in my favor for what did I see as I turned around? A large blue tarp. I grabbed it and laid it out as flat as I could beside the passenger door. I grabbed Cristy by the collar of her dark red shirt and pulled her onto the tarp below. She hit it, not with a loud thud, but with more of a flop.

I closed the car door and got a good grip on the corners of the tarp. I began to pull her towards the door to my house. Damn, was she heavy! The hardest part was getting her over the steps leading from the garage to my little hidden sanctuary inside. She almost slipped off, but I stopped, repositioned her body, and pulled her slowly into my living room.

As soon as I got her safely inside, I closed the door to the garage and sat on my couch to catch my breath. I needed the break before I began pulling her again. Next time I decide to hunt a super-sized meal, I'll remember to buy a large wheelbarrow or wagon first!

As I sat there, staring at her large plump frame, I thought of all the possibilities there were for me to use each of her body parts. Her fat could be rendered to flavor other meats. Her skin was far less hairy that Jeffery's had been, so it would fry up beautifully. And of course, her meat could be used it so many delicious recipes.

For tonight's dinner, I was thinking a nice roast with her cheeks would be lovely. I could even make it a stew if I quickly whipped up gravy to slowly cook the meat in. The possibilities were endless. I, finally, resumed my quest and pulled her into the kitchen.

When I looked at my table, I realized I had a new problem; how do I get her hoisted into position? Usually, my catches are light enough to stand up and plop them right onto the surface, but Cristy was going to be a challenge.

I sat her up and put one arm underneath each of hers. I tried to pick her up that way, but it just wasn't going to work. I flipped her over onto her stomach and lifted her front by pushing her onto her knees. While I had her in that position, I quickly got myself under her and wrapped her arms over my shoulders, like a piggyback ride. It took everything I had, but I got her up off the floor and plopped her onto the table.

She lay across the middle and, I swung both of her legs up and over. I had to catch her head before she fell off and placed both of my arms under hers. I pulled her into the final position so that she lay in just the right spot. I grabbed a kitchen chair and sat down beside her to catch my breath.

I was slightly disappointed in myself. I had ample time to plan for all of this, yet the thought of how to get her into the house and onto the table never crossed my mind. It was definitely a learning experience I could take and use the next time I hunt for a full-meal deal.

I went back out to the garage and grabbed a large pile of rope to secure Cristy's hands and feet. I first tied them together, and then I tied a piece from her hands to the floor, doing the same with her feet, so she wouldn't be able to flail around.

Being that I've been killing for quite some time now, I installed special metal hoops into my kitchen floor to secure my catches. The table was also secured to the floor. The only thing I couldn't figure out how to do myself was setting up a drain directly under the table for all the blood. The first couple of killings, I had a huge mess to clean up, and it wasn't fun at all. I investigated the process of installing a drain and realized it just would not work in the floor.

So how did I remedy the blood problem? It was quite simple actually, when I sat down and thought about it. I never had visitors other than my prey, so I simply took out the kitchen table and installed the kind of table they use in morgues! The one I got had a place to hook a hose to it so you could send the fluids directly to a drain. I simply hook a long plastic tube to it when I'm using the table for my catches and run it into my basement. The blood flows right into the drain my washer uses! It's simple, yet effective.

After I got her all tied up, I removed all of her clothing with scissors and prepared my marinade. This is something for which I remembered to plan.

I got my big metal tub out and poured all of the ingredients into it. I stirred it up well, making sure everything was incorporated, and began to slowly ladle it over her entire body. I used my hands to make sure it got into all of her crevices and rolls. Being that she was a larger woman, I made sure to make extra so I had a little left over. It's very useful to baste the meat with while it's cooking.

After I got her covered all over, I sat down and waited for the marinade to work its magic. It would take at least a few hours. I made sure all the doors were locked and laid down on the couch for a short nap – a well deserved one, if I may say so myself.

I woke up in the middle of the night to the sound of screaming. My dinner was awake. It had been a few hours since I fell asleep, and I was sure she would be nice and flavored. I walked into the kitchen and reached into my pantry. As I was grabbing my apron, I heard Cristy cry,

"What the hell is going on here! Let me go!"

I saw her looking down at her naked body as she asked what was covering her. I didn't reply. My mother taught me not to play with my food, and talking to it is surely not a healthy habit.

I put my apron on and pulled my slow cooker out of the cabinet below my sink. I, then, went back and grabbed two skillets from the same area. Cristy began to scream for help, but lucky for me my nearest neighbor lived a couple miles away. No one would hear her screams. No one would hear anything at all.

I plugged in the slow cooker and grabbed a few ingredients out of the refrigerator. Carrots, potatoes, celery, and onions. I grabbed a knife and my cutting board and began to chop up the veggies. Cristy began to struggle, trying to loosen the ties on her hands. Poor, stupid woman, I'm very good at tying knots and knew she wasn't going anywhere.

The more she screamed, the wetter my mouth became. Nothing in the world tastes better than freshly chopped meat. The crap you get at the grocery stores has been sitting on the shelves for God knows how long, but my meat was always carved from living flesh. I know where it came from, and I know how appealing it can be.

I plopped my chopped vegetables into the slow cooker and filled it with just a touch of water. I, then, went to my fridge and grabbed a tub of left over fat from my last victim. I scooped a couple of tablespoons of it into the frying pan and added some flour. A nice rue would create thick, delicious gravy. All I needed now was some blood to flavor it with. Raw blood has a metallic taste to it, but if you cook it a little, it's quite appetizing.

I pulled open the drawer on my sink and grabbed my sharpest knife. I only used this knife for my "special" meals, and I sharpened it after every use. It could cut straight through frozen food and was perfect for filleting a full, fatty body of meat.

I went over to Cristy and as soon as she saw it in my hand, she let out a terrible scream. I hadn't even cut her yet, and already I was having fun! She kept wiggling, fighting the inevitable.

I slid the knife down her side until I reached the point right in the middle of her shoulder and her hip. I cut into her deeply and held my measuring cup underneath the gash. Oh, how she yelled! I only needed half a cup of the crimson liquid, and it had to be fresh.

I learned the hard way that storing blood in the fridge is a huge mistake. It coagulates and somewhat curdles when it leaves the body. It's not rotten, but tastes like it should be. Fresh blood always tasted the best.

As I stirred in the red flavoring to my rue, all I could hear was Cristy in the background, yelling out things like, "Why are you doing this?" or "Let me go, you crazy witch!"

Of course, I didn't answer, I just continued to prepare for my meal.

The rue was good and thick now, and all the metallic taste had been cooked out. I poured in into the slow cooker with all my vegetables and added some salt and pepper. All I needed to do now was add the meat.

I wanted to make a roast with her cheeks, but with all the squirming she did when she first saw the knife, I knew I was going to have to secure her head somehow. I wanted to get a nice, clean cut of flesh from her face, and it would be impossible if it wasn't immobilized.

I walked back into the garage and grabbed the duct tape. When I came back in, I couldn't help but giggle. Cristy was trying to untie her hands while I was gone, but all she did was make the knot tighter around her wrists. I found it cute that she actually thought she was going to get out of this. So naïve.

I strolled up to the table and stood right beside Cristy. All her crying had made her mascara run down the side of her face, some of it on those delicious cheeks of hers. I'd have to make sure to wash them well before they went into the stew.

She frantically glanced down and saw the duct tape in my hand and began to sob a bit louder than before. I began to rub her cheeks, saying a light "Shhh" to her as I stroked them.

She could only whisper, "Why are you doing this to me?"

I began to wrap the tape around her head and the table; she began to scream again. I had thought of putting some of the tape on her mouth, but I figured it would just get in my way. Now don't get me wrong, I loved the sounds of screams, but it made it very hard to concentrate on getting a perfect cut. Tape might get in the way, but if I put something in her mouth, not only would it stop the screaming, but also the opened position would push her cheeks out, making slicing them off a bit easier.

After I had her head secured with the tape, I went to the fridge and looked for something to shut her up. An apple sounded too cliché, plus she could bite right through it, but an orange would suffice. I grabbed one that I thought would fit in her gaping hole and sauntered back. She started to ask me another redundant question, and I stuffed the orange in as far and as tightly as I could. Now all of her screams and stupid questions were nothing more than muzzled whines, like a dog would make in the summer heat.

I grabbed my sharpest knife and began to study Cristy's face. I wanted to make sure I had a good angle on her cheek muscle. Cristy's eyes looked as if they were going to pop out of her head. She began to sob even louder through her makeshift gag, and tears began to stream from her eyes.

She tried to wiggle her head, but I taped it good and tight. She wasn't going anywhere, and I was finally about to have my dinner. I placed the knife on the crease of her cheek near the eye and nose. She let out a sound like the squeal of a baby pig. All I could think was how ironic?

I began to slice into her, rocking the blade of my knife back and forth ever so gently. The makeshift gag did very little to muffle the sounds of agony, but kept the cheek in the prime position for my incision.

My knife sliced through it ever so quickly and smoothly. I placed the cheek on a plate and went back for the other one. It came off her face just as easily. Her muffled screams of pain remained constant.

I took the two cheeks and filleted off the skin from both of them. I, then, rinsed the meat and placed it into my slow cooker. As I was nestling them in the vegetables, I realized I had more room than meat, so I looked back to Cristy to see what else I could use for my masterpiece meal.

Her eyes were now half closed and blood was pouring from her face. As I gave her a look over, I paused at her thighs. Compared to the rest of her body, they looked lean and tender. A couple of nice slices would go great in the stew.

As I was just starting to cut into her right leg, she began to shake violently. She was going into shock and all the movement was ruining my cuts. As much fun as I was having with her alive, I had to stop the convulsions.

I ran to the sink and pulled out the biggest knife I had. I returned to Cristy and plunged it as deep as I could into her chest. The shaking finally stopped, and her eyes began to bulge in disbelief. Yet she looked at me with a stare of relief, as if she were thanking me for putting her out of her misery.

I had never really had anyone look at me like that before. I didn't quite know how to take it. It made my stomach tingle with both joy and regret, joy for killing her, and regret for killing her before I wanted to. Either way, she was dead now, and I had a dinner to fix.

I finished cutting, filleting, and skinning the meat and placed it in the slow cooker. I turned it to medium heat and sat down by Cristy to wait for the cooker to do its deed.

I was tired, hungry, and still confused by the look she had given me. I didn't like it at all. I got up to inspect her body again, and her eyes were still open, continuing with that look of relief. It felt like she was glad I killed her. Usually, I would concentrate on the sounds my catches would make. The screams and cries for help is what excited me about killing. But this time, I just had to see her eyes. It almost took all the fun out of my evening until the aroma of the simmering meat filled my nostrils.

The stew smelled like heaven, but Cristy's body was starting to let off a rotten stench that was ruining the experience. I untied her from the table and set up the tarp on the floor again. I pushed her off the table and onto the tarp, grabbed the corners once again and dragged her into the downstairs bathroom.

Getting her in the tub was easier than getting her on the table. One good heave, and she plopped right in. I closed and locked the door behind me. After dinner was ready, I would finish cutting off the meat from her bones, freezing it for later, like I did with Jeffery. But for now, I had a kitchen to clean up.

I mopped, scrubbed, and bleached every inch of the room, along with the trail of blood I had left by dragging her into the bathroom. By the time I finished, dinner was just about ready.

I washed for dinner in the upstairs bathroom and put on my red velvet shirt, black dress pants, and a pair of black heels. I didn't get to have a meal this special very often, so I wanted to make it an event.

I set the table with a plate of fine china, a beautiful crystal wine glass, my finest silverware, and a single lit candle. I turned off the slow cooker and removed the lid. The smell of Cristy's perfectly cooked cheeks and thigh engulfed my nose and made my knees weak. It smelled so delicious.

I removed the meat and plated it beside the vegetables with a bit of the gravy on top. I sat down, poured myself a tall glass of Cabernet, and relaxed for a well deserved feast fit for a queen. After three months of hunting, weeks of preparation, and hours of cooking, I was finally having my dinner with Cristy.

PERFECT MOTHER

BY

MORELLA LA MUERTE

A History of Disappointment

It is difficult for an ugly child to be anything but a disappointment to a perfect mother. My mother was almost impossibly beautiful, and she excelled in every one of her pursuits. She was a brilliant scientist, although her work was unorthodox. It is more difficult, in any case, for a woman to get her theories taken seriously by the scientific community. She was also a gifted artist – a sculptor who created the most incredibly lifelike waxworks. But where she believed she should have been hailed as a pioneer, she was reviled as a crackpot, much the same as her parents before her had been. She was bitter and resentful, and she took out her frustrations on me, her unlovely dullard of a daughter.

I was always the polar opposite of my mother. Where she was brilliant, I was merely smart enough to obey commands. When she was my age she had already read all the great classics of literature, had an adult understanding of mathematics and the sciences, and was an accomplished artist. I sometimes begged to be allowed to go with a governess or tutor to wile away the afternoon at the cinema rather than spend the day studying. I had a greater than average understanding of the sciences, but it was nothing compared to the brilliance of my mother. My understanding of mathematics was but adequate, and my foolish drawings appealed to nobody but myself. My slow-witted nature was always sorely bewildering to my brilliant mother.

When it came to beauty, Mother was exceedingly radiant. She was fair of face, blessed with striking amber waves of hair, and had great, dark eyes like limpid pools. She made herself all the more enchanting through the skillful use of a make-up kit purchased straight from Hollywood. She truthfully proclaimed that neither man nor woman could resist her charms.

It should then come as no surprise that she was ashamed to have given birth to an ugly creature, such as I am. I possessed the same charm as a Raggedy Ann doll come to life with my unruly orange-red curls, staring black eyes, and blotchy, ruddy-cheeked complexion. Mother and I could not possibly have been more opposite.

I was born Anthos Malah Peacock Quaranta 12 years ago on Feb. 3, 1945. Anthos means "flower" in Greek, and Mala is a Sanskrit word for "necklace." Thus, my name means "a necklace of flowers." Mother always told me that I was a hideously ugly baby, and she hoped if she gave me a beautiful name I would eventually blossom. So far I have remained a homely, untalented embarrassment to the brilliant, beautiful, and artistically gifted Doctor Victoria Peacock.

My father, the late Wullem "Wum" Quaranta, died in battle less than a month before my birth. He was the son of Líadán Holguín, a Spanish actress, and Isaac Quaranta, an Italian concert pianist who became a spy for Germany during World War I. My grandfather was shot for treason following a brief trial. My grandmother committed suicide as soon as my father was old enough to fend for himself.

My mother, Victoria Oenone Jacob Peacock, was born to be a scientific genius. Her parents were fourth cousins, the products of a long line of explorers and theorists in the worlds both seen and unseen. Her mother, Oenone Pocok, postulated biological engineering theories that were rejected as both inhumane and insane. Her father, Jacob Peacock, was a brilliant, Oxford-educated chemist whose wild theories regarding the creation of a serum to allow virtual immortality made him the laughingstock of his colleagues.

Mother's parents committed suicide by self-evisceration on New Year's Day 1921, literally spilling their guts to the unreceptive scientific community which they blamed for driving them to poverty and despair. The gruesome moment was immortalized on film. The couple hired an unscrupulous filmmaker to document their suicide and deliver the macabre motion picture to grandfather's colleagues at Oxford as punishment for their derision.

Mother was just 12 years old at the time of her parents' suicide, and she swore as soon as she was old enough to resume their work, she would prove their detractors wrong. She was raised after their deaths by a distant cousin who conveniently died after expressing her disapproval of Mother's involvement with my father.

Had the cousin not passed, she could have petitioned to have my mother removed from the will for her defiant behavior. However, with the cousin out of the way, Mother was the sole heir to her parents' will, which consisted of their home and everything in it. She was also heir to the cousin's modest fortune, which she invested wisely and within two years began making a sizeable return. At this point she began her experimentation using her parents' formulas in earnest.

As if Mother's laboratory were not already a terrible enough place, she hung a portrait of her parents there to make the atmosphere all the more Draconian. I always felt as if I needed to behave so properly in their presence, lest they should see fit to punish me. They were, to put it mildly, quite a severe-looking pair.

Grandfather Peacock was a long-limbed, heavyset gentleman with a ruddy complexion and copious ringlets of dark red hair. Pupils resembling violet jewels glared from his bulging sclera. His countenance seemed that of a madman, and I often had nightmares wherein he came to my room and drained me of my life in the manner of Dracula.

Grandmother Peacock seemed the very antithesis of joy. Her ugly, nervous face reflected a deep-seated evil. She had sleek magenta hair and wicked green eyes, glaring from beneath a perpetual frown. She reminded me of the wicked queen from Snow White, and I hated her instinctively. I was glad I had never known either of these terrible people, and, as I got older, I realized that Mother's own malevolent personality must be the result of their neglect and maltreatment.

Father and Mother were married for less than a year when he was killed in battle. Theirs was a passionate and volatile relationship. They were polar opposites. Father was emotional, a stereotypical hot-blooded Italian, according to Mother, who herself went several steps beyond the famed British "stiff upper lip" attitude. Mother was not calm, composed and collected. She was cold. She was a very angry woman but her anger did not burn, it caused frostbite. She rarely struck me, and when she did it was never hard enough to leave a mark, but I felt the chill of her disappointment in me every day of my life.

"Would that I had the sense not to think with my loins the night I met that hot-headed Italian," Mother often lamented. "Then I would not have been cursed with the disappointment of an ungrateful and intellectually inferior child, such as you."

"I gwateful, Mummy," I remember a very tiny me pleading. "I sowwy I inferimur."

It was near the end of my third year when I realized nothing I could do would ever make my mother happy, and I ceased pleading for her affections. I simply obeyed her as best I could, fully aware that I could never make her love me. Most of the time my only hope was to avoid her wrath by obeying her every command without question. I also learned that praising her efforts might earn me a brief moment of affection, though she was incapable of compassion, let alone love, which she considered a weak and useless emotion.

Art and Science

Mother was a perfectionist not only in the scientific field but also in her art, and it paid off. Every detail of the wax figures she created was perfect. I do not mean perfect in the sense that she only created beautiful, flawless people. I mean perfect in the sense that they were exact duplicates of her models.

I always held out hope she would one day teach her technique to me. After all, it wasn't as if she had a myriad of choices for a progeny to whom she could pass her knowledge. I was her only child, and though it was apparent this fact did not at all please her, there are in this Universe some truths that even she was incapable of altering.

My mother's first wax sculpture was created to honor my father. I felt an instinctual affection for the man, which was as strong an emotion as the extreme dislike I felt for my thankfully unknown maternal grandparents. Father had a cherubic face, though his was rather a gaunt figure. He had deep blue eyes and copious waves of blue-black hair.

His wax doppelganger's left arm was held with the elbow bent and the left hand turned inward just below his face. His right hand was extended in such a way that it invited me to grip the fingers lightly when Mother was not around. I wished the war had not taken Father from me before he had ever held me in his arms. I felt that unlike my mother, my father would have loved me in spite of my flaws. Whenever I met my father in dreams he was kind, yet he seemed terribly sad.

There were other waxworks, most of whom I had known throughout my childhood. The women had primarily been maids, tutors, or governesses. Some of the men had been my tutors, but most had been introduced as colleagues of Mother's. Many of these colleagues had become her lovers. They treated me with varying degrees of affection.

One of them was a chaplain from a nearby town who had been relieved of his position for his heretic opinions. His name was Dean Head, which I always thought an amusing name and could not control my giggling the first time he introduced himself. This earned me a slap from my mother, but Dean spoke in my favor.

"No, Victoria, there's no need to strike the lass," he gently admonished. "It is a funny name, so it is. Chaplain Dean Head, founder of a new school of religious thought, based firmly on scientific principles. I am a radical thinker, my dear, so your mum and I are two of a kind. I hope you and I will be great friends."

The wax sculpture of Dean stood gazing thoughtfully toward the corner of the room, as if he were contemplating the nature of God. Physically, he reminded me of my father. He was a tall, willowy man with unruly black hair and violet eyes. By nature he was uncomplicated and possessed an amazingly strong zest for life. The only time I had ever been happy was in his presence.

I supposed that Mother must have instilled a bit of her own morose nature into each of these works, for Dean's face was drawn and gaunt, which was very unlike the man I had known. Although he was a thin fellow, he was always in robust good health, jaunty, and joyful. Unlike some of my mother's other lovers, he liked children. He called me "my kidda," and I found myself hoping for my own sake that he would be my stepfather. For his sake I wished that he'd take himself as far from Mother as possible, which he finally did, two years after meeting her.

I couldn't blame Dean for leaving, though I often found myself wishing he would have taken me with him. I think he would have stayed in spite of my mother's extreme fluctuations in mood if she had only been true to him. But she had many assistants, and by the time I was 10 years old, I was aware she was having affairs with most, if not all of them — mostly the men, but I did once see her kissing one of her female assistants as if they were lovers. I kept this knowledge to myself. I've no idea what she would have done to me if she realized I knew.

Most of the assistants were college-aged, but some of the lads looked to be only a few years older than myself. Once Mother was through with them, they never returned. She always made wax sculptures to commemorate them. Mother broke many hearts over the years. If Father had not died in battle, he surely would have divorced her for her philandering.

Mother planned to sell her immortality formula at an extremely high price once she perfected it. I was sure she was correct in assuming people would pay any price for immortality. So far, her formulations brought only disfiguring death fraught with suffering.

She usually brought me in to dissect the corpses of her subjects while she threw herself into research to improve the next batch of formula. I never had a cat, dog, bird, rabbit, rat, or monkey for a pet. Instead, I saw countless numbers of these creatures before me on an operating table. I would expose their internal organs so that Mother could discern the extent and type of damage done by her serum.

Some of her specimens had their organs liquefied. In other cases, young animals aged and died in a matter of minutes. Some suffered internal hemorrhage, and at other times, certain processes essential to life simply failed. One formulation caused the iron base of the blood, hemoglobin, to turn to zinc. The skin of the unfortunate animal given this poison became dead white, as if it had been bled to death. When I drew the scalpel over the skin, the blood that came out was white and chalky. I always felt sad for Mother's specimens, but I could not allow myself to become emotionally involved if I were to keep my sanity.

"We do this in the name of science, Anthos," Mother would remind me each time I was called upon to dissect one of her victims.

I would agree, all the while wanting to scream that it was she, not I, who was responsible for administering the deadly formulations to these creatures.

"You do it in the name of your brand of demented pseudo-science," I wished to tell her. "You administer these formulas to countless victims without regard to how your potions make them suffer. Do not name me as your co-conspirator, for I would never behave in such an unethical fashion."

I said nothing as I drew my scalpel across the bulging abdomen of her latest victim. It was clear that all the cells in this monkey's body had lysed, leaking fluid into its tissues and causing its trunk and extremities to bulge.

I often thought of running away but wondered where I would go. Mother kept the house locked up like a fortress. The perimeter of the grounds was surrounded by a 7 meter tall wall equipped with alarms to alert her to the presence of any intruder. These alarms would also have informed her of anyone attempting to scale the boundary from the inside. Besides, climbing the wall without equipment would have been a nearly impossible task.

As I wrote in my journal, I was a prisoner. I detailed a fantasy of one day escaping this death camp and being made a hero for turning my mother over to the police for her insanity and cruelty.

The Discovery

One morning I discovered Mother had taken on a new assistant, an exotic young woman named Jamila Van As. I could tell right away the poor deluded girl had fallen deeply under Mother's spell. Jamila was strikingly beautiful with her deep blue eyes, red-brown hair, and rosy cheeks. She said her mother came from the small Middle Eastern nation of Jordan, and her father was of Dutch ancestry. She was kind to me, and I did not wish to see her wounded by Mother's cruel criticisms and unrealistic demands the way everyone who comes into Mother's sphere eventually is.

I wished that I could tell Jamila to go away before it was too late. I knew that no matter how much Mother gushed over her in the beginning, it would be impossible for her to care for the girl – not as a surrogate daughter, not as a respected colleague, not as an assistant, and not as a lover. Mother used and disposed of everyone eventually — everyone except for me. I assumed, and in truth prayed, that I would one day outlive my usefulness to her and be sent away.

Jamila said she was 18 years old, but I didn't believe she could be much older than 16 — a mere four years older than I. I knew one day soon there would be another waxwork in Mother's showroom. This new waxwork would be a beautiful maiden with dark mahogany hair and olive skin. Her blue eyes would have the same look of sadness and terror that all Mother's sculptures held. Perfect though they were otherwise, they always possessed an unsettling look of dejected shock.

During dinner, Jamila expressed her wish that the animals didn't have to be harmed in the experimentation process. She said she understood that sometimes these things must happen, though, in order to make scientific advances. She praised Mother, saying how honored she felt to be working with such a great scientist.

Mother in turn told Jamila how inspired she was to meet a beautiful girl who chose to use her mind rather than allow her appearance to carry her through life. She said that Jamila might be the most beautiful girl she had ever seen, and reached under the table to caress her thigh. Jamila blushed and gave a little giggle as Mother leaned over and gave her a kiss near her mouth. I excused myself from the table, having lost my appetite even for Blancmange, which is my very favorite dessert.

At about 9 p.m., there came a soft rapping on my door. I knew it couldn't be Mother, as she always knocks loudly in case I have fallen asleep. I was fairly certain the cook had gone home, so I rose and opened the door to see who might be calling. There stood Jamila with a tray containing tea and two dishes of Blancmange.

"I hoped you might be feeling well enough to enjoy dessert now," she said. "You looked extremely pale when you left the table."

My eyes welled with tears, and I swallowed hard.

"Thank you, it's very kind of you. You're the nicest one who's been here since Dean."

"Was he one of your mother's assistants?" Jamila asked.

"He was her fiancé. I hoped he might be my father. My father died in the war before I was born."

"Yes, that's what your mother said."

Her voice was so soft, her manner so gentle. She was too good for Mother. I needed to tell her that she must leave for her own sake, before she too was hurt the way Dean and so many others had been.

Instead I said, "Jamila, you're so very kind. I would like you to stay here and be my friend."

"I would like that too," Jamila replied. Then she smiled and a starry-eyed, faraway look came over her face as she spoke of Mother.

"Your mother is so brilliant and so glamorous. I can't believe she chose me to be her assistant. I'm somewhat like you — my parents are dead, too. They were killed in a plane crash. You're lucky that your mother is still alive, and now she's made me feel very special, as well.

"She visited the biology class at the orphanage school and said she was seeking the best of the best to assist her with her work. She thought I was that choice, even though I'm not the sharpest in my sciences. She said she saw something special in me."

"You are special, I can see that," I said. "The trouble is, Mother can sometimes be very harsh. She can hurt people's feelings terribly and not even care. All of her other assistants have left suddenly never to return. I don't want her to upset you that way."

"Well, she is a perfectionist. But she seems very fond of me. Perhaps, for me, it will be different."

I wanted to scream that it wouldn't be different, but I knew it wouldn't do any good. I needed to find a way to prove to Jamila that she needed to get as far away from this place as possible, before she became another victim of Mother's heartlessness.

"I hope you're right," I said. "And thank you for the Blancmange and the tea."

There was another tap at the door, and Mother entered. She smiled broadly.

"I thought I might find you here, Jamila," she said. "How perfectly lovely of you to check on Anthos. Are you feeling better, my darling daughter?"

"Yes, I am now," I said.

"Anthos has a very delicate stomach," Mother said. "Fortunately, it doesn't stop her from dissecting the specimens. Jamila, love, I need to see you in the laboratory so we may discuss certain issues critical to your employment with me."

"Of course, Dr. Peacock," Jamila said.

Before rising, she leaned over and kissed me on the forehead.

"Good night, Anthos," she said. "I'll see you in the morning."

I squeezed her hand and bit my lip. After Jamila had floated from the room on steps so light as to be nearly inaudible, Mother turned and gave a predatory grin and conspiratorial wink.

"She is a beauty, isn't she?" she proclaimed. "And quite bright, which is a bonus. I simply cannot abide a simpleton, no matter how comely he or she may be. Well, dear, it's time for all good children to be off to dreamland. I'll see you in the morning."

Mother's kiss left sticky pink lipstick on my cheek, which I wiped away as soon as she was gone. She was becoming bolder, making little effort to conceal her true purpose for the assistants she brought into our home. I was her only real underling these days. The others were there to fulfill shameful desires.

"I won't let her do it to Jamila—I simply won't!" I swore to myself.

After 15 minutes had passed, I crept into the darkened hallway. As I had hoped, there was no one on either the second or main floors. I slipped into the cellar where I heard the voices of my mother and Jamila.

"Oh, Dr. Peacock, I'm deeply flattered that you are so overcome by my beauty," Jamila said breathlessly. "But this…it's wrong, isn't it? For two women to be lovers, I mean?"

Mother and Jamila were seated on the sofa just outside the sculpture exhibition room. When Mother leaned towards Jamila, she reminded me of Dracula in the movie scene where he corners the flower girl and leans over her, covering both of them with his cape.

"That may be what the rest of the world says, my sweet," Mother sighed, "But a love this strong cannot be fought. You feel it too, don't you, Jamila? Oh, please, tell me you feel it, too. My heart would be broken if you didn't feel it."

"Oh yes, Dr. Peacock. I've never known anyone like you before. You're so beautiful, I simply don't feel worthy!"

Mother brought her face to Jamila's and kissed her mouth. I felt bile rising in my throat. Fortunately, the laboratory was open, and I slipped inside. Mother had carelessly left her notes on her desk. I began looking through them for anything incriminating enough to convince Jamila she should escape the clutches of this perverse madwoman before it was too late.

"Her heart would be broken, my foot!" I snorted. "It simply isn't possible, for she doesn't possess a heart to break!"

Mother's notes began in 1941 when she reached the age of 21 and the title to her parents' home passed to her following the death of her cousin. It was at this time she began in earnest to try and perfect the immortality formula her father had left undone.

I leafed through the journals for some 15 minutes. There was page after page describing the deaths of animal specimens, up until the entry for Jan. 17, 1945. As I read, my hands began to shake, and a little cry escaped my throat.

"He wasn't killed in the war at all. You...you murdered him!" I gasped.

17 January 1945

Wum is due to return to the front tomorrow, so tonight is the night that I test the formula on a human subject. I poured two milliliters into Wum's nightcap. He was none the wiser until his organs began to turn to wax within him, but by then, it was too late. The process took only an hour. He first began to sweat, and then his breathing became labored. He complained of feeling sick to his stomach, as if he had swallowed a tub of clay. Then he spoke no more, and slowly the life drained out of him.

24 January 1945

The army fools came and went today, believing my husband to be a coward and a deserter. I care not. I am happy to find that like the animals in the previous experiments, Wum shows no signs of decay. I have put him on display in the room near my laboratory that I may continue to observe him for any signs of change. I like him much better this way — obedient and quiet!

Sweat poured from my brow, and my breathing became labored. I felt as though my stomach were filled with sludge. Of course, this was simply a reaction to the terrible truth I had just discovered. My mother had murdered my father and Dean and all of her other assistants and lovers, as well. I needed to get this information to the police. But first I needed to be sure that Jamila escaped the madwoman's clutches.

I felt as if I had been drugged. I plodded towards the door, my legs feeling as if they were made of lead. I could hardly move. The journal felt so heavy I could barely carry it. It took all of my strength to pry open the door. Mother, however, pulled it open for me.

I gasped as I saw Jamila slumped on the couch, gasping for breath. Her blue eyes were wide with terror.

"Ah, Anthos—you found my notes," Mother said. "Dear me, it looks as if that big book is terribly heavy for you. I'll take it now. You don't look very well, my girl. Why don't you go sit on the couch beside your new friend?"

I couldn't fight—I could hardly move at all. It felt as if I were drowning.

"Why?" I gasped as Mother pushed me onto the sofa. "How could you?"

"Oh, Anthos," Mother sighed. "It's all in the name of science. How can I ever complete my parents' research when traitors threaten to stop me from my work at every turn? Your father called me mad. He threatened to turn me over to the RSPCA for my unauthorized experimentation on the specimens. Dean had the audacity to tell me I was a bad mother and threatened to tell the police I was abusing you. Isn't that absurd? And one by one my assistants became ungrateful, calling me inhumane and refusing to care for my…well, I'll just say, my womanly needs. You were the only one I could trust not to expose me — until I saw the latest entry in your journal. Really, my dear, did you think you had any secrets from me?"

I'm sure my eyes reflected my surprise. I kept my journal hidden in a small cutout panel in my closet behind my clothes and several boxes. I never dreamed she would look there. I realized too late how wrong I was in my belief that my mother never paid attention to me.

"How sharper than a serpent's tooth it is to have a thankless child," Mother lamented. Her wicked face was blurry in my failing vision. I felt something brush against the tips of my fingers and realized that Jamila's hand had fallen against mine. I forced my hand over to hold hers.

"Just like sisters," my mother gushed. "I knew the two of you would get on nicely. That's why I mixed the formula into the remaining Blancmange. I suggested Jamila bring it up for the two of you to share. She's so perfect that I almost couldn't bear preserving her so soon—but the beauty of love in early bloom always goes rotten sooner or later. Besides, she would never have understood my need to sacrifice my treacherous daughter."

As the world went dark before my eyes, I heard my mother's final words to me.

"Now everything is perfect in my world. I have the perfect husband, perfect child, and a group of wonderful, perfect lovers and cohorts. None of you will ever leave me or betray me, and you will all remain young and beautiful. It's a shame the precise formula for the Immortality Serum continues to evade me, but my father's Preservation Serum is perfect in every way!"

VALLEY

OF

THE GODS

BY

MICHAEL D. GRIFFITHS

Damn, it was hot. But what else could you expect being in the deserts of southern Utah in June? My wife and I had fled here, this desolate yet beautiful place, this Valley of the Gods. No rotting flesh bags came here. Why would they? They were searching for ways to quench their cannibalistic desires and little else. There wasn't even so much as a small town within 40 miles of here, and even the living dead would be hard pressed to hike through these leagues of jagged cliffs.

A raven made a strange guttural caw as it passed overhead, flying to the butte that held Balancing Rock. Despite how many times I had seen the looming high mesas, they still filled me with wonder. The narrow spires gave the impression of figures, which reminded one of forgotten gods. The vermillion cliffs surrounded us in every direction, a fortress of solitude and silence. A perfect place to hole up during this plague of death, save for perhaps one thing – we were slowly starving.

We had gathered as much food as we could before we fled, but when the walking dead are eating your neighbors, you don't have to time go shopping. My wife and I tried to be conservative with what we had, but soon we were forced to consume the few local animals we could find.

The only reason we had survived even this long was our discovery of a natural spring. As bizarre as it sounds, in the middle of this arid desert, a small spring flowed out over some limestone like a miracle. When my wife Loni had spotted it, she had held me as tears poured down her face.

"We're going to live," she had cried, and back then I had agreed. But now we had sunk down to levels I would have never thought possible.

We have each loved the little critters that populate the southwest, and it broke our hearts when our driving hunger required us to start consuming them. Loni, once again, had tears pooling in her eyes when we were forced to eat our first tadpoles. The frogs were next, but even these didn't last long. The spring only ran for maybe an eighth of a mile before the desert sands reclaimed it, but it did draw other animals. I was able to catch a few snakes and even a bird or two, but soon it became apparent that we were fighting a losing battle. We were holding on, but we both silently realized that we wouldn't be able to go on this way.

Another issue we were having was our quickly dwindling firewood. Since we needed to boil our water before drinking, this was also a severe need for us. The desert shrubs provided enough fuel for us to make this happen, but as the weeks passed, I needed to forage further and further from camp.

One day, when I was returning with an armful of chaotic twigs, I heard Loni screaming for help. Dropping the sticks, I began to sprint back to camp. As I approached, the screaming only increased in volume. Topping a hill, I saw that a zombie was clawing at our tent. It was already half shredded and from the sounds of things, Loni was trapped inside.

All my weapons were in the main camp, save my dagger, but I didn't have time to retrieve any on them. I tore down the incline in three oversized strides. Water splashed wildly, as I raced through the stream. Loni was still screaming, which I hoped was a good sign. Drawing my double-edged dagger, I started to yell in the hopes of distracting the animated corpse. It wanted Loni and couldn't have cared less. It did notice when my hiking boot took it in the face.

It looked up at me. Its milky eyes were liquid death. With a reptilian hiss, it came at me spraying black phlegm as it stumbled through the tattered remains of our tent. I stumbled back a step and promptly fell off the 4-foot incline that dropped down into the stream. My butt landed in the water, and my left elbow landed on a rock.

The elbow hurt worse.

My only salvation… the zombie's spill was almost as nasty as mine. He rushed towards me, but totally ignored the drop off. He came crashing down on top of my legs and for a moment, I feared I might have received an accidental bite. This wasn't the case, but the zombie was quickly attempting to rectify that shortcoming. I stabbed forward with my dagger aiming for his eye, yet only managed to cut a jagged tear across the right side of his face.

It was clawing at me and going for a bite, when it was suddenly pulled off me. Loni had it by the ankles. It was distracted enough that this time my dagger did take it in the eye. It finally collapsed in a jet of gore.

"Oh my God, Emery. Are you okay?"

"Am I okay? How about you? Did it get you? Are *you* alright?"

She looked over herself once more as if uncertain as to the truth of her words. "No, he didn't get me. I'm fine. Other than a few bruises that is."

"Yeah, I might have you beat there," I said, rubbing my elbow. But my eyes were lingering on the foul corpse lying beneath me.

"It seems strange that one of them would show up at our spring," she said past a worried face. "I thought you said they would never come out here."

"Well, I suppose they will show up everywhere eventually. Still, it's a big difference between seeing one lone zombie after a month and the large hordes we barely escaped from before."

"But what does this mean? Why now?"

"It only means one thing: the zombies around these parts won. There are no humans left in the little towns, so they are slowly wandering away in search of new victims."

"So there might be more?" Even in fear, I found her beautiful and knew I would do anything to protect her.

"This means a lot of things, honey, not the least of which is that anything left behind in these towns is up for grabs. We could use getting some weapons better than an axe, and of course, a few hundred cans of food would be nice."

"But Em, the fact that all we have is an axe is a good reason not to go to town. These people had guns, and they are dead. How do you think we would fare?"

"But we just saw that the zombies are off searching. Maybe they have left the towns. Sure some are around, but if we try for a small town where there weren't too many people to begin with…"

"I don't like that idea. Could we just stay here longer? I'm sure you'll bag a deer soon."

"With what, my homemade spear? Listen, if it looks too crazy when we get there, we will just leave. But even besides food and weapons, there are loads of other things we need to live out here. We left our home so quickly, and I'd love to get more tarps, tables, a saw, wood, all sorts of things. We could make this place far safer with a little more gear.

Taking her into my arms, I said, "Come on, Loni. We knew this day was coming. We don't really have a choice. We'll just have to be careful."

She snuggled into me and shivered despite the desert heat.

*   *   *

It was a quiet drive to Bluff, the town we had chosen to hit. Bluff wasn't too large, on the best of days, and was about a one gas station town. It was my hope this would make it perfect for our needs.

We spied a zombie stumbling along the road more than a few times. Every time this happened, I could feel Loni tense. We both hated what our world had become, but what could we do?

"You would think we'd see someone," she said, as the clutched the armrests until her fingers turned white.

"There must be people around. In an isolated place like this, the packs wouldn't be huge enough to take out everyone, but the people left would be holed up or hiding. There would be no reason for them to be out here."

My words seemed to help her; even if I wasn't sure I believed them myself.

It was about a 50-mile drive to Bluff; so besides everything else, I knew that getting gas would be something we would need to do. As we drew near, the zombies grew in number. It was still nothing like the cities or even the mid-sized town we were from, but for just two people that didn't have one gun between them, it was certainly enough to make us worried.

"So the plan is: food, gas, tarps, and any extra weapons we can get a hold of." My words were full of confidence, but as the zombies began to lurch towards us, they rang hollow and were replaced by a whispered, "How are we going to do this?"

By the time we reached the outskirts that held a few businesses, we had an undulating parade of at least two dozen zombies following us. It wasn't too much, but more than enough, and others were appearing each minute.

Cold hands slapped at our car as we passed, leaving angry red smears. Tangled bloody teeth gnashed, and as always, the horrid moaning filled the air.

I thought Loni might have been silently crying, and I knew I had to think of something. A simple Rambo-style approach wasn't going to cut it.

"Okay, I have an idea," I said, as I slowed the car.

"What sort of idea? Why are you driving so slowly?"

Then, I started honking the horn.

"Oh my God. Emery! Aren't there enough out here already?"

"Don't worry, I have a plan. I'm going to lure them all out of the town. Then, when they are all far enough away, we'll hurry back in and grab the goods. I think it will work. If enough of them make it back, then we can always…"

My voice trailed off when our car went over a cattle guard with a load bang. Looking down, I saw that it looked like someone had removed every other runner from the cattle guard. "I wonder…"

"What are you – Emery get back in the car!"

Grabbing up my wood axe, I said, "Hold on, let's see how well these shits do with this jacked up cattle guard. I might be able to finish this right here."

"Please don't. It's too dangerous!"

"If I can kill them all then this whole town is ours."

I think she was getting a weapon of her own ready, but I needed to focus on the first three zombies that were nearing the cattle guard. I knew that cattle were too stupid to figure out how to cross these metal grids, but I wasn't sure how well they would work on zombies. Sure these freaks were probably not even as intelligent as a cow, but their feet were longer, so the whole thing was still a toss-up.

The first one made it a few steps before it slipped through the rails and slammed down to his waist. It was a male zombie, and if there were ever a doubt about them not feeling pain, it was instantly dispelled when his groin smashed into a cattle guard rail with a loud snap. It was painful to see, but didn't keep me from batting the guy's head off with my axe.

Three more came and, with the help of the altered cattle guard, I was able to take them out easily enough, but as the main horde approached, I grew concerned. At first, I held my own, swinging my axe until sweat poured off me in thick threads.

Then, things went south.

The cattle guard was becoming clogged with bodies, and the other zombies were now able to just walk over their fallen fellows. I wanted to run, but if I turned my back I was afraid they would get to me before I could reach my car.

Loni screamed and I shouted, "Get behind the wheel and get ready to--" And that was when the first shot rang out.

I was startled when the zombie's head to my right exploded in a shower of gore. Another and another fell. Not questioning my salvation, I hurried into the passenger side of my ride. Loni needed no encouragement and sped away.

We spied the black Ford and the two guys standing in the bed with rifles. Once we arrived, one of them, a man, maybe 30 with a faded old cap hopped to the ground and yelled, "Come on, we got a safe place."

Then, without waiting for a reply, the pair sped off towards the north side of town.

We came to some kind of mansion surrounded by a 5-foot brick wall. It had a steel gate, at which two zombies tugged. Two loud shots silenced their moaning. The passenger leapt out and opened the gate. Once the truck was safely inside, we were waved through.

The engines were turned off, the gate was locked, and we finally had a chance to take our rescuers in. The driver approached us, shaking each of our hands.

"Hello, there, great to find others who have made it through this mess. I'm Mitch, and this here is my pal, Bobby."

On closer inspection, I saw that Mitch was probably closer to 40 than 30. His hair was beginning to both recede and gray. He somehow had managed to retain his beer gut through the apocalypse, but he had a nice enough smile.

His buddy Bobby might have been more on the shell-shocked side and only mumbled a greeting. He was in his late 20s, also a bit stocky and tended to keep both his long, tangled blond locks and half of his face hidden under the shadows of his straw cowboy hat.

Mitch laughed. "You two look like you haven't seen a good meal in quite a while, although I have to say the effect does look good on you, miss."

I thought that was a bit of a strange comment, but we went ahead and introduced ourselves before proceeding into the mansion and enjoyed the biggest meal we had eaten since before all this hell started.

* * *

After sharing a tense dinner, where we did more staring than talking, the plain meal was interrupted by the sounds of the zombies' moaning growing louder in volume.

"So they are just on the other side of that wall?" I said.

"Yeah," Mitch said with a grin. "We picked this place well, huh?"

"Doesn't that drive you crazy?" Loni asked, but I was thinking about something else.

"You mean this place isn't yours?"

Mitch had been looking at Loni, but his jaw snapped shut and after a glance at Bobby, he turned towards me.

"Nope, this isn't our place. It used to belong to 'ole Gunny, but when we saw him walking around with half his neck torn out, we figured he won't mind if we moved in." Then with an edge, he added, "Is that okay with you?"

"Yeah," I said, lifting my eyes towards him, while trying to watch Bobby's expression at the same time. "I suppose I might have done the same thing. If we're going to survive we need to use all the resources we can get."

Mitch broke out into a wide smile. "Good, good, glad to hear you say that. We couldn't agree more."

Loni was giving me a nervous glance, but despite this I said, "Um, okay. So, ah…I guess considering everything, I suppose we are going to need to stay here tonight."

Like always, Mitch did all the talking.

"Of course. As if we'd throw you out there in the dark. Come on, we have plenty of room, right Bobby?" His friend just nodded. "Shoot, we got bedrooms we barely even looked at yet. You can take your pick."

I tried to smile, but the situation was so odd, I'm not sure I pulled it off. Outside, the moaning seemed to increase in volume.

"That sure is generous of you guys, but can I ask you a question?"

"Of course, fire away."

"I'm not an expert on your town, but it doesn't seem too big, and I imagine many zombies were killed before the takeover, and I'm sure a few…victims were eaten beyond repair, so why can't you two just sit on the wall and wax everything that moves?"

141

"Interesting question. I have a few things to say on the subject. Firstly, hell, the plague only started a few weeks ago. We are still trying to get our shit together and figure out what we should be doing. Secondly, and I tell you this in confidence, one of the reasons we are letting all the walkers roam the streets is to keep scavs out of here. Some of the stuff might be hard to get, but the way I look at it, Bluff is ours.

"Now, don't get me wrong, I'm happy you two showed up, and we could probably use some other decent folk, but I don't want just any loser that wonders by thinking this town is up for grabs. So in some ways, they're our guards."

"Strange concept, but I guess it makes sense. So, uh, you'd want us to stay here?"

Keeping his eyes locked with mine, Mitch said, "Sure, why not?" He gave a little laugh, "Unless you have somewhere better to go."

I could see the whites of my wife's eyes, but answered, "Not right now we don't, so, ah...thanks."

"No sweat. Now, Bobby, why don't you show them to their rooms."

*   *   *

After leading us down a dangerously dark corridor, with only his flickering taper to show us the way, Bobby left us in the doorway of what must have been a guest room. A thick comforter covered a Mission-style bed, reminiscent of the Santa Fe theme. After a few forced pleasantries, odd stares, and a couple of grunts, Bobby left the candle with us and took his leave.

As soon as the door was shut and Bobby's clunking footsteps had retreated, Loni threw herself into my arms.

"I wish we'd stayed in the desert. This place is horrible."

"The place itself isn't that bad. At least we're safe."

"Are you sure? I'm frightened. I don't like how those men were looking at me. I'm afraid of them."

"I hear you. With the law gone, there's always the chance that people might just start making up their own rules."

She shivered against me. "I hope they aren't thinking anything along the lines of see, want, take."

I tried to laugh, but it sounded hallow in the stygian room.

"Come on, honey. These guys might be a little socially inept, but I don't think they're serial killers or anything."

She pulled away, but kept her chocolate eyes locked to mine. "I wouldn't be so sure. Can that guy Bobby even talk? I feel like we have entered into some Dawn of the Deliverance, here"

I laughed again, this one more relaxed.

"Yeah, they're goofballs, and I doubt they're the type of guys we would be normally sharing a few beers with, but they may grow on us. Besides, there really aren't that many zombies here. If we can clean out this town, then we could have a real chance. I'm sure a hick place like this will have loads of guns. We can get food, even another ride if we needed to. Once we are set up, then we'll have more options."

"If you say so." She was hugging her arms around her slender form while she talked. "I still don't like it."

"Come on, baby, what do you wanna do? Sneak off in the dark and try to make it through a few dozen zombies without us even having a gun?"

"No...I..... just promise me that you won't let them get weird."

"I promise to protect you. Don't I always?"

She said, "Yes," but as the candle made dancing tiger strips of darkness across her face, I wasn't sure if she really meant it.

*   *   *

Wiping the sweat from my brow, I looked out over the field of rotting death that lay before us. It had taken a little convincing, but I was able to talk Mitch into just going ahead and clearing out the rest of Bluff. There might have been about 200 zombies still walking the streets, but after a morning of almost constant gunfire, nothing moved other than a stray tumbleweed and the growing number of circling vultures.

"Well, I guess we can just grab what we want now," I said, as I moved closer to where Mitch and Bobby were standing on the roof.

"I suppose you could say that," Mitch grinned. "This is our town, but we're willing to share, right, Bobby?" His friend nodded. "We're all in this together, right, Emery?" he continued while slapping me on the shoulder.

"Oh, yah," I said.

I was about to go on, when Loni called up from below. "Are you guys finally done?"

"Yeah, I think so," I answered.

"Good, I made us all something to eat if you wanna head down here."

143

"Thanks, darling," Mitch called. "That's quite a woman you got there," Mitch said, addressing me. "Quite a woman."

*   *   *

Later that night, as I relaxed in bed and tried not to worry about the fact that the book I was reading covered a lifestyle that would no longer be possible, I heard a scuffle in the hallway. Loni had just gone to use the restroom, and I jerked up. *Could a zombie have somehow gotten inside?*

Grabbing up a pistol along the way, I rushed out into the hallway. Shadows owned the narrow passage as I hurried in the direction I had heard the noise. Rounding the corner, I was shocked by what my eyes beheld.

Before me were both Bobby and Mitch. Bobby was closer and had a shotgun leveled at me before I even understood what I was seeing. Mitch had a pistol in one hand and Loni in the other. He was keeping her in a half headlock with his hand clamped over her mouth. Her eyes were wide with horror, which was understandable when he pressed the barrel of the pistol against her temple.

"Hold it right there, Emery," Mitch said. "Just play this cool, and no one needs to get hurt."

"Get hurt! You are the one with the gun against my wife's head! What the hell are you doing?"

"Now, you just calm down. Haven't we shared everything we have with you? By God, we've shared the whole town with you. The least you could do is share the one thing you got with us. We wouldn't need her every night, just once in a while to take the edge off, until we could find a couple of women for ourselves."

"You're sick! Let go of her right now!"

"We may be sick, but I think you are the one that needs to let go of something – your damn pistol. Drop it or I drop her."

Mitch put his pistol against Loni's leg. I don't need her walking for what I want, and she'll have a harder time running away with one leg." We locked eyes for a long moment. "Don't give me an excuse to take you out of the equation, boy."

My pistol clattered to the floor.

"Good boy, glad to see you're being smart. I like you, and I'd like for us to get past this and still be able to work as a team."

"Screw you, Mitch."

His face grew tense. "Don't make me regret my choices, boy. Bobby, go grab that pistol."

Moving closer, Bobby tried to keep both his gaze and his shotgun pointed at me as he stooped over to grab my fallen pistol. Sensing my intent, Loni began to struggle, and that was when I made my move. My foot lashed out, knocking the shotgun's barrel to the side, and I drove in close, keeping Bobby between Mitch and me. A second later, my dagger filled my hand. A second after that, it found a new home in the left side of Bobby's chest. The big man stumbled back with a groan. His body hit the wall and, then, slowly slid down it, dead before he reached the floor.

"Bobby! Bobby! You son of a bitch!" Mitch's pistol was pointed at my face. "Give me one reason I shouldn't just kill you where you stand."

That was when Loni bit down on his hand while pushing his gun arm up towards the ceiling. Shots rang out loudly in the enclosed room and bits of plaster rained down on them as they struggled. I attempted to move toward them, but had only made it a few feet before Mitch shoved Loni against the wall. Her head connected with a metal candle stand, and she crumbled with a short gasp.

"You piece of-"

"Watch it, boy." His pistol was once again pointed at my face. "I'm beginning to think you two are more trouble then you're worth."

"What, you just want to live here by yourself?" I couldn't care less what Mitch wanted, but at the time I figured keeping him talking was a better alternative to have him pump me full of holes.

"No, I'll keep her, but it's you I'm uncertain about. You think you can behave?"

"While you rape my wife?" As soon as the words escaped my lips, I knew I shouldn't have said them. From the look on his face, I knew this wasn't the thing Mitch wanted to hear.

"Yeah, I guess that would be a hard road. Well, it was nice knowing you, kid."

As he leveled his gun, I was wondering if there were any chance I could dodge to the side and …

That was when Bobby's animated corpse reached out and grabbed Mitch's leg. Mitch might have thought his friend was still alive, at least until his teeth tore out the man's Achilles' tendon.

There was a scuffle and shots, but I barely paid it any attention for I was scrambling for my pistol. "Oh, no," I heard Mitch moan. "Am I going to become one of them now?"

"Nope," was all I said, before my pistol roared to life.

The smoke hadn't cleared before I sprinted over to Loni. "Loni, baby, are you okay?"

At first I thought the worst, but then her eyes fluttered open "Are we safe?"

I smiled. "Yeah, about as safe as one can be in a world full of zombies."

*   *   *

"So, that is how Loni and I came to be in possession of this choice stronghold. I'm glad that you have found us. Sure we get zombies here from time to time, even groups of them, but we are so far off the main routes that there hasn't been anything we couldn't handle, yet. We might be running out of food and ammo one day, but for now we are okay. Loni is raising chickens, and we even have a little garden."

"So you're welcome to stay, as long as you remember my one rule. No matter how long you stay here or how cute Loni may look working in the garden in her little shorts. Hands off! Loni is mine and mine alone, and if you don't want to end up like the others you remember that.

"As long as you keep that in mind, I'm sure we'll be great friends."

HIPS

BY

WILLIAM TODD ROSE

It was dark when she awoke. For a moment she laid in the sleeping bag with her eyes closed and listened to the shuffle of footsteps out in the hall. She could hear the heavy doors of the other cells being opened, one of the new girls sobbing softly, the murmur of conversation as her captors made their rounds . . . just like always.

Every day, the same sequence of events played out as if she were nothing more than a character in some macabre loop film. Judging by how muffled the sounds were, she knew she would hear seven other cell doors swing open before they made it to hers. As the squeaking of hinges grew louder, so would the terse commands of their keepers. The same set of orders repeated in voices that sounded emotionless and bored. Day in. Day out.

Her bladder felt as if a heavy stone had grown in it overnight. The stone had sharp edges that raked against the soft, unprotected lining of the organ, flaring with pain as she struggled to hold it in. A little wooden bucket sat in one corner of her cell, but even with the sleeping bag pulled up over her face she could still smell it: the stench of stale piss and caked-on shit, so thick that it seemed to lodge itself in little chunks in the back of her throat. A steady stream of urine would only make matters worse, churning yesterday's waste into a frothy, brown sludge and releasing even more of the noxious vapors. No, it was better to wait. Before they left her cell, they would empty it into the drum which sat across the hall. If not clean, at least it would be *cleaner.*

All part of the routine.

She finally opened her eyes and pulled the sleeping bag down to her shoulders. The view that greeted her was the usual brick walls that glistened with condensation and the concrete floor with its Rorschach stains of various bodily fluids. Her cell was no larger than a broom closet, and the only light came through the small, barred window on the wooden door . . . and even then only when torches had been lit in the hall. The wall opposite the door also had one of these windows, but beyond it was a darkness so complete that she could only hear the things that shuffled on the other side.

That would change soon, however. It was also part of the daily routine. The moment her door opened, they would be at the window, grasping through the bars with hands that looked shriveled and mummified in the dim light of the cell. With fingernails worn down to ragged splinters, they would reach through and claw at the air, scratching at the bricks as if they could somehow erode the rough mortar through persistence alone.

The creatures had deteriorated to the point that they no longer had an odor, but anytime a "freshie" was added to the group, there would be weeks where the stench of decay overpowered even the toilet bucket. Somehow, that was the worst part of the ordeal: smelling the greasy, sweet reek of rotting meat and knowing that once it had been someone just like her. Someone who had learned to cope with life in the cells as best as she could. Someone to whom she'd spoken, perhaps, through the bars on their doors. Someone who was no longer useful . . . .

"Assume the position, Mole."

The voice was closer now, maybe only four doors down or so.

"I said, *assume the position, Mole!*"

The voice was more annoyed than angry. But if the unseen woman continued to resist, things could turn bad quickly. She'd heard (and felt) the beatings before: the dull thud and smack of sawed-off broomsticks against thighs, the cries of pain, the tears and sobbing and pleading apologies.

"Just do, it." she muttered. "Make it easy on yourself, Mole."

She felt her face grow warm and her stomach churned in a nauseating mixture of disgust and shame. *Mole.* She'd actually called the woman that. Like their captors, she'd stripped away every fiber of personality from her fellow prisoner with a single word. It was a word that reduced a living, breathing, thinking *person* into nothing more than a single characteristic. It was a word that left her mouth feeling so dirty that she would rather drink her bucket of waste than utter it again.

She, too, had a name once; but now she was simply Hips. Like her mother and boyfriend, her name had disappeared into the mists of time and memory. Sometimes, while the darkened hallway beyond her cell echoed with snores, she would lay in the gloom and whisper that name over and over. As if it were some sort of mantra that could magically teleport her from this dank dungeon to some distant place where she would feel the warmth of sun on her skin and hear birds chirping overhead. Without fail, though, it always took her mind back to that last day of freedom. To the day she lost everything . . . .

They were hunkered down in a burned out storefront, hidden behind the charred remains of the front counter. The sun had set several hours earlier, and a darkness had fallen across the town that made it seem as if they had been plunged into the void of space. The days of street lamps and the soft glow of curtained windows were over. No headlights splayed across the soot-stained walls, no winking neon or stop lights cycled through their array of colors. And on that particular night, there wasn't even the pale luminescence of moonlight to chase away the shadows.

With the darkness came silence, as well. She'd never realized how noisy society was until it had all been taken away. The humming of air conditioners, traffic four blocks over hissing through rain-slick streets, the muffled beat of music seeping through the walls of bars and clubs – all those things were missing now. The million other tiny sounds her ears had learned to take for granted had been replaced with a silence so complete that only a high-pitched ringing filled her ears.

And, it was really the quiet that worried her most. They had run their hands along the cinder-like edge of the counter and smeared the dark ash across their faces and arms commando style. They'd curled up beneath a black tarp Jeremy had found a few days back, had tried everything within their power to pass themselves off as just another cluster of shadows. So, in a sense, the darkness was their ally. Her boyfriend, however, had a tendency to talk in his sleep. In the bedroom of their apartment it had been nothing more than softly muttered gibberish, not even loud enough to wake her if she were sleeping. But out here that same sound would be like a loudspeaker broadcasting in the night: *we're here, we're hiding over here, come get us, come quick . . . .*

Which was one of the reasons sleep came in short, quick bursts. Even though she was so exhausted that her muscles felt as if they were made of overcooked spaghetti, she had to be ready to clamp her hand over Jeremy's mouth, to push the words back into his throat if she could. She had to be ready to keep her loved ones safe.

She didn't have to worry about Mama, however. About two weeks earlier, they'd been attempting to sneak through a heavily infested area just outside of Redfield. There were rumors of a FEMA rescue station nearby, and her stepfather, Denny, had insisted on scouting the route ahead of them. They'd followed about 50 yards behind and hid behind dumpsters or wrecked cars when he'd form his hand into a fist and then move on when he'd wave.

Start and stop. Duck and hide, picking their way through the rubble and debris of a once proud society. But then he'd been pulled down by a pack of corpses that seemed to appear from nowhere, ripped apart right before their very eyes. Sometimes she'd still see him in her dreams: the way he fought and clawed and punched even as his knees buckled from the force of the assault . . . the bright, crimson arc of blood that spurted with slow-motion clarity as teeth pulled strands of flesh and muscle from a throat no longer capable of producing sound. He'd been a good husband and decent stepfather but, in the end, had made a horrible scout. He should have pushed his ego aside and listened to her suggestions instead of simply shrugging them off. Maybe if she'd been the one running point, things would've turned out differently.

But she'd learned quickly that in this new world regrets could quickly get your ass killed. You had to focus on the here and now, to push memory into the farthest corners of your mind and bury it beneath the weight of more pressing concerns. Food. Clean water. Shelter and survival.

The future operated on the same principle. In her previous life she'd had dreams: she'd finish college, get a job with a decent newspaper in a medium-size town, get married, and have kids eventually. At some hazy point on the timeline of her life, the grandchildren would come bursting through the front door with squeals of *Grandma!* She'd shower them with hugs and treats and smile serenely at the man by her side . . . the man whose face she'd seen morph from the smooth flesh of the young into a wrinkled mask of experience.

But things had changed, hadn't they? Hopes and ambitions were now exclusively short-term. Her ambitions had been reduced to making it through yet another night alive, of finding that mythical pocket of society that had somehow been untouched by the insanity that had swept over the world like a tsunami of death and mutilation. Life had been reduced to an almost constant state of *now,* and those who dared to dream too long would quickly find themselves wrapped in the darkness of a sleep from which they would never awaken.

The world had changed. And she, in turn, had been forced to change with it.

The sun had just begun to paint the eastern horizon with streaks of amber and orange when she heard it: a scuffling sound from outside, so soft and furtive that it was almost lost beneath the rhythmic lull of her companions' breathing. Footsteps? The sound of well-worn soles sliding over concrete and asphalt?

She closed her eyes and tried to listen for the sounds to repeat, to lock in their distance and general location. But her heart hammered in her chest with such force that she could only hear the whooshing of blood as it surged through her veins.

The cold hand of fear squeezed her stomach and caused bile to shoot up through her esophagus and flooded her mouth with stinging bitterness. Beads of sweat dotted her forehead, and the muscle below her left eye twitched like a caged bird longing for flight. She held her breath, remaining perfectly still, listening, praying.

Maybe it had only been the breeze, or a yellowed scrap of newspaper, perhaps. Maybe it was a small animal. Dogs and cats were few and far between these days, having been hunted almost to extinction by the same masters who'd once showered them with toys and treats. They were rare, but not entirely unheard of.

Could that be it, then? Nothing more than a mangy cur scavenging for carrion?

She took a breath through her nostrils so slowly that it took nearly 10 seconds for her lungs to fill. She could smell the musty scent of age within the store, the smoky ghost of the fire that had gutted this place and refused to leave its haunt, and the sharp bite of dried sweat. If the stench of rotting flesh existed outside the shattered shop window, it was masked by these other odors.

But surely the reek of a rotter would've overpowered them? It had been so hot lately that the sun-bloated corpses who staggered across the landscape traveled in a cloud of fetor so repugnant that even the flies shunned them.

Had she imagined it all? Perhaps she'd slipped into sleep for a fraction of a second, and her mind had amplified the sound of the tarp shifting into something much more sinister?

That had to be it. The dead were notoriously noisy, caring not for stealth or cunning. While it was true that they didn't grunt or growl or groan, they were clumsy for the most part and prone to knocking over precariously balanced piles of rubble or kicking old bottles as they shuffled forward. Surely a freshie or rotter would've tripped across the string of tin cans she'd tied between the splintered telephone pole and an old parking meter by now. They weren't smart enough to avoid traps, after all. Not even such primitive early detection systems as hers.

Mere feet away, something thumped against the floorboards of the store, and every muscle in her body tensed.   *Fight or run? Shit, how many of them are there? Shit, shit, shit . . . .*

A long, slow creak as the wooden planks flexed beneath the weight of the intruder.

Just one. Has to be. More would be nosier. I can deal with just one. I know I can.

Her hand began crawling across the floor as if of its own accord, its fingertips searching for the cool reassurance of the tire iron.

Two blows. Quick crack to the skull to stun it. Then plunge the business end into the eye socket, go for the brain, use all your strength, all your weight, drive that fucker home.

The muscles in her arms and legs had begun to quiver with a mixture of fear and adrenaline. Her heart thudded out a cryptic message in Morse code, and her throat felt as if it had somehow expanded to allow more air to flow into her lungs.

You can do this, girl. You wake up Mama and Jeremy, and they'll be dead before they've even cleared the cobwebs outta their minds. You have to do this.

Her fingers wrapped around the smooth metal of the tire tool, and she lifted it from the floor so slowly that it almost seemed as if she suspected it would disintegrate if hoisted too quickly. Though her palms were warm and slick, the weight of the weapon immediately caused her breathing to even out. *Drop that fucker fast and then get the hell outta here.* Opening her eyes, she saw a dark shadow against the golden glow of sunrise on the wall. The silhouette was human shaped and grew larger with each beat of her heart. She couldn't lie to herself any longer: they were not alone in this old store, and the time had come to walk the tightrope between life and death.

She sprung from the floor with the speed of a striking serpent and vaulted across the counter in a single, fluid move. In her mind, a shrill battle cry trilled through the stillness of the morning, and she felt the spirits of a thousand Amazonian warriors raise their spears and shields in solidarity. In reality, however, she was as silent and swift as sudden death. Only her eyes reflected the intensity of the rage that boiled within her, the grim determination of a woman who would *not* "go gentle into that good night."

The man across from her scrambled backwards as his hands flew up in an open palmed display of surrender. His eyes grew wide beneath his curly bangs, and he continued backpedaling as his hoarse voice stammered words so quickly that the syllables all ran together.   "Wait! No! Alive! I'm alive! I'm living, here!"

For a moment, his pleading didn't register in her mind. She continued her assault. The tire tool was raised above her head like the sword of a charging samurai and, like those legendary weapons, seemed to demand a taste of blood before allowing itself to be lowered.

The man's hands shot to the rifle slung over his shoulder and snapped it into firing position as his knees braced himself against the force of the attack.

"Damn it, I'm not one of them!"

His sharp tone cut through the haze of battle, and she stopped so suddenly that momentum almost caused her to stumble forward. They stood facing each other for what seemed to be an eternity: she with the tire iron poised and ready to strike, he with the bore of his rifle staring at her like a dark, unblinking eye. "Please, I don't want to shoot you. But I will. I swear to God, I will."

"You're . . . you're really alive?"

"No, I'm the smartest damn zombie that ever existed. What the hell do you think? Of course, I'm alive."

She felt a hand on her shoulder and a familiar voice whispered in her ear.

"It's okay, sweetie . . . "

She'd been so focused on her attack that she hadn't even heard him stir. But it stood to reason that the flurry of activity would've awakened him. Mama, too, most likely.

"Look, folks, I'm here to help. I really am."

Together, the two of them lowered their respective weapons. She was breathing heavily now, her chest heaving with each breath, and for some reason tears had begun to make the world around her swim in and out of focus. She blinked rapidly, trying to focus on the bearded man in the tattered clothes whom she'd been mere seconds away from killing. But he wavered as if she were viewing him from the other side of a waterfall, and the first tear had just begun to leave its warm path down her cheek as he unclipped the walkie-talkie from his belt.

"Eden Team, this is Serpent Six, over."

There was a hiss of static and then his voice again.

"Serpent Six to Eden Team. Come in, Eden Team. Over. Serpent Six this is Eden Team. Over."

The voice was thin and soft, but it was the voice of someone else like them. Someone left alive in a world ruled by the dead.

"Eden Team, I have three survivors. Two female, one male, none apparently infected. Repeat . . . I have three survivors. Over."

"Serpent Six, rendezvous at Alpha Base One at oh-nine-hundred hours. Reanimate activity in sector seven high. Advance with extreme caution. We'll notify The Garden that the mission was successful, and we're coming home. Over."

"Copy that, Eden Team. Serpent Six, out."

There hadn't been much time for conversation, but she'd learned the man's name was Donnely. He was apparently nothing more than a small cog in a much larger machine – what the man on the other end of the radio had referred to as The Garden.

The Garden, Donnely had explained, was a collective that had established a fortified outpost about half a day's walk from their current location. Whereas the dregs of humanity seemed content with cowering in the shadows like frightened animals, The Garden had loftier ambitions. They were going to rebuild society, reclaim the coveted position at the top of the food chain, and re-establish mankind's dominance over the world.

The human race, he said, had been decimated, and the undead far outnumbered the living. But in the future they envisioned the tide would be turned. Children would be trained as efficiently as soldiers. Once their numbers were great enough, they would rise up against the undead in one, final battle. Within 15 to 20 years, tops, the world would be theirs again, and the blight of the living dead would be no more than a chapter in history books yet to be written.

It had sounded so promising: a place where they would be sheltered from the horrors of the outside world, a society that still functioned, that sent out teams to find those still left alive and bring them back . . . no wonder they referred to themselves with terms like *Eden* and *The Garden*. True, their ambitions sounded lofty. But at least they still had goals and plans. At least they could envision a world that consisted of something more than picking at the carcass of civilization like nomadic scavengers. At least they had *hope*.

So, they had followed this man, Donnelly. She, Jeremy, and Mama had allowed him to guide them through the maze of mangled cars and toppled buildings. They had slipped through the wreckage of the city like ghosts, skirting around enclaves of rotters so skillfully that the dead never realized they were there. For the most part, they progressed in silence. But every so often, when Donnely decided they were well out of harm's way, they would stop for a quick rest. During this down time, they would whisper to one another, and she slowly began to grasp the full extent of The Garden's plans.

"To beat your enemy," Donnely had told them, "you first have to understand him."

He was part of Eden Team, whose job was to search out those wandering the wastelands that would be able to assist in repopulating the cities of the earth. But there was also a group he referred to as The Tree of Knowledge. Their entire purpose, he said, was to study the undead menace. But they didn't just study the ways in which they could be dispatched. No, The Tree of Knowledge wanted to know everything they could about their adversaries.

"Everyone knows a bite will kill your ass and bring you back. But did you know that any exchange of bodily fluids will do the same damn thing? You kiss someone who's infected, for example, and get even the smallest amount of spit in your mouth, and you're done for."

When he spoke about The Garden and its various projects, his voice rose slightly in pitch, and the words came more rapidly. Breathlessly, he told them about the actual gardens where they grew crops, the kitten nurseries with their self-replenishing sources of meat, and the various ways they had of collecting and purifying water. The entire time, his green eyes shone with the light of the true believer.

His enthusiasm was as contagious as any of the corpses in this God-forsaken land. As they pressed on, her mind was filled with images of what The Garden would be like – how she would never have to know the sharp pangs of hunger or the fear of darkness again. Perhaps she and Jeremy would be able to recapture the sort of life that, just hours ago, she was sure they had been robbed of. Only, hopefully, it would be better than she'd ever dreamed.

Her stepfather had never really approved of her boyfriend. He'd said Jeremy was weak and unfocused, that she could do so much better than a guy whose major goal in life was to beat the most current level of whatever video game he was playing. And, on some level, she'd kind of agreed with Denny . . . even though she would never outwardly admit it. She'd silently hoped that someday her boyfriend would tire of being just another telemarketer tethered to his cubical by a headset. Maybe he'd start to dream of management or even actually creating the games he loved playing so much. A little time at the gym wouldn't have hurt either . . . even before fresh food had become as rare as gold, Jeremy had been thin and gangly. He'd been kind of like a tall, pubescent boy, really.

But maybe The Garden would have the positive effect on him that had somehow been lacking in their previous lives. Perhaps there he would find something he was so passionate about that his eyes would spark with excitement the way Donnelly's did. He might even decide that he wanted to become part of Eden Team and those thin arms might bulk up with the same sinewy muscle that strained at the sleeves of their guide's T-shirt. Not that she wanted him to be *exactly* like their new-found benefactor. She did love him for who he was, after all. But a little maturity wouldn't hurt, would it?

After what seemed like hours of walking, the group finally crested a small hill that overlooked a valley lush with trees and a patchwork of multicolored foliage. The sun was hanging low in the sky but the temperature had already begun to climb which caused her skin to be coated with a sheen of sweat. From this distance she could just make out a stream that snaked its way through the valley below. Its waters sparkled as if millions of pixies bobbed on its surface, and it was all too easy to imagine how cool that water would be as it lapped against her sunburned skin, how good it would feel as it quenched the dry harshness of her throat.

"Wait here."

Donnely's command had pulled her thoughts away from the meandering creek and back to the cluster of camouflaged tents just within the grove of trees before them. Three men walked out to meet him, each with a rifle slung over his shoulder by a thin strap. All of the men were similar in build to their guide: muscular, seemingly well-fed and healthy, and obviously selected for Eden Team because of their athletic physique.

However the center of attention seemed to be a short bulldog of a man with a neck so thick and brown that it could have passed for the trunk of a small tree. As the others spoke, this man kept shooting glances at the newcomers through his spectacles, and something about his gaze had made her feel like an insect beneath a microscope.

She shifted her weight from foot to foot and kept discovering new patches of skin on her arms and face that needed scratched. Something about this little man and his cold, hard eyes made her uneasy.

"Must be their leader," Jeremy said. "Kinda looks like a general, huh?"

She'd nodded in response, maybe uttered some non-committal answer . . . she couldn't be sure. All she knew was that, for reasons she couldn't understand, she now felt as uneasy as if they were standing among a group of ravenous rotters. But that was ridiculous. These people were here to help, right? They were Eden Team. From The Garden.

The group of men disbanded, Donnely disappearing into the woods as the others walked slowly toward them. The one Jeremy had referred to as a general seemed to be smirking slightly, and she'd gulped hard, trying to tell herself that it was simply thirst that made her feel as if her airway was constricting.

Maybe if they'd actually said something, she would have felt better. But, no. General Bulldog and one of them men stopped several yards away from them and seemed to study the small group with their eyes. At the same time, the other man circled around them, and for some reason the image of a pack of dogs came to mind. It was the way they would circle their prey, cutting off any means of escape before lunging into their attack.

But that was silly. Of course these men would be wary. The world was full of people who saw the apocalypse as a handy excuse to simply do whatever the hell they wanted. Rapists, murderers, thieves: as the number of survivors had decreased, the sins of those left alive had grown exponentially. It made sense that they would be very careful about the people who were brought into their fold.

It was all entirely logical. But logic did little to assuage the nervous tightening in her stomach and even less to silence the voice in the back of her mind which whispered that something just wasn't right.

General Bulldog's eyes studied her for a moment, and for some reason she felt the same way she had when she'd walked through the din of catcalls and innuendo of construction workers. Like she was nothing more than a piece of meat, something to be had and discarded.

"Useable. Good hips."

His voice was gruff and abrupt and somehow sounded as if he were passing judgment on her. She immediately felt herself stiffen as her hands balled into fists. She wanted to spit some caustic remark back at him, but her mind balked and left her simply standing there with her mouth agape.

The little man's eyes darted to Jeremy, and for a moment he almost seemed to wince.

"Weak. Bad stock."

Then onto Mama.

"Too old."

There was a moment of silence before the man spoke again.

"Tree of Life has an adequate number of test subjects. These two are useless."

It happened with the quickness of a lightning strike. One moment, these two groups of people were simply standing on the hillside staring at one another as a cloud passed across the sun. The next, General Bulldog and his underling had their rifles shouldered as if by magic. Two shots rang out and echoed through the valley below, startling a flock of birds into flight as twin puffs of spent gunpowder filled the morning with their sulfuric odor.

Jeremy and Mama's heads snapped back as a crimson mist seemed to spray in slow motion from the dime-sized holes that had appeared in their foreheads. Their bodies crumpled to the ground, falling atop one another while unblinking eyes stared at the boots of the men who'd killed them.

She'd screamed and turned to run then, spinning around just in time to see the stock of a rifle racing toward her face. There was a flash of pain, and dark spots that had exploded like antimatter fireworks in her field of vision. She felt the sensation of falling backwards and then nothing but darkness.

When she came to, her forehead throbbed as if her heart had taken up residence just above the bridge of her nose. Her entire face ached, and she could feel something tacky on her bangs, something that felt like half-dried glue. Reaching up, she winced as her fingertips brushed her wound. Streaks of pain radiated from a central point, and her head immediately felt as if it had tripled in size. She was nauseated, as if her stomach were on the verge of purging what little food it contained, and she viewed the room she was in as if through a fog. But even so, she realized that the dark stains on her fingers were partially congealed blood.

"Just cooperate."

The voice was familiar, but not overly so. Where had she heard it before?

"It'll be easier if you do."

She turned her head toward the source of the words, and it seemed as if it took the world a fraction of a second to catch up with her. But when it did, she saw Donnely. He was on the other side of the door, looking in through the little window with his hands wrapped around the bars. For a moment he became nothing more than a blur before snapping back into sharp focus.

"You should feel honored, really. They don't select just anyone."

He seemed to be looking everywhere but directly at her. As if he couldn't bring himself to meet her gaze.

"Wh . . . where am I?"

Her voice sounded as if it were coming from the end of an infinitely long tunnel and only the stabs of pain that accompanied the movement of her jaws convinced her that it was her own.

"The Garden. You're safe now."

Something about his tone sounded almost apologetic or as if he were trying to convince himself of his own statement.

She closed her eyes for a second and was suddenly back on the hillside. She saw Jeremy and Mama lying in the grass, their blood mingling in a collective pool below them. Unmoving. Silent. Dead.

Her eyes snapped open and, even though it hurt like hell to do so, her brow furrowed as she glared at the man on the other side of the door.

"You bastard. What they hell have you done? What the fuck . . . ."

But then she was sobbing, her back heaving with tears as her fingers pressed against her temples and bubbles of snot erupted from her nostrils.

"I'm . . . I'm sorry. It had to be done. For the good of all. For . . . humanity. See? There's a greater good. A higher purpose. But for what it's worth . . . I am sorry."

That was the last time she'd ever seen Donnely. In the beginning, she'd entertained fantasies of him returning in the middle of the night. She'd had dreams of keys rattling in the lock and the door swinging open to reveal him silhouetted by torchlight, ready to whisk her away from this place and make amends for the evil he'd brought upon her.

But that was so long ago, and she now knew he would never return. On some level, he probably did feel bad for his part in what had happened. But she couldn't help but remember the look in his eyes as he'd described the work done here. She'd rightfully identified it as the passion of a true believer. Any guilt that kept him awake at night was undoubtedly overshadowed by the zeal of his belief.

The door to her cell swung open, and two men shuffled inside. This morning it was the ones she thought of as Fred and Barney, which meant that Larry and Curly would be making the evening rounds.

Barney glanced down at the clipboard he held in his hands and thumbed through the pages with bored detachment.

"Says here her last period was two weeks ago."

Fred nodded and propped his sawed-off broomstick against the wall.

"Assume the position, Hips."

In the beginning, she'd fought. She'd scratched and bit and kicked and ripped out clumps of hair. She'd been beaten until it hurt to take a breath, had been held down and forced to take part in the routine no matter how much she squirmed and writhed. She'd had breakfast and dinner withheld. Even though it was the temperature and consistency of warm puke, it was still food . . . and she'd gotten tired. She was so tired of the purple and green bruises, of trying to sleep when it felt as though her ribs had been kicked by a wild mule. No matter how hard she fought the result was always the same.

Donnely had been right – it was much easier just to cooperate.

And so it was that she closed her eyes, bent over in a wide-legged stance, and gripped her ankles. She imagined that she was back in her little apartment, Lady Gaga was on the radio, and Jeremy was bitching about some cock-knocking camper who'd just picked him off three times in a row. Outside, an ice cream truck called to children with its pied piper jingle, and the scent of curry drifted from the Singh's apartment next door.

She tried not to let the cold glass of the rectal thermometer shatter the illusion as it invaded her body, tried to convince herself that she was only gritting her teeth because Jeremy had launched into another curse-laden tirade against the sniper who'd become the bane of his existence.

The DJ on the radio was calling for sunny skies with a 10 percent chance of precipitation. But then his voice melded with Barney's nasal whine as she felt the thermometer glide out of her most secret of places.

"Congratulations, Hips . . . you're ovulating."

She heard one of them crossing the room, cursing beneath his breath as he picked up the waste bucket with a slosh.

"Hard to believe someone so pretty can smell so damn bad. Shit."

She kept her eyes closed as she stood upright, continued envisioning her apartment, the potted plant by the door, the opening notes of *The Entertainer* as her cell phone lit up with Mama's number.

It had been Fred complaining about the bucket. Which meant Barney was currently bringing in the gruel that passed as breakfast. As if on cue, the smell of the meat and vegetable slop overpowered the curry of her dream world.

"Eat up, Hips. You're gonna need your energy."

They both laughed as if they'd heard the joke the DJ had just made about lesbians, potpourri, and open cans of tuna. Then her door creaked shut, there was the click of the lock, footsteps, and the entire scene replayed itself in Scar's cell.

She bit her bottom lip and tried to take a long, slow breath. But the air seemed to stick somewhere in the back of her throat.
Ovulation.

She knew what that meant. Within an hour, there would be a stream of men coming through her cell. Each one would have his way with her. Each one would fill her with millions of tiny swimmers, some of which were destined to trickle down thighs that would soon feel raw and stingy. For the next few days, she would know practically every man in The Garden. multiple times. Some would border on brutality with their savage thrusts and the twisting of her nipples. Others would behave as if this were simply another chore, no different than cooking the slop or slaughtering the cats which went into it. A select few would be shy and apologetic, each telling her that she had to understand that there was a greater good.

They had to repopulate the world after all. They had to outnumber the dead. They had to have children who would grow into soldiers. They had to keep the gene pool as diverse as possible.

Within a few months, her fate would be decided. If their seed didn't take purchase, if her belly didn't begin to balloon out and her monthly flow come to end, then she would be declared barren. She didn't know exactly how it would be done, but the end result would be the same. She would end up on the other side of this cell, in the darkness with the other rotters, just another subject for The Tree of Life to experiment on.

She opened her eyes and saw their hands reaching through the bars of the wall's window. Flaky skin, some deteriorated to the point that strands of muscle could be seen beneath patches that had been eaten away by time. They grabbed and grasped with mindless enthusiasm, seeking purchase that would never come.

But the living *would* come. And come. And come.

To them, she was nothing more than an incubator, just another breeder in a long row of nameless women.

She walked over to the hands, keeping just out of reach and inciting them into a frenzy with her presence.

Those men had killed Jeremy. They had killed Mama.

They'd locked her up and humiliated her on a daily basis. They raped her countless times all in the name of procreation.

And they'd kill her, too, if she didn't produce a child soon. But what if she did? Nine months of respite? Nine months of being in the maternity wing before being transported back to this dingy cell? Wouldn't it be worse then? Knowing that there was better food, more comfortable quarters with no chance of beatings for fear of damaging the fetus? It would all begin again – the daily inspections, assuming the position, the monthly violations.

The hands were so close that she could see the little black specks beneath what was left of the fingernails. They clutched at the air, seeming to squeeze invisible stress balls with sheer abandon.

Even now Donnely, and others like him, were probably out there, scouring the countryside. They searched for fresh stock – for new victims, for more women to defile.

How long would this go on?

"No more."

Her voice was a soft whisper but was filled with more resolve than the loudest shout. She could still fight back. She could bring the entire Garden crumbling down, could utterly destroy all they'd worked so hard to build. And it would serve the bastards right.

She extended her hand quickly before she had a chance to lose her nerve. Thrusting it into the darkness, through the bars on the little windows, squeezing her eyes shut.

It didn't hurt as badly as she thought it would. The bite was quick and felt no different, really, than the time she'd been nipped by the neighbor's Chow as a kid. Wrestling her arm free from the rotter's weak grasp she immediately wrapped the open wound in the hem of her dirty smock and applied pressure. Blood blossomed on the fabric like a rose in a dirty field of snow, but it had been nothing more than a flesh wound. Within 15 minutes, the blood had clotted, and she licked the iron tasting flecks from the tip of her finger. If anyone bothered to ask, she's simply say she'd jabbed a splinter from the door into it. But no one would. She knew this as surely as she knew the contagion was flowing through her veins, poisoning her healthy cells with the infection of the walking dead.

"Bring it on, fuckers!" She shouted so loudly that her vocal cords felt strained with the words. "Bring it fucking on!"

At the same time she heard another voice, this one echoing through the corridors of her mind instead of the hallway with its series of cells and captives. It was Donnely's voice, culled from her memory.

"Did you know that any exchange of bodily fluids will do the same damn thing? You kiss someone who's infected, for example, and get even the smallest amount of spit in your mouth, and you're done for."

So let them come. Let the parade of rapists begin. She would spread her legs and would welcome them into her body. She would take every single man in the colony if they sent him. She would exchange bodily fluids with each and every one and let them have their way.

She would have her revenge.

From down the hall she heard a door swing open. She heard a male voice doing an off-key rendition of Snoop Dogg's *Sexual Seduction*.

Laying back on her sleeping bag, she closed her eyes and waited for him to enter her cell.

"My name is Alejandra," she whispered.

"My name is Alejandra."

BLACK SNOW

BY

ELIZABETH REUTER

Bianca Butler loved fairy tales, and *Snow White* had a special place in her heart. The image of a girl with skin pale as snow, hair black as ebony, and lips red as roses was so romantic she'd been captivated by it since childhood. When she married her prince (a handsome Wall Street banker named Jeffrey) and became pregnant, she went to bed every night praying for a child like Snow White.

*White skin…black hair…red lips…*Oh, the romance! The beauty! The purity of such a child! Bianca went to sleep at night and dreamed of a little girl dancing through newly fallen snow, thick black curls up in pigtails and bouncing merrily round her rosy cheeks as she giggled and spun around.

When her child came into the world nine months later, it was mostly what Bianca had wished for: its hair was black as ebony, and its skin white as snow. Only two tiny details were off.

First, it was not the child's lips, but its eyes that shone red. Though they normally looked brown, in certain lighting a red sheen would glint around the edges of the iris. Bianca didn't admit it aloud, but she never wanted to meet her child alone in a dark alley.

The second aberration was the child's gender. Rather than the beautiful girl Bianca had hoped for, she gave birth to a beautiful boy.

And he *was* beautiful. Though neither Bianca nor her husband Jeffrey had any interest in the name Angelo before seeing their child, they both agreed no other could fit him once they'd seen his face. Bianca quickly learned to expect (and enjoy) the comment, "My God, he looks like an angel!" from anyone seeing him for the first time. She took pleasure in their expressions when she said they'd guessed his name. Those exclamations remained an almost weekly occurrence throughout her shortened life.

Angelo was an unusual child, so calm that Bianca wondered at first if he had some sort of disorder. He neither cried nor smiled, but instead let his red-tinted eyes wander around any space he occupied, as though memorizing every crack in a wall, every cloud in the sky, every feature on a person's face. He made no sound, no coos or cries.

Bianca rarely saw her husband, but one night when he came home from work early for the first time in four months, she seized the opportunity to talk about how unsettled Angelo made her feel.

"I don't think he's normal, Jeffrey," she whispered. Angelo couldn't understand words yet, and was asleep in his room. But Bianca felt she needed to keep her voice low. Somehow she knew he heard every word she said and forgot nothing.

Jeffrey looked at her incredulously from the other side of their kitchen table, a forkful of roast beef halfway to his mouth.

"We're alone for the first time in months, and that's what you want to talk about?"

He never returned home early again. Bianca knew Jeffrey meant his absence to be punishment for not paying more attention to him, but she wondered if he had another reason for staying away. Somewhere, in the back of his mind, did Jeffrey fear their son, too?

When he was 1 year old, Bianca put Angelo into the bathtub without realizing the water was scalding until she touched it herself. Angelo hadn't let a sound pass his lips, but sat motionless in the water as his skin turned red. By the time Bianca lifted him out, crying apologies and desperately trying to remember First Aid training for burns, blisters were raising on his pale flesh.

Angelo stared at his mother as she called her doctor and drove him to the Emergency Room. His eyes flickered from brown to red to brown again as Bianca's little Toyota sped under street lights that lit up the car one second and left it in darkness the next. In the ER, as the doctor spread ointment on his flesh, he acted the same. He just stared until Bianca wanted to run away so she never had to see those huge, penetrating eyes again.

I'm watching you, those eyes told her. *I know who you are.*

One evening when Angelo was 2 years old, Bianca was cutting carrots to use for dinner soup. She turned to grab a kitchen towel with the knife held loosely in her hand when she saw Angelo in the doorway. He stood shaded in the darkness of the hall, red eyes shining like two bloody wounds. Bianca screamed, sure some wild beast had come to rip her throat out. When she swung her arm up to defend herself, she felt pain as the knife sliced into her right thigh.

The sight of the blood seemed to fascinate Angelo, and he walked toward his mother in steps much too composed for a toddler. Bianca looked at her son and couldn't move, her chest heaving with suppressed, panicked sobs. It was her son approaching her, she could see that now. Why was she still so frightened?

Angelo had been able to use individual words, even a few simple sentences, for quite some time, but he said nothing as he bore down on Bianca.

When he dug his chubby fingers into the cut in her thigh and brought the blood to his mouth, licking it like some exotic delicacy to be savored, she knew why her fear refused to go away.

After that day she often spotted Angelo hiding in shadow around the house, gazing at her as though waiting for something, those red, red eyes following her movements. Sometimes she looked at him, and he'd just wave at her unabashedly. Other times she'd see him from the corner of her eye and turn to get a better look, only to find he'd disappeared.

Firmly, she ordered herself not to think about it, because after all, Angelo hadn't hurt her. *You're acting hysterical over nothing,* she told herself. *Stop it.*

When Angelo was 3 years old, Bianca gave birth to her second son. She hadn't intended to have any more children, but then came that night when Jeffrey stumbled in at two in the morning, drunk and glaring at her so intensely she hadn't dared to protest. God, how he had smelled! With his hair tangled like barbed wire and his clothes a wrinkled mess, a bottle of Jack Daniels in his hand with half its contents slopped down his front, Jeffrey had looked like a psychopath escaped from some slasher movie come to take her life.

Firmly against abortion as Bianca stood, she refused to terminate the resultant pregnancy. Nine months later Caleb popped out and proved to be as beautiful as his brother with that same black hair and pale skin, though his eyes were a normal shade of brown. Caleb's behavior also proved different from Angelo's. Upon being taken from the womb and slapped, he started to cry, and then settled contentedly when placed in his mother's arms. Bianca was surprised to hear this was normal baby behavior; when he'd begun crying, she'd almost stopped breathing in shock. She'd forgotten what a child's cries sounded like.

Bianca was more than a little worried about bringing Baby Caleb home. Her eldest son frightened her, really frightened her, though she denied this to herself on a conscious level. One wasn't afraid of their own children – that wasn't how the fairy tale she'd promised herself she'd live was meant to go.

Angelo's reaction was a relief. When Bianca sat down on the living room couch and, using all her will power to show no fear, invited Angelo to sit next to her and meet his baby brother, Angelo began to study Caleb's face intently.

"Let me hold him," Angelo said. His sentences were remarkably well formed for his age, making him sound adult. Bianca had never been inspired to try baby talk.

"Ah, I think you're a little too small to support his head properly, dear."

A small crease appeared between Angelo's black eyebrows, the closest he'd ever gotten to showing upset feelings. A bolt of fear made Bianca shudder; quickly trying to ease him, she said, "Why don't you hold his hand instead? Here, look, your brother wants to say hello!"

Angelo reached out with caution that was far more mature than his years. When Caleb's tiny fingers closed around his own, Bianca was amazed to see the first smile that had ever crossed Angelo's lips.

"He's perfect," Angelo said. The look in his eyes threw Bianca back to a year ago in her kitchen, and she wondered why his expression now should remind her of the predatory way he had tasted her blood.

She pushed the thought away. She had a perfect family. She had her manly prince of a husband, and now two beautiful children who loved each other. This was exactly the way her life was supposed to turn out.

Angelo and Caleb grew up close; closer, in fact, than Bianca had known brothers could be. The usual sibling rivalry and childish tantrums simply didn't occur between them. Angelo was a kind, patient guide, and Caleb an adoring, faithful follower. Bianca worried sometimes about just how devoted Caleb acted and how easily he believed anything that came out of Angelo's mouth. But she decided to believe that was just the way children behaved. Goodness knew some of the silly things she'd accepted as true when she was their age.

Sometimes Bianca would wake up to check on her sons and find Angelo standing by his brother's bed, staring down at Caleb and gently stroking his cheeks or forehead. Once, when he caught his mother looking, his gaze came sharply up, and Bianca knew without words that she'd been told to *get out.*

She got out. Everything was fine, she told herself as she hurried back to bed. Perhaps Angelo fixated on his brother a bit more than a normal sibling would, but that just meant Angelo loved Caleb more deeply than most little boys were capable of loving. There was nothing to worry about.

How strange, Bianca thought as she reached her room. *I'm shivering, and yet it's so warm out.*

When Caleb grew old enough to walk, Angelo began taking him on all day expeditions around the neighborhood. He told Bianca that he wanted to show Caleb the world, to introduce him to the unique way Angelo saw things since Caleb lacked his powers of observation. Bianca asked where they went, and Angelo became vague. *Here and there.*

Nothing wrong with that, Bianca told herself. After all, Angelo was such a bright boy. Why shouldn't Caleb get the benefit of his elder brother's experience?

Angelo didn't have any friends, and for the life of her Bianca couldn't understand why. He was handsome, polite, and intelligent. Even anti-social people tended to have somebody, someone, anyone. Why did Angelo never so much as mention a single person except Caleb in an affectionate way?

He hit puberty and his beauty began to mature, attracting stares from people of both genders and all ages. This made Bianca nervous, but Angelo showed no more interest in any of his would-be admirers than he did in playmates. That made his mother nervous in a whole different way.

"Angelo," she asked him when his 15th birthday drew close, "Who do you want to invite for your birthday party?"

He looked startled, as he hadn't had a birthday party in 10 years, nor shown any interest in one. Bianca hoped he didn't realize she only asked to find out who his friends were.

"Just Caleb," he said after a moment. Then he turned away from her as though he couldn't be bothered to think about the question any longer, or the woman who had asked it.

Bianca frowned as he prepared to leave the house. "No one else?" she asked.

"No. No one else."

Bianca wondered if she should go after him and ask again, but then she told herself not to read too much into his solitude. Sometimes when two people became very close like Angelo and Caleb, they didn't pay attention to others around them for a while. Angelo would have friends when he was ready.

Soon after, Caleb brought home a friend for the first time, a cheerful boy named Mark from school. The two boys spent the afternoon playing video games on the floor of the Butler living room, squealing with laughter as they tried to outrace and outfight each other on the small screen of the Butler's flat panel Sony TV.

When Angelo came home and saw his brother with Mark, he froze in the doorway.

Bianca, who'd stood in the kitchen at the time, later convinced herself she hadn't seen what she thought she'd seen. She told herself that she'd been quite far away from Angelo and hadn't gotten a good look at his expression. How silly could she be, to think that such naked hatred and jealousy would ever appear on Angelo's face! Why, he barely showed any expression at all, usually. He'd only smile or frown once every other month or so.

Yet Bianca couldn't shake off her uneasiness. It was normal for siblings and good friends to feel some measure of possessiveness, but that look had been beyond anything Bianca had ever seen in real life. Stronger even than the look her first boyfriend had given her when he'd found her in an empty classroom at school with another boy's hand up her blouse in 9th grade.

It doesn't matter, Bianca told herself firmly. *It doesn't matter because I didn't see what I thought I saw. Angelo never gave Caleb that look. I made a mistake.*

About a week later Mark left his house to go to school and never made it there. No trace of him, not a scrap of cloth nor a lock of hair, was ever found.

The night Mark's parents announced him missing by hysterically calling everyone they knew, Bianca watched Angelo console the distraught Caleb and told herself over and over again that he couldn't have had anything to do with Mark's vanishing. She tried to focus on the compassion Angelo showed, the way he held his brother close and stroked his hair and back, and told herself that Angelo was indeed an angel, her angel. No angel would do such a heinous thing as murder a child.

For all she knew Mark fell into a ditch somewhere, and no person had done anything to him. Yes, that made sense. Mark had been gangly, all elbows and huge feet, and hadn't struck Bianca as very bright. It had to be Mark's own stupidity and clumsiness that was at fault, not her son.

Caleb buried his tear-stained face into Angelo's chest, and for a second, Bianca saw her elder son's mouth curve into a smile. Disquiet washed over her, scattering her fragile surety — had that smile been as triumphant as it looked? But no, no, Angelo was just smiling because Caleb had finally stopped crying. Her perfect son would never do anything…inappropriate.

Caleb never brought home another friend.

Some nights, when Bianca couldn't sleep, she heard panting and groaning from the brothers' room. They were passionate sounds that she faintly recognized as sexual, even though she and Jeffrey hadn't been intimate since conceiving Caleb. There were whispers in the dark, soft sounds that Bianca could have passed off as talking except that gasping always followed. She heard huffing and bed springs squeaking, and little whimpers and pleas that cut through the night air.

Bianca heard them as plainly as she heard the TV on her dresser. She heard when Caleb squealed *Angelo* and when Angelo whispered things like *beautiful* and *need* and *love* just a little louder and more forcefully than the rest of his words.

Caleb began acting much less lively at the same time the noises began. He grew thin and wan, so that he looked less like an angel and more like a ghost. Bianca thought if she took her eyes off of him for too long, he might disappear. His temperament changed as well. The cheerful, curious boy he had been disappeared, seemingly overnight, replaced by a sullen, joyless lump. He was a hunk of empty flesh that barely got up unless someone forced him and then acted as though it was a tremendous effort just to cross a room.

Whenever Angelo reached out to touch him, Caleb flinched.

He's just a teenager, Bianca told herself, *most teenagers are moody and don't like their families.*

Still, she decided the time had come for them to spend a little less time together. She informed her sons they were getting too big to share the same room; 16 and 13 was plenty old enough for them to have their own space. Caleb looked at Angelo without saying a word, obviously expecting his elder brother to answer for them both. Whatever Angelo said, Caleb would abide by. Bianca despaired to realize she had no influence at all over her youngest son anymore. Had she ever had any?

"That's all right," Angelo told her, not bothering to look at Caleb or ask his opinion. "There's no need to go to all the trouble of moving and re-arranging and making space. We're okay where we are."

Caleb looked back to his mother and nodded. The law had been laid out. There was no more to be said, even if he did have a haunted, defeated look in his eyes that Bianca knew deep down would remain forever. It would be a scar on his soul.

No! Bianca told herself, *No! Don't be dramatic.* Whatever reason Angelo had for not wanting to let Caleb out of his room, it couldn't be anything bad. Angelo and Caleb probably just sat up at night and had brotherly talks or played video games. They had so few friends; naturally they wouldn't want to be separated.

And so what if they did engage in a little bit of unusual activity upon occasion? Children experimented naturally, didn't they? In her childhood, Bianca had explored new boundaries and shown curiosity with friends on occasion. That was what children did, and it was perfectly normal that her sons should do the same. That is, if they were doing anything – which they weren't.

The next day, Bianca bought the most powerful sleeping pills and the thickest ear plugs she could find. She used them every night. Even in a perfect world a person needed a sound night's sleep.

Bianca knew her sons spent a lot of time wandering around town, and she sometimes wondered if they went to any particular place. Some nights when they came home Caleb would be shaking, and Angelo would have blood under his fingernails. Bianca wouldn't think anything of it during the day — she trusted her boys, after all! — but there were some mornings when she woke up, screaming from nightmares full of blood and torture and dismemberment.

How unpleasant, she would think as she huddled against her headboard and trembled. Perhaps it was a reaction to something she'd seen on TV.

She discovered her sons by accident one day on her way to pick Jeffrey up from work. Though she knew he'd wrecked his car, she was a little surprised he'd called her for help. Jeffrey rarely came home to sleep any longer; it wasn't unusual for him to spend several days out. Bianca preferred it when he did. Her fairy tale marriage was easier to maintain when he wasn't around (not that there was a *problem* with that, it was just what happened to couples as time went by, perfectly normal).

Bianca planned on swinging by Dave's Auto Shop on the way to see just how badly her husband had damaged his car. To her irritation, she missed her turnoff and wound up turning onto the next off ramp instead, eventually exiting onto a poorly-maintained, nearly-abandoned street without another car in sight.

She passed by an old, stooped woman with sagging jowls and wild, stringy hair sitting on the side of the road. Bianca couldn't see the woman very well, but somehow she felt the woman's eyes on her, deep blue orbs that examined her very soul and found it wanting.

You're a bad mother, Bianca Butler! A bad mother!

Biting her lip to keep from screaming, Bianca fought to keep her hands steady on the wheel as panic jerked at her gut. She pulled the car over to the curb as soon as the old woman was out of sight just long enough to slap herself as hard as she could. A bad mother, what a ridiculous idea! Her sons were clean and well fed and brought home excellent grades. She was a fine mother!

Shaking her head and favoring her stinging left cheek, Bianca took deep breaths to calm herself and looked around. Overgrown grass lined the road along with debris from other drivers unlucky enough to have come this way. There was the occasional deserted, crumbling building that had probably housed businesses back when people still lived in this area.

It's amazing how quickly terrain can change, thought Bianca as she drove slowly on, watching for the next turn back onto the highway (it would be easy to miss on this mess of a road). She was still so close to her house, little more than a mile away, and yet she felt like she'd stumbled into another country.

It was, thus, that much more surprising to see a familiar dark head disappear into a rusting former garage half-a-block ahead.

If Bianca had been sure that she'd seen one of her sons, she would never have investigated, but she wasn't sure who she'd seen, and curiosity compelled her to look closer. She pulled up to the side of the garage, stopped the car, and pulled the key from the ignition. She didn't know why she was being so cautious and quiet. If it wasn't her son inside, she could leave. If it was her son, there would be nothing to fear.

The garage door was rusted shut, but the business entrance beside it was open and almost falling off its hinges. Bianca pushed through without making any noise by putting pressure on the side. Once in the doorway, she blinked to adjust her eyesight to the dark.

Then, she screamed.

Oh God this isn't real, this can't be true I'm having a nightmare, I'll wake up any second...

In the gloom sat Angelo and Caleb, the latter sitting behind the former and clinging to his back. Before Angelo lay a large cat, a discarded syringe, and many, many sharp objects.

Bianca entered just in time to see Angelo slice into the cat's midsection. It gave a drugged kick of its fat grey legs, and Bianca prayed that whatever Angelo injected it with took away pain, as well as motor function.

All around her boys were signs they'd cut into plenty of animals before this one. Spots of blood, chunks of fur, toolboxes and gloves; all were scattered around, denying Bianca any chance to pretend she looked at a one-time fluke or anything other than regular, premeditated torture.

When Bianca screamed Caleb's first response was to scoot even closer to his brother and hide behind him while Angelo maneuvered himself between Caleb and the door. It was hard to say which brother looked more surprised when they saw who had found them, but Caleb grew fearful while Angelo's usual non-expression slid quickly back into place.

Angelo disentangled himself from Caleb and strode to his mother, authority in his every step. It wasn't until he slapped her that she realized she was still screaming.

"I — oh glory, Angelo, what are you *doing*?"

"Calm down," said Angelo. His breathing was regular and even, and if Bianca had dared to feel for his pulse, she felt horribly certain it wouldn't be a beat faster than usual. "You did this same thing in high school science, didn't you?"

"S-science?"

"Yeah," said Angelo, ignoring the struggles and mewls of the cat behind him. Blood flowed from its split belly and onto the floor, spreading out towards Caleb's sneakers. Looking down and shuddering, Caleb scooted backwards until he'd squashed himself into a far corner. "I just want to see how things work."

Bianca hesitated. It was a terrible excuse, and her rational mind found a million holes in it, but...

A science project, of course! A smart boy like Angelo would want to learn more than his teachers could teach him in school. Studying by himself showed initiative, a determination to better himself that most young men didn't have. Good for him.

Bianca began to calm down until she looked past Angelo's shoulder to see Caleb. One look at him broke her heart.

There was a sick desperation on his face that was even more disturbing to Bianca than the cat's struggles. His eyes were wide and his body trembled. His gaze pleaded with her for help.

He was trapped, Bianca realized, as trapped by Angelo as she was by her marriage. Angelo dominated him so completely that Caleb didn't know up from down unless Angelo told him which was which. Angelo's actions scared Caleb as badly as they did her. So here and now, he was begging her to have the strength to be strong for him. He needed her to be strong because Angelo had carefully prevented him from being strong on his own.

Save me, he cried, without saying a word.

Bianca felt a rush of anger at Caleb. How dare he put her into such an uncomfortable position? It was just selfish!

Angelo gently took his mother's chin and forced her gaze back to him. She studied his perfect features and sighed; her anger melted away, replaced by a feeling of peace. No one so beautiful could be bad.

"Go home, now," said Angelo, voice calm and soothing and eminently reasonable. "We'll be home in time for dinner."

Angelo knew her well. It was all about being home in time for dinner, all about calling her sons by pet names, and kissing them goodbye when they began each new day. All about going through the motions of being a fairy tale family.

Bianca took one last, brief look at Caleb. He sat frozen, huddled in on himself in the corner, throwing away whatever dignity Angelo had left him to implore his mother, his last hope, to save his soul.

Bianca turned away from Caleb and left the garage. She kissed her husband on the cheek when she picked him up and did not tell him what she'd seen.

By nightfall, she'd decided she hadn't seen it at all.

It was on Angelo's 21st birthday that reality intruded into Bianca's life. The day started out well, quiet but fun. With Caleb just graduated from high school and Angelo free of university classes for the afternoon and evening, the three of them had been able to go out to dinner to celebrate. Caleb rarely spoke as Angelo and Bianca chattered about his algebra classes and her cooking experiments, but grinned the whole time like a dog anticipating some great treat, barely able to contain itself for excitement. Bianca felt happy to see him light up that way, since Caleb usually seemed so gloomy. Perhaps he looked forward to his post-graduate life.

At 8 p.m., Bianca took her sleeping pills like always before going to the kitchen for a glass of warm milk. She noticed that she felt tired more quickly than usual, but it wasn't until her hand grew so numb she dropped her glass that she realized something was wrong.

Bianca stumbled over to the counter, struggling to keep her vision from blacking out completely. Heedless of the shards of broken glass scattered about the floor, she reached out and grabbed the phone hanging by the sink, her vision wavering in and out.

Angelo's hand reached from around the doorway like a disembodied limb flying out from the darkness, and pulled the cord from the wall.

Bianca began gasping, her lungs struggling for air that had been so easy to take in only moments ago. She collapsed to her knees as Angelo dropped the phone cord to the ground, strolled further into the kitchen, and opened the refrigerator. "Caleb, do you want a sandwich or mac-and-cheese?"

Bianca fell onto her back and stared up to see Caleb follow his brother in with his shoulders hunched and his head lowered. He told Angelo that he wanted mac-and-cheese, but his eyes were only for his mother. They were so full of hate Bianca felt her chest burn.

Bianca understood. She had abandoned him his whole life. She'd let him be enslaved by his brother, and this was his revenge.

Bianca felt strangely relieved. No more sleeping pills or long days of pretending her husband wasn't avoiding her. No more sudden stabs of guilt that came to her randomly and brought her to her knees with pain. No more worries about holding her family together. All those choices had been taken away from her, and for a single, glorious moment she felt liberated in a way she hadn't since Angelo's birth.

But, then, Angelo grabbed his brother's arm and pulled Caleb to him. Angelo kissed him like a starving man feeding from Caleb's mouth. Bianca saw Caleb's posture droop in resigned surrender and knew he would always be Angelo's dog. He had given up all hope the day she'd turned away from him in the abandoned garage, and though he hated Bianca for it enough to help Angelo kill her - or had it been his idea?- there wasn't enough hate in the world to set him free. Angelo would go out into the world and do abominable things, and Caleb would follow him, and fall with him, when they were brought down...if they ever were.

Bianca didn't feel liberated after Angelo released Caleb. There would be no peace for her in this life or the next. She began to see fire erupting and spreading from the corners of her kitchen, the fires of Hell come to claim her.

Hyperventilating, wanting to scream but unable to gather the strength, Bianca tried to deny reality one last time. This had to be an accident, a mistake, a dream...but she couldn't lie to herself any longer. She died moments later with her eyes wide open to the truth and her fairy tale in ruins, Hellfire swallowing her soul. The last thing she saw was Angelo, holding Caleb to him and staring down at her over his shoulder, red eyes dancing with derision and a promise of tortures to come.

CABIN

FEVER

BY

J. FRANKLIN EVANS

It was supposed to be a vacation.

I'd just lost my job and hadn't been able to find another. My wife Becca was the sole breadwinner in our household, and she didn't let me forget it for one second. Still, this was a chance to escape our troubles, at least for a few days. It was a chance to get away and sort things out.

Of course, we were piled into Clarke's brand new huge SUV, along with his wife Sandra, heading for God knows what.

Clarke was my best and oldest friend from 8th grade. He'd been my constant companion for all of these years – the one human being who knew me and all of my secrets both good and bad.

Clarke had the keys to the cabin in the mountains owned by Nick, his boss--my former boss--near a stream where, he said, one could experience the best trout fishing in the state.

It was a long drive to our destination – six hours – and we had to park next to the road which was still a couple of miles from the front door. We, then, had to unload our baggage and carry or drag it up a path, through the woods. It was not going to be an easy start to our serene tranquility.

The road wound through some hilly country with mountains towering on the horizon. The cabin was old, Clarke had told us, saying that Nick had inherited it from his father, who had, in turn, inherited it from his father. Clarke and Sandra had spent quite a lot of time there over the years.

When we did finally arrive, it was easy to tell nobody had used the cabin in a very long time. Opening the door kicked up a cloud of dust, and a squirrel on the roof started scolding us for invading his property. The air inside was stale, and there were cobwebs everywhere.

We estimated it'd take three trips altogether to get our baggage from the car, but after that we could relax and begin our vacation. We were in the middle of our second trip back, all of us carrying bags, fly rods, or back packs, when disaster struck.

Clarke was in front, and I was behind him. Becca followed me with Sandra bringing up the rear. We were at a point where the forest encroached on the path with trees and brush so thick we couldn't see anything off to either side. It was only a couple more hours until sunset. Cicadas sang in the trees, and the heat was beginning to wear on us.

"Why is it so bloody hot?" Becca asked.

"You can't take a little heat? It's good for you," I said in a not-so-nice tone.

"This is a vacation," Becca replied. "I don't go on a vacation to be miserable, Bruce. I go on a vacation to have a good time. I go on a vacation to relax. I don't go to hike 800 miles, uphill, to some tiny little cabin with a portable potty and no shower just so you can not catch fish for a couple of days."

"Becca--," I started, but she ignored me.

"It's a good thing we brought some beans with us. We won't be counting on you bringing dinner home. You're just not that good at bringing home the bacon, Bruce, we all know that. Of course, maybe bringing the beans along wasn't the perfect solution since there is only the one bathroom."

"Damn it, Becca, what do you want from me?" I asked. "What could I possibly do to--"

Sandra screamed. It was a quick noise that sounded like it was cut off. I spun around and saw the bushes close to where she'd been moving violently. Then, they stopped. I thought I could hear something rustling in the brush, rapidly growing fainter. We all stood there for several seconds, unable to figure out what to do. I heard her scream again, already quite some distance away. It was an awful sound, full of despair and terror. I had never heard anything like that before.

"Sandy!" Clarke shouted, running back past us, getting to the point on the path where she'd been. He pointed at the ground, looking at us, shock on his face.

"There's blood here! Sandy!" He ran into the bush, following her path.

Becca turned to me. "What do we do? Do we help him?"

"Let's get to the cabin," I said. "It's almost dark, and maybe we can find some flashlights or something to help us search."

As we trudged onward, my mind wandered back on how my demise had begun.

*   *   *

I was in my tiny office during a routine day. Nothing special going on when it had started.

There was a knock on my door as I sat at my desk doing research for one of our clients online. Clarke came in, followed by Nick. Nick closed the door quietly.

185

"Uh, Bruce, we need to talk." Nick said. He seemed nervous as he and Clarke sat down in the cheap chairs I had been given to use for visitors. Clarke wouldn't look at me.

"What's up?" I asked, trying to sound cheerful, knowing, though, that on this most routine of days, I was about to get some really bad news.

"It's about the BAK account," Nick said.

"What about it? Their new rep rocking the boat?" I asked.

Clarke shifted in his seat, looking at me, finally, a solemn expression on his face. "He called me, Bruce. He wants to work with me from now on."

"What?"

BAK was our biggest account. According to Nick, it was our only account--the bowing and scraping that went on in our office when their rep visited was a bit of an embarrassment, I thought.

"He wants to deal with Clarke," Nick said. "It's what he prefers."

"So you're taking the account away from me," I said. It wasn't a question.

"Yes," Nick said, and as I stared back at him, he simply shrugged.

"I don't know why," Clarke chimed in. "I'm so sorry. I haven't even talked to them, so I don't know why they want to make a switch. I especially don't know why they are insisting on dealing with me."

"I need you to forward anything you have on the account that isn't on the network servers to Clarke ASAP, Bruce," Nick said. "He needs to be brought up to speed. I want you to know this is no reflection on your work. It's always top-notch. This is just what the client wants."

If it were any other client, they would have been told to stick with the account executive who had been assigned to them. Anybody else would have been told to shove it.

Not BAK, though. No way. What they want, they get.

Nick got out of the chair and looked in my direction. "You've still got the Imprector account, along with Zipmann Glover. That'll keep you busy. I'll be in my office."

Nick left, closing the door quickly, but quietly, behind him. I looked at Clarke who was leaning back in his chair.

"I know this is a blow to you, Bruce," he said. "Look, Nick's going to be in his office, and quitting time is in an hour, anyway. Why don't you head down to Kelly's, and I'll join you there in a little while?"

A drink or three or five sounded good to me then. I got up, a bit weak in the knees. "Sure," I said. "I'll see you there."

"Sure thing, buddy," Clarke responded, walking with me across the floor outside my office, through the maze of desks of junior executives, interns, and assistants to the elevators. I pushed the button and turned, seeing everyone at a desk looking at me. I wondered if they all knew somehow. I felt like it was written on my face.

The elevator doors opened, and I stepped in, turning back to see Clarke standing there staring at me, a faint smile on his face, and I suddenly remembered that, in my shock at getting the bad news, I'd forgotten to log off of my computer.

"Clarke, could you log me off?" I asked.

"Sure thing," he said as the doors started closing. "See you in an a bit."

*   *   *

After a short debate about possibly returning back to the car or continuing on to the cabin, the cabin held its luster since it was closer. We wanted to get out of the open as quickly as possible. We made it just as the sun seemed to disappear behind the mountains. It went from weak daylight to pitch-black in minutes.

We hadn't brought the fuel for the generator yet so our only ability to see came from our flashlights. I opened the baggage we already had, but only found some food and water.

"Why did we come here?" Becca asked me over and over again, while we dug through the luggage, looking for I don't know what. "We don't even like fishing."

"Oh, would you please just shut the hell up!" I said when the door opened, causing us both to jump.

It was Clarke. His expression was blank as he came into the cabin and sat on a bunk, seeming not to see us for several moments. He was bloody, sweaty, and scratched, probably by branches from the bushes he'd gone through. He was filthy.

"Did you find her?" Becca asked.

He looked at her, his eyes finally focusing.

"Yes," he said, and it sounded like his voice came from a great distance away. "A hollow tree. She was at the base of a big old hollow tree. It had her arm up inside of it. I could hear it chewing . . . she looked at me, Bruce. She looked at me. Her mouth was moving, but she couldn't even scream. It was eating her alive. It was . . ."

"Shhhh . . .," Becca said, but Clarke went on.

"It pulled her into the tree a little further. I could hear it. I could hear that thing eating my wife, Bruce. Her bones . . . she looked at me . . . she tried to say something, but she was in so much pain . . ."

He let out a sob and stared at his trembling hands.

"Do you know what it is?" I asked.

"I didn't see it. It's inside the tree. I can find that tree again, though."

Clarke started looking around the room, finally seeing a bag he'd brought that we hadn't opened, yet. He got up, went over to it, opened it, and ripped through the clothes inside until he found what he was looking for.

It was a revolver, a .38, I'd guess, nickel-plated.

"You didn't say you were bringing a gun!" Becca gasped. I wanted to hit her.

"All kinds of bastards hide out in these woods," I said, instead. Clarke looked at me for a moment before running out of the door, slamming it behind him.

"Clarke!" Becca shouted after him. At that point, I did hit her. I couldn't help it. She needed it, though.

My knuckles stung, and Becca had blood in her mouth. But she shut up, looking at me, shock in her eyes.

"Now be quiet, and sit down," I said. I got up and dropped the bar across the door.

"You're locking Clarke out there?" she whispered to me.

"Better him out there with that . . . whatever . . . than having that thing able to just walk in the door," I hissed back at her. "And if we stay here and stay quiet maybe it won't find us. Do you understand?"

There must have been something in my tone because she nodded. I got up and started going through drawers and closets, as quietly as I could, seeing what else was there, figuring there was nothing else useful in the baggage.

I found the shotgun in the back of a closet. It was ancient, a single-shot, and when I broke it open there was one solitary cartridge in it. It was coated with dust, and the powder was probably stale, but it was better than nothing.

This sucker was huge, though, probably a 10-gauge. One shot from this thing would take out a grizzly, I figured. I thought of Clarke out there, with his little .38, and me in here, with my big old shotgun. I sadistically found that a little humorous.

Yeah, I snickered about that for several minutes.

*   *   *

It was my 21st birthday party when I'd first met Becca.

I was a junior in college – I came back to the apartment I shared with Clarke to find it decorated for a surprise party. It was all Clarke's idea.

Like a lot of parties on a college campus, we had a lot of gate crashers. Becca was one of them – she had come with some friends of hers. We all got drunk and loud, and the party broke up around 2 a.m. when the cops shut us down. Clarke took Sandra and went into his room, leaving me to fend for myself.

Becca had told the cops she lived there because her ride had bailed on her. I offered to take her home – she lived on the other side of town. But she saw how drunk I was and declined. She really had no choice but to crash at my place.

I didn't mind, even though we were both too drunk to do much fooling around that night. Instead, we lay on some blankets on some dingy old carpet and talked.

"That guy, Clarke," she said. "He lives here with you?"

"Sure," I said. "We've known each other for years."

"Is that his girlfriend he's with?"

"Yeah. She used to be my girlfriend, but she dumped me for him."

"Jesus, Bruce. You let him get away with that?"

"What do I care? He's my best friend. I was just looking to get into her pants. He's more serious."

"Serious? Really? Think they'll get married or something?"

"I think it's possible," I said.

She sighed. "Damn, he's good looking. And he's charming."

"So? What does that have to do with anything at all?" I asked.

Instead, she just looked at me a moment before turning over on her side, her back to me, and going to sleep. I did likewise and forgot all about her until the next morning when her vomiting in the bathroom woke me. That was when I felt sober enough to take her home.

We'd been together ever since. What an inspired beginning to our wonderful relationship.

*   *   *

"We should save the flashlights," I whispered.

Becca was shining her light around the cabin, looking for who knows what. "I don't like sitting in the dark," she hissed back at me.

"We're on top of a hill," I said. "The light probably shows for miles around."

"It'll give Clarke something to see," she said. "He's still alive, I just know it."

"Maybe, maybe not," I said. "But I think that thing out there can also find us. Do you understand?"

"Bruce, Clarke just lost his wife. He's gonna need us. He's going to need someone to comfort him, to help him get over--"

"Jesus, please shut the hell up," I whispered back at her. "Clarke will be fine. You just need to keep your mouth closed and turn out that light. Do you understand?"

"Fine," she said, and I heard her click off the light. It quickly got so dark we could barely make out each others' silhouettes. "Now what?" she asked.

"We sit here. Quietly. And wait until dawn."

"Oh, God, Bruce. Are you crazy?"

"You have any other suggestions?"

She didn't say anything, which was answer enough.

*   *   *

I sat at the bar in Kelly's for hours the night I managed to get myself kicked off the BAK account. Clarke never showed. I did manage to get really drunk, though – the barkeep took my keys, and I took a cab home.

I was braced for a tongue lashing from Becca, but instead she was sitting on the couch, reading a magazine. The TV set showed the local news. She looked up when I came in, accepted a kiss, and went back to reading while I went to change.

There was something odd in the bathroom, I thought, but in my alcohol-dulled senses it took me a while to figure it out.

The toilet seat was up. I went back into the living room, anger beginning to boil up inside me. "Who was here?" I demanded.

Becca looked at me, alarm on her face for a moment. "Why do you think anyone was here?"

"Because unless you haven't taken a piss in the four hours since you've been home a man has used the toilet." I said.

"Uh, it was the cable guy," she said, after a couple of moments. "It was out when I got home. I called, and they had a guy in the neighborhood, so he came right over. He asked to use the bathroom while he was here. It only took him a few minutes to fix whatever it was. He just left right before you got home."

"I see," I said, settling onto the couch next to her, picking up the TV remote and flipping through the channels, deciding to let the matter drop for the moment.

"I was watching that," she said.

"No you weren't. You were reading. I'm sure there's a game on here somewhere."

"You've been drinking."

"No, I haven't. I'm just tired," I responded.

It was almost word-for-word the conversation we'd had for the past few years every night. She got up and went into the bedroom, taking her magazine., I knew she'd be reading until she fell asleep.

Instead of moving to the bed, this one night, I dozed off on the couch and stayed there until morning. When Becca woke, she said nothing, not even waking me as she got herself ready for work.

I waited for her to leave before beginning my own morning, making sure the toilet seat was down when I left the house.

*   *   *

It had been dark a couple of hours. Becca and I both settled onto the floor, backs against the wall, as far away as we could get from the door and the windows. The shotgun lay across my lap.

Suddenly, I heard six rapid pops. It was probably Clarke's gun going off. Then, silence.

"Do you suppose he killed it?" Becca whispered to me.

"He'd try to come back if he did," I whispered.

"It's dark out there, and he's probably lost in the woods," she said. "Maybe we should call for him or something. Maybe that's why he's not--"

"Why do you care so intently anyway?" I asked. "What's this man to you?"

"Bruce, he's in danger out there!" she whispered. "He's your best friend! Aren't you worried about him even a little bit?"

"Sure," I said. "But why are YOU worried about him, Becca?"

"What the hell are you say--"

She never finished her sentence. The window on the other side of the room shattered, and she screamed once, briefly. Then, she was gone, dragged several feet through the air and outside in less than a second.

I could see in the moonlight blood on the jagged shards of glass still left in the window pane. Glass littered the floor, along with more blood. I heard her scream a couple more times, each time further away. I took a deep breath and let it out, slowly, feeling calmer and more content than I knew I should. I just sat there quietly, waiting for dawn.

*　　　*　　　*

It was another after-work night at Kelly's. Clarke made an appearance this time, joining me at the bar.

"Sorry about the other night, Bruce," he said, slapping me on the back when he got there, settling onto the barstool next to me. He held up a single finger at the bartender, who put a glass of beer on the bar in front of him without a word. "New guy at BAK has started in on me already. He's not letting the grass grow, let me tell you."

"Keeping you busy, are they?" I asked.

"Sheesh. Demanding bastards, aren't they? They want this, they want that, and they want it now. I've come close to telling them to stuff it more than once. I don't know how you put up with them as long as you did."

"Thinking about asking Nick to put somebody else on the account?" I asked.

"Not yet," Clarke said. "I think I can get a handle on their new rep. He seems to know what he's doing, and we speak the same language. I'm just blowing off steam, you know? How are things with you? We never get the chance to hang out anymore."

"Okay, I guess. Becca and I are--"

"Oh, speak of the Devil, there's Clyde. I'll be right back."

He got up and left me sitting there, going to talk to the new BAK representative who had just come in.

It was okay, though, because I had my gin martini to keep me company.

*　　　*　　　*

Quiet. The silence outside was almost a physical thing. Like a big, hulking monster in and of itself, sitting out there, daring anyone to bother it.

193

I wasn't about to make a sound. Anything – even a hastily drawn breath – would probably be as loud as a cannon shot.

I sat on the floor, back against the wall, shotgun in my lap, as far away from that shattered window and the door as I could get. Of course, there was another window on the wall above me. But it wasn't shattered. It was closed, and I was willing it to protect me against whatever was out there. It needed to protect me against whatever had taken my wife. Becca was gone.

We had been married for about eight years. No children – Becca had miscarried during the first year and hadn't gotten pregnant again. It was a hard time for her and for me, too. I don't think we'd ever gotten over it.

Clarke had always had better luck with women than I did. He also had more friends than I did – meeting people, talking to them, making them feel at ease, was always easy for him. He should have gone into politics. He never did.

Sure, he had his faults, but who doesn't? He more than made up for them with his virtues. I mean, yah, he would take things without asking, sometimes returning them, sometimes not. He would get drunk and hit on my girlfriends. But I always remembered that when I'd needed him, he'd been there for me when no one else had been. That more than offset the problems.

Even if Becca had . . . the image of that raised toilet seat came back to my mind. Cable guy. Right. Like that <u>ever</u> happened.

Still, Clarke and Becca? The idea was ridiculous. Even though Clarke had never made it to our little after-work get-together, things like that happened, right? I knew better than anyone the stresses of that job, of dealing with BAK and those other clients. Things have a tendency to come up at the last possible second, even when you're heading out the door. It happens all the time.

It was so quiet outside, but I wanted to hear a noise, anything, anything at all, to give me something to focus on besides the turmoil in my mind.

I didn't get my wish. The quiet went on for a thousand years it seemed.

*   *   *

When I got to work that fateful day, the door to my office was locked. I tried my key, but it wouldn't work.

I felt a hand on my shoulder. It was Clarke.

"Nick needs to see you," he said.

"Okay," I said. I knew right then that it was going to be bad. But for the life of me, I couldn't figure out what I'd done.

Nick's receptionist told me to go right in. Nick was sitting behind his desk when I opened the door.

"Come on in, and close the door, Bruce." he said.

I did as he asked, settling into the big, comfortable chair. It was so much bigger and more comfortable than the visitors' chairs in my own office. Nick looked at me a long while, his eyes narrowed almost to slits. He rocked back and forth, holding a pen in front of his chest, toying with it in his fingers. I could hear the antique clock he kept on a shelf against the wall ticking away.

"There's a problem, Bruce," he finally said. "A big problem. With the BAK account."

"What sort of problem?" I asked. "And why aren't you talking to Clarke about it? He's the exec on that account now."

"This is from your time handling it," Nick said. "There are . . . irregularities."

"What kind of irregularities?"

"The accounting kind," Nick said. "Did you think we weren't going to notice?"

"I'm sorry, Nick, I don't know what you're talking about," I said.

Nick snorted, and I realized then that he was really angry. I'd never seen him angry before.

"It's too late for you to play dumb with me. You're caught. You got greedy your last day handling that account, Bruce, and that's what nailed you. You were embezzling from that account, and when your access was being revoked you decided to triple your usual take. It was too big to hide. All I can say is thank God we put Clarke on that account before you bled it dry."

"Nick, I still--"

"Oh, for God's sake, shut up, Bruce. You're only insulting my intelligence and making yourself look bad. Now, we're not planning to prosecute, but you're fired. We'll ship your personal belongings to your house from your office, but as of now you are no longer welcome here. Turn in your corporate ID at the security desk and leave the premises. Now."

"But that last day---" I remembered, right then, turning, seeing that I hadn't logged off of my computer, Clarke standing there, smiling at me.

I remembered Clarke not showing up for our after-work get together.

"Please, Bruce, don't make this worse. Go home. I'm sure you'll turn up something. Plus, you get to keep the money you stole from us. It's a sweet deal, I'd say."

There really was nothing else to say. I got up, a bit shakily, and made my way out of the office.

I was in the parking deck, getting into my car, when Clarke slid up behind me in his own new car, a really huge SUV.

"Hey, Bruce, I heard what happened," he said. "Let's meet down at Kelly's for a burger and a beer, okay? You can talk to me about it."

"Sure," I said, not really knowing why.

*   *   *

We sat in a booth, me nursing a beer and a burger, Clarke slurping down some oysters on the half-shell. I thought over my suspicions about him and, then, dismissed them as ridiculous. There was no way Clarke would submarine me. He just wouldn't do that.

The mostly likely scenario was someone hacked my password and accessed the accounts that way. It happens all the time. At least that's what I kept telling myself.

"Man, that sucks," Clarke said, taking a sip of his own beer after gulping down yet another mollusk.

"It came out of nowhere," I stammered. "What the hell is going on?"

"Anybody who would accuse you of embezzling obviously doesn't know you," Clarke kept going. He gulped down another oyster after dousing it with hot sauce. "You've been my best friend since eighth grade. All through college. You looked out for me; you were always there for me. You helped me get this job. Without you I don't know where I would be, Bruce, and that's a fact. It really pisses me off that someone would treat you like this."

"I'm thinking of suing," I said.

"Hmmm . . ." Clarke muttered, chewing a mollusk while he thought. "I don't know about that. They can terminate anyone for any reason, you know. Plus, they didn't make their accusations public, so you can't accuse them of slander."

"But they aren't right!" I said. "I didn't steal anything! Nick thinks I have all this money when I don't! I have no idea what happened to it!"

"Shhhh!" Clarke patted my arm. "Maybe there is some legal recourse, I don't know. But I feel pretty sure that if you pursue it, Nick will press charges, and you'll find yourself arrested."

"Damn it," I felt like my hands were tied behind my back. "You're probably right."

"I know I am. I think I know Nick pretty well. He's a vengeful little bastard. I think you'll find yourself a new job pretty quickly. You've got a good reputation on the street; lots of people out there know you. Someone will snap you up as soon as they hear that you're available."

"They're going to want to know <u>why</u> I'm available," I said. I took a bite of my hamburger--it was cold and a little greasy.

"You can tell them that your former boss was a real SOB," Clarke just kept going. "He's got a reputation, too, you know. People who work for our clients know what he's like. Hell, I get people telling me all the time that they can't see how I keep working for him. I had lunch with Clyde at BAK just today and he said . . . . sorry. I guess that's a sore spot right now."

"Don't worry about it," I said.

"You're my mentor, Bruce, don't you ever forget that. I'll tell anybody who asks. Everything I learned, I learned from you."

"So I can use you as a reference?"

"Sure thing, buddy. Sure thing."

The waitress brought our check, and he grabbed it.

"I'll take this," he said. "After all, I'm the one who's working, right?"

*   *   *

I heard something moving around outside the cabin.

It didn't sound like it was getting closer or even further away. It was just something rustling through the underbrush. Casually moving around out there, not worrying about being noisy.

It went on for some time before my curiosity overcame my fear and I got up, as quietly as I could, to take a peek through a corner of the window.

At first I could see nothing at all. I'd never seen darkness so complete before – the moon wasn't even visible now, going down behind a distant mountain.

At last, my eyes acclimated, and I saw something move, just inside the tree line. I watched it for a long time before it started to take shape, and I could make out details.

It was a deer, grazing on something a few feet away. I guess it was a doe – it didn't have horns, and I think that time of year the bucks all have horns. She didn't notice me as she stood there, chewing on something tasty she'd found growing on the ground, just a few feet away.

I watched her for some time. I'd never actually seen a deer in person before, and she was the most beautiful, graceful creature I'd ever laid eyes on.

Then something slammed against the window right in my face, causing me to fall backwards onto the floor, almost soiling my pants.

It was a raccoon, masked face pressed against the window, looking inside, holding onto the wall with its paws while it played peeping tom. It was a cute little bugger, I thought, when my heart finally stopped hammering and my breathing slowed to something approximating normal.

The raccoon glanced around, quickly, and then let go, dropping to the ground. I could hear the deer running away through the forest, and I imagined the raccoon was doing the same.

I resumed my former position, shotgun held across my lap, deciding not to move until dawn no matter what I heard outside or how curious I became.

*   *   *

"I think Becca is cheating on me."

Clarke had agreed to meet me at Kelly's, and we sat across from each other in a booth, a beer in front of me, a Scotch-and-soda in front of him, and a big bowl of salted peanuts in the middle of the table between us.

"Really?" Clarke asked. He had a handful of nuts almost to his mouth and paused when he said that, looking at me. "How sure are you?"

"I just got that feeling," I said. "I can't describe it, but she's been acting . . . really squirrely. Plus, there have been other things."

"Like?" he asked, tossing a peanut into his mouth.

"Little things. The toilet seat being up when she's been the only one in the house all day. The smell of a strange man's cologne. And I found a condom wrapper in the trash."

"Bruce, I don't think--"

"We don't use condoms, Clarke," I heard my voice rising in volume.

"Maybe it got there some other way. You know, some kids on the street, doing it in their car, and just tossing the wrapper into the bin outside the house. Because you know if they just tossed it onto the street the Nazi Neighborhood Watch would write down the license plate and report them for littering."

"Sure. That's entirely possible except this was in a trash can in the house," I continued

"Oh," Clarke said, chewing absently. "Uh, do you have any ideas who it could be?"

"No," my voice was now losing a little control. "Nothing concrete. I have my suspicions, but nothing I can really put my finger on."

"I see," Clarke said. His eyes seemed to grow distant then for a while, and I knew he was thinking. "What will you do if she is and you find out who she's been cheating with?"

"I'll kill him," I said, and my voice didn't waiver on that note, as I stared straight into his eyes.

Clarke was in the act of eating a peanut, and he choked on it, coughing. Finally, he took a sip of his drink to wash it down. He continued coughing and gasping for a while after that.

"You okay?" I asked, and he just waved me off.

"Kill him?" he gasped. "That's crazy, Bruce!"

"Crazy?" I heard my voice going up again. "What's crazy is her cheating on me, after everything I've done for her. After all the indignities I've endured, all the things I've done to put food on our table. Now she's bedding down with some other guy and pretending that nothing's happening. That's what galls me more than anything else, Clarke--she's shameless. She looks me right in the eye and lies."

"If you did find something out, how would you kill the guy?" Clarke asked. "I'm just curious."

"I bought a gun today. A 9 millimeter Beretta. Of course, I have to wait three days before I can pick it up, but that's no big deal to me. I've waited this long, I can wait a couple more days."

"What do you mean you've waited this long? You think this has been going on a while?" Clarke looked pale and sweaty, I'm guessing because of the painful and recent experience with the peanut.

"I think it's been going on for quite a while," I said. "I just have that gut feeling. That it's been going on for years, maybe."

"Look," Clarke muttered, leaning forward. "I have an idea. Let's get away for a few days. I've got the key to a cabin in the hills. Nick's cabin. We can all head up there, do a little fly fishing, sing a few camping songs, get away from it all for a while. What do you say? You, me, Sandy, Becca, all of us. For a couple days."

"I don't know, Clarke. Nick probably won't be happy with my going up there. And, I mean, me being cooped up with her on the trip there, then being with her in the cabin, nowhere to go . . ."

"We, you and me, will be fishing most of the time. And what Nick doesn't know won't hurt him. Come on. It'll be good. Maybe you can get a better idea of what's going on with her. Observe her, up close. It'll help you make some decisions, won't it? Really, you don't want to do anything rash, something that you'll regret for years and years and can't ever undo."

I thought about it, eating a couple of peanuts, washing them down with my warming beer. "Sure," I finally responded.

"It'll be like the old days," he said, brightening a bit, like he was looking forward to it. To be honest I was too--Clarke was right, it had been too long since we'd taken a trip together. He held up his fist, and I bumped it with mine.

"You have always been such a good friend to me, Clarke," I said, choking back tears. "I don't deserve you. I don't know what I'd do without you."

"I can say the same thing, buddy," he grabbed me, giving me a hug.

He, then, coughed and wiped his mouth with the back of his hand. "I can say the same thing."

*   *   *

I finally worked up the courage to go through my own baggage, finding this little tape recorder I always carry with me. I'm guessing if you're listening to this you found it, too. The battery seems to be fresh. I hope I'm talking loud enough for the mic to pick me up.

I can hear something moving around outside. I would call out to see if it's Clarke or maybe even Becca, but something's stopping me. Fear, maybe. Whatever it is, it isn't making much noise – only the occasional stick breaking or leaves rustling. If I listen very intently I think I can hear something that sounds like sniffing and snorting. Or maybe that's just my imagination.

So I sit here on the floor, the shotgun pointed at the door, cocked and ready. I can hear something just outside, something on the porch, something turning the knob. When that door opens, I'm going to pull the trigger. It's the only way – this thing, whatever it may be, it's just too fast for me to do this any other way. Whatever comes through that door is going to get itself shot before I can even decide what or who it is. Whatever is out there will not stand a chance.

I hope like hell it's Clarke.

BORIS AND THE NEIGHBORHOOD WATCH

BY

WEDNESDAY LEE FRIDAY

Part One: The Arrival

Things were looking up for me at the time of "the incident." I hadn't had an episode in months. The job was going well. I had a great girl, one I wanted to marry. Mom was even starting to trust me again. I almost felt, dare I say it, normal. Then, it all went to hell. It got away from me so fast, and I couldn't remember how I got to where I was. The only thing I remember for certain is that I loved my girl.

The lawyers got me all that lawsuit money while I was still in the hospital. I used my share to buy this house. It meant nothing without my girl. Without her it was only a monument to what I did not have, what was taken from me—not intentionally, but taken all the same. I hadn't set foot inside my house yet, and I loathed every inch of it.

That doctor said I've got to trust myself, to get on with things. She didn't really explain how, just ordered me to do it. All of them suggested things that could never happen: going back to work, finding a new girl, calling Mom to see how she was. I didn't see the point of making a life outside the hospital. I couldn't imagine I would ever know how. Anyway, it was just a matter of time before something happened, and they sent me back.

It wasn't my fault. I'm supposed to tell that to myself no less than four times an hour. It's what they call an *affirmation*. I call it a ridiculous waste of time. I do it just to spite them, to prove that this crap doesn't actually work. There's nothing that can make my life happy again. I don't even know what I'm still doing here. Most people would be relieved to know that I was gone.

Connie said I might as well go and see the house I worked so hard to fill with furniture. I wasn't actually convicted of anything, so they let me use a computer in the hospital. I suddenly had all that money, so I bought a washer and dryer, couches, a big TV, even a refrigerator. It never really occurred to me that I might buy things like that new. Fridges just came with the apartment, washer/dryers were down the hall, TV's got handed down friend-to-friend. This was all totally surreal.

Mom thought she was being gracious by unpacking everything and setting it up for me. She told Connie she wanted to *help out in any way she could.* Sure…as long as it didn't involve actually being in the same room with me, or talking to me, or writing me a letter, or sending anything, or e-mail. Any *other* way she could. Who could blame her though? I'd put her through so much already.

Connie offered to ride with me. I told her she didn't have to. Connie had a way of looking at me. It was the way you'd look at a lost dog or a crying baby you didn't know. Part pity, part annoyance. I wished she didn't have to be confronted with the fact that stories like mine exist in the world. She didn't deserve such misery foisted on her. She said it was *all in a day's work.* She suffered; I knew she did.

I'd never been in a taxi before. Taxies were for the wealthy and the drunk, so far as I knew. It was clean, air-conditioned, and smelled strongly of pine. I counted 14 "No Smoking" signs while the driver listened to some maddening radio drone. It played nothing but terrible news spoken in a complete monotone. How could anyone keep their voice so level and calm talking about bombings and explosions and bloody coups? Why would anyone would make *that* the background noise of their workday? I really wanted to get the hell out of this cab, but I didn't feel ready to go "home." It didn't even occur to me that I had a choice.

The house looked exactly like I pictured from the outside. Sunshine yellow siding, plants in little window boxes, blue curtains over the white-paned double-hungs. They say blue fades faster than any other color. I like blue, though. If I actually lived long enough to need new blue curtains, I could certainly afford them now.

A yellow post-it note was fixed to my new front door with a piece of Scotch tape, sort of invalidating the purpose of post-it notes. *"Claude is the Neighborhood Watch Leader. Will be by to visit. –Connie*

PS. Happiness is finding joy in the unexpected!"

Jesus, Connie. *Joy in the Unexpected.* That's a laugh. Wait, Claude? That sounded vaguely familiar. But there must be a million Claude's in the world. I peeled the tape off the front door and tucked the note into my pocket. Sometimes Connie's flaky advice turned out to be damn useful.

Connie told me over and over that I should get a cat or two. No way. I eventually told her I couldn't because my new furniture was too nice. She agreed with that logic, not realizing I got leather furniture just so she'd stop bugging me about the Goddamn cat. There was no telling what kind of horrible thing could befall an animal unlucky enough to be under my care.

I opened the door and clapped my hands twice, activating the stupid clapper Mom insisted on installing for me. *The wave of the future*, she called it. My ass. Three matching orbs illuminated the room, propped up on stylish brushed metal poles. There were a few of what could only be described as "tasteful knick-knacks" here and there. It could have been much worse. Knowing Mom, this place could have been loaded with a bunch of Chia Pets or Hummels.

The curtains were wide open; exactly the way Mom liked them. She's always had some sick obsession with *letting the light in*. How smart is it to tie back the only protection your home has against the cancer-causing heat lamp known as The Sun? Not very. I pulled them shut for privacy and because the cool darkness felt good on my skin. Take that, potential cancer!

The room was pretty much as I'd imagined. Thick blue carpeting under black leather couches, tasteful glass end tables, and a fish bowl that, upon closer inspection, housed a little plastic manta ray. It was funny, its motorized little tail propelling it in a tiny circle. Other than that desperate bit of whimsy, the room looked like it belonged in a magazine.

I carried my only suitcase to the bedroom. The door opened with a pronounced creak that was oddly satisfying, almost comforting. This looked like a bedroom in a doll's house: bed with that fluffy cloud mattress from TV, ridiculous flowered comforter on top, and one big pillow, right in the middle. I made double sure that my bed would never look like it had two distinct sides. I made Connie tell Mom about that over and over. I honestly believed for a time that if I took away the reminders of my girl that her face would stop plaguing me--that I wouldn't see her absolutely everywhere. She was always there, a million times an hour, every hour of every day. I knew she would never go away. She wanted to remind me, torment me, never let me forget what I did to her. She was right to do it.

I clapped my hands again, and two lamps identical to the ones in the living room came on at once. All my breath left me instantly. Purest horror confronted me, throttled and assaulted me. I tried to scream. The terror gagged me into silence.

I shut my eyes tight, knowing the scene would be different when I opened them. Dr. Rand told me that many times. *It's part of the illness, and you're smarter than it is. Close your eyes, count to 10, open them up again. Everything will be fine.* I started counting fast. One, two, three…I slowed myself down. It might not work if I counted too fast. Four…five…six…I really wanted to look now. I can't. Listen to the doctor, that's what you paid her for. Seven…eight…nine, I don't want to look. What if it's not gone?

I opened my eyes again. Shock. Panic. Fear. Disbelief. It was happening all over again. I would never escape it.

Dr. Rand's voice came back again, louder. *You KNOW the difference between reality and fantasy. You CAN talk your way through a delusion. It just takes practice.* Clearly, I had not practiced enough. She kept saying it was normal to see things, part of the illness that eventually fades. I didn't believe her. I still don't.

It was torture to stare at it, but I could not move. It was HER. But…not her. My girl in that same blue dress she died in. She was lying still in my bed, her blood darkening a wide swath on the blanket. Dead.

Beaten. Limp blonde hair covered her face. I was glad I couldn't see her eyes. Her expression must have been horrible. I was sick, sweating, dizzy. Was it happening again? I couldn't stand it if it were. No…please, please no.

I touched her, still warm. She looked like she might get up and walk away any second. My poor girl. Something far away told me I should do something, call someone. I couldn't. Blinded by stinging tears, paralyzed by panic and horror. I wept like a child, vaguely glad there was no one alive here to see me.

A bloodied baseball bat was propped on an open drawer in the nightstand. My God! Her. The bat. The knowing. It flooded back so clearly. That feeling of being absolutely sure she wasn't *her* anymore. She was a demon. I saw it in my girl's face…no, not HER face, the other face. The terrible one. Like in a dream, a nightmare. I did what I had to then, to help her. I really thought I was saving her. Hitting and hitting—killing it so it couldn't take her. Now I wasn't sure of anything. I never should have left the hospital. More tears. *Run.* A voice gave me the most obvious answer. *Just leave here, and never come back. You have all that money, just run for it.* It was the only thing that made sense. *clap clap* Lights off. Run.

Part Two: The Diversion

"Welcome Wagon!"

A smiling jackass who looked like a linebacker swooped down on me the second I closed the front door. I darted past him, ready to break into a sprint. I was ready. It would be miles before my legs gave out from under me. But the blond behemoth jogged after me, catching up effortlessly.

"My name is Claude, your friend Connie said I should come over and say hi!"

He held out his hand for the shaking. Something inside me told me not to take it, not to trust him. It felt so familiar. The fear, the paranoia. It only led to one place. I had to calm down. I had to just shake his hand and walk away. Run. I could go back to the hospital. I could find Connie, and tell her what happened. She'd believe me. She'd help me. She was on my side.

"Hi, yeah…the uh…neighborhood watch guy," I watched my own hand nervously as I shook his, terrified that it would be spattered with blood. I could see only one single drop. I could smell it, I was pretty sure. Claude didn't notice.

"Nice to meet you," I told him. "I really have to be—" he laughed and shushed me with a waiving hand gesture. I wiped the dot of blood on my jeans, fervently hoping he was too dim to notice.

"Neighborhood Watch, Welcome Wagon…it's all the same job really. Making this block a safe and happy place! Oh, you need to come inside for a beer. We just installed a tap."

Before I could step backward, Claude swung a burly arm around me and dragged me toward his house. Its outside was pale blue with yellow shutters, but otherwise identical to mine.

"C'mon, you look beat. Moving in takes a lot out of you, no?" Claude laughed forcefully. I thought for a moment about ducking out from under his over-muscled arm and making a break for it. What was he gonna do? Chase me down? I tried to take a deep breath, but my lungs felt heavy and full of holes.

He hurried past a nondescript living room and kitchen, briefly pointing out a picture of him standing next to a small woman with short brown hair, and two thoroughly average-looking children. A few other photos were tipped over so that the flaps on the backs rose feebly in the air.

The basement was, apparently, our final destination. It was obvious why Claude was anxious to show it off. Instead of the dart-boards, pool tables, drum sets, and mini-fridges that occupied most basements, this one boasted a wet bar beneath a huge aquarium. It stood opposite a fantastic jungle habitat that radiated bright, hot light. The clear blue tank with three circling ocean rays was instantly calming. The aquarium was built right into the bar, and served as its backdrop. Sparse pink coral and the rays were all it contained. If I intended to live, I might have to pick something like this up. It was relaxing in its sheer simplicity.

"Check out THIS beast," Claude pointed to what was easily the biggest snake I'd ever seen. "This is Boris. He's a green anaconda. Only the most serious herpers keep these." I didn't know what the hell a *herper* was, but this snake gave me chills. All I could think of was this monster wrapping itself around unsuspecting native people, squeezing them to death in absolute silence.

It was a dark, mottled green that was probably the exact color of its surroundings in the wild. Its girth was enormous. I doubted I could even get both hands around it. It could murder me in an instant—that much was clear. Everything in the world was conspiring to terrify me. The snake had weird, top-set eyes and nostrils, and was covered with black rings. I couldn't say for sure how long it was, but it looked almost as long as my front yard.

I wanted to ask him why the hell anyone would keep such a gruesome animal right in their home. I didn't. I didn't want to get him talking. I just needed to get the hell out so I could think.

"Don't like to blow my own horn," Claude gave a laugh that was almost a guffaw, "but he's pretty cool, huh?"

"Yeah, he really is. Listen--" he responded by holding up one finger, telling me to wait just one second. My host stepped over to a full bar and fiddled underneath it before retrieving two chilled mugs. Wispy tendrils of frozen smoke wafted gently off them. Smiling broadly, Claude expertly filled the mugs with reddish-brown lager.

"Nothing better on a bright, sunny day than a frosty mug, eh?" He handed me a beer, and we both took a drink. It was mellow, but with a bitter finish--obviously some kind of local microbrew.

Claude's eyes were fixed to the gargantuan snake that was easily as thick as his thigh. He went into a long explanation of how every so often some African villager goes missing, and they find him in the belly of some huge, distended snake. He guffawed again like a half-witted teenager. Claude was disgusting. How could anyone find humor in someone dying?

"You know, as impressive as that animal is, Boris only kills to eat— never for sport, personal gain, never just for the fun of it. The only animal that kills for pleasure is man," he said, as if trying to deflect from my unspoken comments.

"Uh huh," I nodded noncommittally. Claude reached up toward a section of hinged glass at the top of the enclosure. The snake's massive head thumped the opening, wanting out.

"Only thing worse than a man killing for his own sick, demented needs is that man getting away with it. You know what I mean?" He spoke each word slowly, staring me down. What the hell was this guy's problem?

I didn't speak. I took another swig of lager and watched the hand that could let loose a monster on me at any moment. "Oh hey," he laughed again, "How ya liking that beer?"

"Delicious," I said. Claude was scaring the hell out of me. I was feeling a buzz already. The alcohol content must have been pretty high. 'Course, it was my first drink after more than a year of water, orange juice, and Sprite.

"It's called *Detroit and Mackinac*," Mister Neighborhood Watch motioned to my drink. This guy was creepy. I couldn't believe that such an obvious dumbass would be in charge of keeping the neighborhood safe. He didn't seem remotely trustworthy. "It's a local microbrew I've been into lately. I get these little mini kegs shipped in."

Suddenly I felt so dizzy I almost lost my balance.

"Whoa there, partner!"

Claude pounced and grabbed my arm. Instead of guiding me to the nearby chair, he wrapped my hand around the load-bearing basement pole and helped me stand. "You alright? Why don't I walk you home?"

Walk me home? What was he? My prom date? I was so dizzy, sick. How could one beer make me feel like this? It must be messing around with my meds. Come to think of it, I hadn't had any breakfast today either. A strong, mid-afternoon beer on an empty stomach. I felt myself retch involuntarily.

"No, really, that's fine. I'm right next door," I told him as I held my stomach and tried to make my way up the stairs. I stumbled again, grabbing the railing for balance. I could feel nails rip loose from the drywall. I let go of the rail and almost fell backward until Claude pushed me upright. His irritating guffaw sounded again. There was a definite streak of schadenfreude in him.

"I'm not taking no for an answer, sir. Neighbors gotta watch out for each other, right?"

He half-carried, half-dragged me home. I no longer felt capable of running anywhere, though I was terrified of going back inside. I just wanted to sleep, to dream of my girl again, alive, happy, everything like it was.

"Mind if I use your facilities?"

Claude pointed down the hall that ended in the bathroom, office, and the tainted bedroom. *Just get out. Get out, get out, get out of my house...* I wasn't thinking straight. I could barely move. When I didn't answer, Claude started down the hall, his voice bouncing back toward me. "Oh, is this your office? What kind of work do you do?"

Was he just trying doors at random? What the—? I groaned and with great effort, pushed myself up from the leather sofa.

"Hey! Wait a minute—" my panicked cry came too late.

I threw my hand out uselessly, unable to stop him flinging open the bedroom door. What could I do? I couldn't even run for it. I could barely stand. He might do any crazy thing in the world when he saw—

"Oh, my God," Claude murmured, staring into the bedroom. It must have been ghastly for him. I winced, waiting for the explosion. "Is that a Victrola?"

For the first time, I noticed my grandmother's antique phonograph in the corner of my tainted bedroom. No girl. No blood. Just fresh, clean bedclothes and a spotless room with an old Victrola.

This had to be a joke, a put-on. I squeezed into the bedroom after him. She was gone. No baseball bat, no sad cascade of blonde hair lying in the crimson pool. I could feel the remaining color drain from my face. Could I have imagined it? I don't see how that's possible. I was so sure, terrified even. I remember the fear. It was real. Wasn't it? But I *must* have made it up. It was shock or post-traumatic whatever they called it. What other explanation was there? Unless it was…the demon. The *real* demon. But that couldn't be.

"You gonna be okay if I leave you here?" Claude's voice snapped me back into focus, into reality. I gave him a non-committal shrug, having no idea if I was going to be okay or not.

"You been grocery shopping yet? I can have the wife bring you by something to eat, maybe?"

"No, please, don't go to any trouble. I'm just gonna lie down."

That was a lie. The very idea of lying down in that bed, even going into that room was repulsive. There's no telling what I might see in there next. What the hell was wrong with me? They told me that none of this was my fault. They told me all that therapy crap was supposed to make this better. I told them they never should have let me out. Why didn't any of them listen to me?

Part 3: The Confession

"Kirk, my God! Are you okay? What happened?"

Connie looked worried, no, frightened to see me at her door at whatever the hell time this was. I didn't realize until she answered the door in her pajamas that it was totally dark outside. She didn't even ask me how I found out where she lived. I was much better with computers than I let on.

"Tell me what happened.,"

Her voice was calm, not angry or accusing. She cared about me. She was the only person left in the world who thought I was worth saving. If I were ever going to trust another person again, it would be Connie. I told her all about coming home and finding my girl, bloody and broken in my new bed. How everything was ruined again. I explained how sure I was that she had been there. I touched her. I *felt* her. The blood all over her arms, her hands, like she fought. I remember her feeling warm, sad, still, and *there*. My girl was there.

"We talked about this, remember?"

I nodded, knowing just where she was going.

"We discussed how the medication and the EMDR therapy would lessen the hallucinations and the panic attacks. But Dr. Rand did say that either could reoccur."

But that wasn't what it was. I saw her!

"Kirk, maybe we should go over it again."

Connie wasn't a doctor, just a social worker from the hospital. Her job wasn't to counsel me, just to make things right. She got paid by faceless people in government who believed, in theory, that people like me deserved some kind of social justice.

"The first strange thing I noticed was that splotch on my hand. In a way, it ran up my arms and around my neck. I thought it was trying to strangle me."

I shuddered at the nightmarish memory.

"Yes," she was forcing herself to be calm, so as not to upset me. "The drug interaction was giving you hives. That's normal, Kirk. You remember, Dr. Rand told you it was perfectly normal."

"Yeah, right," I scoffed.

"It is! There are many drug interactions that can give you hives. The pharmacist's mistake—"

"Mistake?" Hardly. A mistake is when you order soup and they bring you salad. This was not a mistake. This was a tragedy, a grave, life-destroying injustice.

"Yes, they told you the pills looked different because they were generic now."

She looked at me piteously. I took their word for it. I didn't research it, didn't check. Just popped their poisons in my mouth according to doctor's orders. I was a sheep, and my girl paid for it in the worst way imaginable.

"It wasn't your fault. You did your best to stay healthy. You never would have hurt anyone otherwise. We've talked a lot about how much you need your medication to be healthy. Remember?"

I nodded, not looking at her.

"You weren't given it. Worse, you were given something that actually hurt you. We talked about manic episodes and the things that can happen."

So what? I wasn't going to be magically absolved just because I didn't mean for it to happen. That wasn't going to bring my girl back or make anything like it was before.

"Tell me what you saw in the bedroom."

She leaned forward, and I looked away from her cleavage.

"I didn't just see her. I touched her. She was warm…but dead and bleeding. Just like when…"

"Say it out loud, Kirk. Say what happened."

"…when I killed my girl. When I hit her with the bat."

The guilt was on me again, the fear. Tears.

"I was so scared. I didn't know what was happening. The terror of…her…"

I was sobbing in front of Connie again. She kept asking questions and trying to reason with me. Doctors knew it was no use reasoning with a schizophrenic, but not Connie. She never gave up.

"But Kirk, if she was really in your house, where did she go? Why wasn't she there when you got home?"

I tried to think back. Where could she have gone? It wasn't just her…it was the blood, the bat – it was all gone.

The anger came on suddenly, sharply, thrusting into my gut. Somebody was doing this to me. Toying with me. Someone who knew what I had done. Once I realized it, it seemed so obvious. How had it taken me so long to figure it out? Claude! It had to be him.

"What?" Connie said fearfully…I hadn't realized I'd been thinking out loud. What had I said? What did she know? It was all so confusing, racing thoughts.

"Kirk, you don't really think that your new neighbor—what do you think, exactly, Kirk?"

She was trembling, her voice shaky.

"I think I'd like to go home."

As I remembered everything that happened since I got out of the taxi, the anger multiplied. Claude stopped me when I was trying to get away. Claude made me go drink beer with him, beer that made me far too drunk. Mister Neighborhood Watch came to my house and into my bedroom for no good reason. Since when does a man want to walk into another man's bedroom? He knew about me, about my girl. He hated me, just like the newspaper people and those muckraking local pundits who thought it was big humor to call me crazy and make jokes about how fun and cushy my life in the mental hospital would be. Bastards! I needed a reason to live, and this would be it. I would *get* all of them.

Part Four: The Mad Dash

"Can you give me a ride home?" I asked her as calmly as I could. She was one of those people who, if you told them you were going to *get* someone, they'd think they had to call the cops. I didn't want to trouble Connie; she believed in people. She was good.

Connie drove down the road, still in her pajamas. The worst part of that night played over and over in my anger-addled mind. I swung the bat. I hit my girl and hit her. Over and over. Each swing felt like a lifetime. The terror. The complete and utter terror of it happening right in front of me. The fear that I would never get my girl back if I couldn't kill the evil thing inside her, everywhere. I loved her. There was no choice. Her screaming in the distance was torture, every second a lifetime of pain. The beast went into terrifying death throes. I raised the bat again. But before I could bring it down, I'd fallen into a black oblivion. I woke up in the hospital.

"Kirk? Are you okay?"

I jerked back into reality with Connie still driving, her open purse hastily tossed between us on the long front seat. In her rush to get out the door and drive me away from her place, she had still taken the time to pack the telltale black case that every staff member carried in the hospital. If I did anything physical that Connie didn't like, she was going to fire electricity into my body by way of a non-lethal taser. Brave Connie.

"I want you to listen to me," Connie said sternly, "Claude doesn't hate you. None of your neighbors hate you. I've met him. I've spoken with him, he didn't even know about your case until..."

"Until?" She had my full attention now. "Did you tell him?"

My heart fell into my gut. Connie. She told the neighbors about me, made them hate me. I'm sure she didn't mean to. Poor Connie believed that deep down everyone was good. When I was ridding the world of that malicious jackass Claude, I'd have to get a swipe or two in for Connie.

"I wanted to prepare him, in case..."

She cut herself off. She wanted to warn them. She didn't want to feel responsible, just in case it wasn't the switched pills that made me crazy enough to hurt my best girl. "In case anybody got the wrong idea about you, about what happened. There's already been such a glut of misinformation. Claude is such a nice man, wanting to be helpful. There aren't a lot of people like that left in the world."

She kept glancing away from the road to give me sympathetic looks. I hated knowing she was so sad for me. She took a hand from the wheel and took one of mine. It felt warm and sweet, no one had touched me nicely in so long. In another life, Connie and me...it could have happened.

"He hates me. I'm telling you. I can see it in his eyes."

I could feel her eyes roll without even looking at her.

"Answer me this, Kirk. Why? What possible reason could he have for wanting to trick you? Or hurt you? Or do anything bad to you? He just doesn't strike me as that sort of person. It so happens that I know a thing or two about humanity."

She smiled like it was a joke, but I don't think it was. Connie really did pride herself on her people skills.

"People don't always need a reason to be assholes," I told her, as if that needed explaining.

"I'm gonna drop you off, but I'll come by tomorrow. You and I can go talk this out with Claude and his wife together. You'll see there's nothing to—"

I stepped out of her car and slammed the door harder than I meant to. She looked up at me, clearly startled. I couldn't think about that now. Mister Neighborhood Watch himself was bounding toward me in the darkness, his arms outstretched as if he was about to hug me.

Part Five: The Confrontation

"Burning the midnight oil, are ya?"

Claude's wide smile looked freakish in the moonlight. He seemed to almost glide around to the driver's side of the vehicle, opening Connie's miraculously unlocked door. "I'm that way myself. Insomnia, I guess. You guys out for a movie?"

His eyes slid over Connie, taking in her penguin-print pajama pants.

"She's just dropping me off."

I wasn't ready to do this yet. I couldn't do anything until I was ready. And Connie shouldn't see it.

"Oh, you two should come over for a drink. The wife could sleep through a plane crash, but I'm bright-eyed and bushy-tailed."

In addition to being a spiteful jackass, Mister Neighborhood Watch seemed to only speak in dumb clichés.

"We really can't," I told him, raising my wrist to consult a watch that wasn't there. Connie sort of half-nodded, half-jerked her head at me. I shook mine back in silent dissent.

"It might be nice to come in for a minute," I said.

I wistfully recalled a time when people didn't constantly push me around. A diagnosis of schizophrenia isn't just about being crazy, it's about not trusting yourself…at least not like you used to.

The grass was wet as we walked over the lawn toward the home Claude shared with his family. I hoped for his sake they really were asleep.

There was no telling what could happen now. The yard felt like it went on forever. Yards didn't seem this big when I was a kid. But then, my neighborhood wasn't nearly this nice.

Connie and I sat on either side of a velvety sectional sofa. It probably used to be nice. But now it was covered in snags, cracker crumbs, and something that looked like an old grape juice stain. Connie clutched her bag to her chest nervously, and I was sure she'd put me down like a charging rhino if I did anything.

"Did you tell Connie about Boris?" Claude asked me as if he and I were chummy old friends. That jerkass wasn't fooling anyone. Connie raised an eyebrow at me.

"Boris?"

Connie's voice was light, curious. Even she was acting as if Claude and I were best pals, as if I was the only one who wasn't in on it. A woman stumbled into the room wearing nothing but a long T-shirt. She jumped slightly when she noticed us.

"Oh! I didn't know we had company."

Claude's wife looked the same as in the photo, except she'd gotten some sun recently. Her skin looked ruddy and reddened, even in the dimly lit living room. Connie, for some reason, couldn't take her eyes off the woman. Claude rushed over to his wife.

"Honey, this is Kirk from next door and Connie."

He gave his wife a knowing look. I knew it! He'd been talking to her about me. It was all so obvious.

"They wanted to see Boris."

The couple whispered to each other in the hallway, before she retreated down the hall and out of sight.

Connie stood up and wandered around the room with a kind of forced nonchalance. Whatever she had expected to happen during this farce, this wasn't it. Hopefully she was realizing what a bad move it was to force me to come here. I was feeling well enough to go to my house. I could sleep on the floor or maybe on that expensive leather sofa. I'd bide my time, wait until I was ready, until I knew exactly what to do. Connie didn't have to know anything about it. She was too special, too good to know about this.

Connie was looking through the framed photos around the mantle on its little shelves. She picked up one in particular, and stared. Her head lowered, and she raised a hand over her face and stayed like that for a full minute, maybe more. Then her hand went out to the mantle for support.

"Are you okay?"

I went to her. Her eyes were red and teary, when they hadn't been just moments before.

"Yes," her voice was low. "I'm going to the powder room. Please don't do anything until I get back."

She squeezed my arm and handed me the frame in her hand. I thought wistfully that nobody really called it a *powder room* anymore.

I looked at the thing that made Connie weepy. A framed photo of what appeared to be a younger Claude and…it was unmistakable. I gasped out loud. My girl. Ten years younger, maybe, and leaning against a young Claude who towered over her by a head. Her bright blonde hair shone in the sunlight, like her smile. Seeing them next to each other, it was obvious that they were related. Their eyes were exactly the same, even though I now knew that one pair of them was good, and the other was evil.

Connie's question from the car came back to me. *Why? Why would Claude hate you. He didn't even know about your case…*

He was a faker, a liar. He did this to me on purpose. He hated me like everyone else. He believed I did it on purpose, or that I should have gotten the chair. People actually asked for that outside the courthouse. They wanted me to be strapped to a chair and burned to death with electricity. People were all evil inside; some just buried it deeper than others. I returned the frame to its former place, face-down on the mantle.

Connie must have left me alone to do what I had to do. Thank you, Connie. Thank you.

"Alright, man, you up for a beer?" The buffoon looked on the brink of another irksome guffaw.

You should have let Boris loose on me when you had the chance, Claude. When I was doped up on whatever poison was in that frosty mug. You think you're such a smart son-of-a-bitch, don't you Claude? I'm onto you.

"Sure," I told him, following toward the basement. The whole way down, my eyes darted everywhere. How would I do it? How would I wipe this mean, nasty bit of filth off the face of the planet? If I took care of everyone who behaved this way, slowly, surely, I could rid the world of hate. Malice and vitriol would breed themselves out of the gene pool. It was the best reason to stay alive. It would almost be worth my suffering to save the world from evil.

There were full, heavy whiskey bottles all across the bar. A weight rack in the corner revealed dumbbells just large enough to bash someone's head in. Then I saw it. It was just behind the bar. My beloved bat. Well, not MY bat, but the one he'd planted for me to see. The one he'd used to push me back to a time when there was only fear, only terror, a time when all I could do was lash out against the evil. Bashing him with it was just, and apropos.

"Hope you're in the mood for something extra strong!"

Claude's unnaturally cheerful exclamation made me wince. Not long now, Claude. Get ready. I took a step toward the bar and took my drink, not daring to touch it to my lips. God knows what was in this one. I tried to take another step toward the bar. I just needed to get behind it. He was blocking my way, pretending he wasn't, leaning in silent menace to keep me from my target. Did he know?

Too soon, far too soon, Connie's furious steps descended the stairs. Claude took a step toward her, clearing me to dive behind the bar and pick up the glorious baseball bat. I squeezed it in my hands, relishing the weight on the end. This would fix it. This would end it. Suddenly, it all made sense. Connie was holding something in her hands. I didn't realize what it was. A flash of blue light streaked the room. I heard electric crackling and a scream of pain. There was a pronounced thud, then silence. I was standing. Holding the bat. Claude lie switching and writhing on the floor as Connie pressed the button down as hard as it would go. After what seemed like a very long time, she stopped and looked up at me. She tossed something yellow and stained on the floor next to the still-twitching Claude.

"They both did it. The wife too. I--" Connie looked like she might cry again. "I'm so sorry," she stammered.

It was a blonde wig, stained with blood. I didn't imagine the thing in my bed. It wasn't my girl. They were tricking me. Just to hurt me. Just to make me pay, and pay, and have to keep paying.

Connie pressed the taser again for good measure. Claude appeared to have peed himself, but otherwise lay perfectly still. I didn't know what to say to her. How do you thank someone for believing in you? How do you express gratitude when somebody gives you back your sanity, or at least helps you remember where you had it last? While I was thinking about that, I didn't really notice that Connie had pulled open the top of the massive snake's enclosure.

"So this is Boris?" she asked, not remotely fearful as its massive, scaly head moved smoothly up the side of its Plexiglas box. I nodded. Connie took my hand and pulled me toward the stairs. She was so much tougher than I realized. She was brave, proactive, forceful, even lethal, it seemed.

I paused just long enough to see all 17-plus-feet of Boris coil around his former owner, who was just then starting to regain consciousness. The last 18 hours of my life were the strangest ever—even after spending a year in the mental hospital. It was profoundly terrifying, exhilarating, shocking. I moved forward up the stairs. I couldn't help thinking that just like Connie suggested, I was finding infinite joy in the unexpected.

JournalStone

THE ROAD OF THINGS TO COME

BY

BENSON PHILLIP LOTT

Sheriff Gerald Keylee knows the identity of the man walking down the middle of the road even before he sees his face.

Simon Fielding: White male, six feet, approximately 160 pounds, brown hair, hazel eyes.

At precisely 11:14 p.m., Mr. Fielding was reported as having escaped from County Hospital (his third AWOL just in the last six weeks). On each of his flights he is found wandering down the shoulder of the Jessup County expressway. His escapes are always sudden, always unexplainable and they always occur in the middle of the night.

Tonight is no different.

Law enforcement in Jessup is held together by a handful of officers. There's hardly any crime. On most nights, only the sheriff and the dispatcher, Debbie, remain on duty. A fellow officer, Ralph Jenkins, is on call and can be alerted to assist if necessary.

Because of Fielding's history, Keylee had started the night's search on the expressway, using his searchlights in an attempt to locate his suspect. At 1:26 a.m., after nearly an hour of driving the same 20-mile portion of road, the sheriff had begun to wonder if somehow Fielding had moved beyond the city limits. He had expressed his concern to Debbie over the radio and she in turn had suggested that he check out some of the back roads near the southern county lines. She recommended one road in particular: Shepherd's Pass.

"And it looks like you were right, Deb," the sheriff says to himself as he pulls his patrol car over to the side of the road. Simon is 10 yards away, venturing the uneven concrete, the pavement ruined from years of neglect.

Fielding is a notorious sleepwalker. He walks the cool pavement barefoot, dressed only in his state-issued hospital clothes. If he were actually conscious, he would undoubtedly be freezing. Fortunately, (or perhaps unfortunately) he is lost in the depths of a dream.

Keylee reaches for his radio. "Deb? It's me. I've got good news."

The speaker crackles. An excited woman's voice asks: "Did you find him, sheriff?"

"Copy that."

"Okay, great. I'll get County Hospital on the line and tell them we found their patient."

"Right. I'll let ya know when I'm en route."

"Should I send Ralph for back up?"

"What for?"

"Just thought I'd check."

Keylee switches off. Next, he opens the driver's side door and steps out of the cruiser to approach his suspect.

Fielding walks in perfect stride, missing every pothole, every pile of loose gravel, as though he were coordinating each step meticulously. This is impossible of course. After all, his eyes are closed.

The sheriff knows from past encounters that he could speak to Mr. Fielding who occasionally would even reply despite his lack of awareness. The trick was to speak to him gently, act polite. And most of all: *show no fear*.

"Evening Simon. Where you off to tonight?"

Simon's eyelids flutter, his head turns ever-so-slightly. The reply he gives is a soft spoken enigma. "The corner of 1st and May."

Keylee swallows and takes a dramatic step forward. "Well, how 'bout I give you a lift?"

Simon halts and Keylee stops with him.

"A lift?"

"That's right Simon..." Keylee places a hand on Fielding's left shoulder and guides him back to the patrol car. He gently places him into the backseat without cuffing him. There's no need. The sheriff straps in his suspect then quietly shuts the rear door. He returns to the driver's seat and puts the car in motion, making a quick U-turn so he can get back to the expressway.

Minutes pass in silence. Keylee glances up and checks his rearview mirror. Mr. Fielding sits motionless, both hands resting in his lap.

Keylee knows the staff at County Hospital will place him in the Disturbed ward once they arrive. "Disturbed" is a high security section on the fourth floor of a six story facility. The two floors above it are also occupied by men with mental incapacities, some of them mild, most severe. To prevent him from escaping again, the staff will undoubtedly monitor him on camera and possibly strap him to a gurney or hospital bed. Electroshocks are out of the question, but heavy sedatives are certain to be on hand. There will not be another escape.

Keylee's thoughts shift to Simon's escapes in general. He suspects someone at the hospital might be assisting him with breaking out, but the real question is why?

Suddenly, the police scanner clicks, the sound of static erupts through the speakers –*sssssssssssssssssssssssssssss*- a voice finally transmits. It's Debbie again.

"Sheriff? You there? How's it going?"

Keylee snatches up the receiver. "Copy, Deb. I've got our mystery man in custody. I'm heading to the Interstate, but it's gonna be minute 'til I get there. He was pretty far out there this time."

"How far'd he make it?"

"Hmmm, about six miles. He was right where you said he'd be."

"Did you ask him where he was going?"

"Yes, ma'am"

"And did he give you that same address? First and May?"

"Sure did."

"God, that's so strange…"

"Yeah well, this whole thing is strange if you ask me."

"Well, just so you know, I ran a search and there's no record of a First and May anywhere in the state. I double checked. I even asked a few locals. Lots of First streets they said, but no May."

"Well, I think it's safe to say our boy's from outta town."

"Yeah, but from where?"

"You know as much as I do, Deb. In fact, I got a feeling you know a lot more. Speaking of which…how'd you know for me to check Shepherd's Pass? He's never come out this way before."

"Just call it a hunch, Sheriff."

Hearing this, Keylee smiles and shakes his head. "Bull. C'mon, Deb. What's the story?"

"Well, Sheriff, I can tell you, but you won't believe me."

"Try me. I got a good 10 minutes to spare before I make it to the Interstate, another 30 to get to County Hospital. So I got plenty of time to debate your wild theories."

Laughter comes over the radio speakers. Keylee checks his rearview mirror again to monitor his man in custody through the Plexiglas divider.

Mr. Fielding is still asleep, his breathing, slow and even. Debbie's voice cuts in, but Keylee misses it.

"What's that, Deb? Sorry. I was checking on something."

"I said I had a dream about it."

"A dream about what?"

"The road. Shepherd's Pass."

"I'm not following you."

"Well, you know the old story about it, don't you?"

Keylee groans into his radio. "Oh boy, here we go. I knew this was coming. You and your old stories..."

"What's that's supposed to mean?"

Keylee sighs, still smiling as he plots his next words carefully. "I guess I'm simply saying that you're...beyond common understanding."

"Well put, sheriff."

"Thank you."

"Anyway...what's your latest? Let's hear it."

"Well, since you're so eager to know, Shepherd's Pass was where they found that doctor."

"Doctor? What doctor?"

"County Hospital's got a history of patients goin' missing from it, Sheriff."

Keylee frowns. He has been on the Jessup County police force for 10 years, sheriff for five. And during that time he has never heard of anyone other than Mr. Fielding escaping from the County's mental ward. Then again, he thought, Debbie has lived in Jessup County all her life. Her father had been a deputy for 36 years. Perhaps she knows something he doesn't.

"It was before our time," Debbie explains as if sensing his confusion. "A good twenty somethin' years ago. Back when Shepherd's Pass was still open."

Keylee frowns. "What's the Pass got to do with it?"

Debbie continues. "A lot of folks in town who were around back then think it's got a lot to do with it actually. They say that road is...of the devil."

Keylee sighs. "Deb, some folks in town say *everything* is of the devil. Cable TV is of the devil. McDonald's is of the devil. Airplanes...of the devil. Hell, Ms. Clarkson accused my cat once of bein' 'of the devil'."

"I know, I know. But this is different."

"Yeah? How so?"

"The doctor, I think his name was Grover, claimed he knew the cause for all the disappearing patients. He said he'd discovered some secret manuscript, some book. Of course no one ever saw this mysterious book and before he could produce it, the good doctor just snapped."

"What do mean?"

"Well, he showed up at the hospital one night, took out a guard and then helped one of his patients escape."

A knot tightens in the sheriff's stomach. *So the hospital had a prior incident of someone helping patients break out.*

"Go on," he says, his level of intrigue rapidly increasing.

"Well, the police were called in, my father included. He said they never found the patient, but they did manage to locate the doctor. And I'm sure you can guess where..."

"Shepherd's Pass?"

"Bingo."

Keylee ponders this information then asks: "So, where is this doctor now, do we know?"

"He's dead," Debbie says flatly. "When they found him on the Pass he was in his car. Apparently he'd been in a terrible accident. The car had flipped over several times. When the medics arrived and transported him to the hospital they said the doctor was delirious. He died a few hours later, slipped into a coma in his hospital bed, then he flat-lined."

"Wow. That's too bad. I would have had a lot of questions for him."

"You and a lot of other people, Sheriff," Debbie remarks slyly. "The hospital was furious that they couldn't press charges. The guard he'd taken out almost died from his concussion. Anyway...that's the story."

"So no one knows what became of the missing patient, huh?"

"No, but you can bet there were some pretty wild theories. That's why the city council decided to close the Pass. Folks in town were scared.

Thought the crazy man might still be out there. And sheriff, you're not gonna believe this next part. The patient? They said his name was Fielding."

Keylee's eyes widen in bewilderment. "*What*? Debbie…why didn't you tell me this before?"

A dead silence fills the patrol car. The radio crackles, hissing with static. Keylee attempts to switch frequencies, but the white noise continues.

-sssssssssssssssssssssssssssssssssssssssssssssssssssss-
"Debbie? Debbie, come in?"
-sssssssssssssssssssssssssssssssssssssssssssssssssssss-
"Sheriff? Are you there?"
-sssssssssssssssssssssssssssssssssssssssssssssssssssss-
"I'm here Debbie. What the hell's happening?"
-sssssssssssssssssssssssssssssssssssssssssssssssssssss-
"Sheriff? Hello?"
-sssssssssssssssssssssssssssssssssssssssssssssssssssss-
"Debbie, can you hear me, copy?"
-sssssssssssssssssssssssssssssssssssssssssssssssssssss-
 "Yeah, I can hear you now. Did you get him?"
-sssssssssssssssssssssssssssssssssssss- (The hissing stops.)
"Get who?" Keylee asks, confused.
"The suspect. Simon Fielding."

What's going on here?

"Of course I got him, Deb. I already told you this. Who do you think we've been talking about for the last ten minutes?"

"Uh, sheriff…" Debbie replies hesitantly. "You haven't called in for over an hour."

Keylee's face reddens. "Deb, what the hell are you doing? Quit playin' games."

"Sheriff, I've been tryin' to reach you for a whole half an hour, but all I've been getting is static."

Keylee's pulse quickens. He gazes out the windshield, losing himself in the beam of headlights reflecting on the asphalt. The surrounding night has consumed all visibility. There is only the road ahead.

"Debbie, what are you saying?"

No response. The radio is crackling again. The hiss of static returns.

-ssssssssssssssssssssssssssssssssssssssssssssssssssssssss-

"Debbie? You there? Can you hear me?"

-ssssssssssssssssssssssssssssssssssssssssssssssssssssssss-

"Deb, this isn't funny…"

-ssssssssssssssssssssssssssssssssssssssssssssssssssssssss-

"Deb…?"

-ssssssssssssssssssssssssssssssssssssssssssssssssssssssss-

The radio clicks off. Silence fills the patrol car, amplifying the hum of the engine as the sheriff looks up and stares at Simon's reflection. His eyes are open now. He's alert…and smiling.

Keylee turns in his seat, releasing his grip on the steering wheel. "Mr. Fielding? Are you alright?"

Simon remains silent as he reaches out and taps on the divider and points to the windshield, his lips mouthing two words: "Look out."

Keylee frowns and his eyes shift back to the road. The patrol car is swerving toward a massive ditch on the left hand side of the pass. The sheriff gasps and he frantically realigns his position on the road.

"Mr. Fielding I need you to sit back in your seat, sir…"

Simon does as instructed.

Keylee calms himself by inhaling a deep breath. "Mr. Fielding? Are you okay back there?"

Simon's head tilts back, his eyelids fluttering faster than before. "Let me out, Sheriff…" His voice is soft, thoroughly absent of malice, yet all the same, it manifests something that causes the sheriff to shudder.

"Mr. Fielding…what's going on?"

Simon's lids peel open. "I have to stop the crash," he says. "I have to stop it…or we'll never get out."

I should pull over, Keylee thinks to himself. *I should pull over and put him in restraints.*

The interstate is less than two miles distance, and this fact deflects his decision to stop. *Just keep him calm. Keep him talking. Find out what's going on.*

"Mr. Fielding? Can you hear me? I need you to explain to me what crash you're referring to."

Simon bows his head. "I'm lost…"

The sheriff shakes his head firmly. "You're not lost, Mr. Fielding. You're right here with me."

Simon reaches up to his face, emitting an agonized groan. "Oh God, I'm lost…so lost…I can't get out…I can't escape it…"

Get to the hospital. Stop screwin' around and get to hospital now!

Keylee floors the accelerator. The speedometer races to 90mph as Simon cries out in terror, banging at the divider. "You have to get us out of here!"

Keylee whirls around. "Sit back!"

Simon ignores him, pounding the plate glass like a man in the midst of torture. Keylee grits his teeth and impulsively reaches for his sidearm. "Sit back in that seat right now or so help me I'll-"

Vvvvvvvvvvvvvvvvvvvvvvvvvvvvvmmmmmmmmmmmmmmm-BMPT!

A loud crash as the hood of the patrol car collides with a thick mound of dirt. Keylee is thrown forward, his seatbelt choking him as the vehicle swerves headlong into a ditch. A spray of white rocks crack against the windshield. The sheriff grips the wheel and stomps on the brake pedal. No use. The vehicle falls directly into the ditch and flips on its side. There's an explosion of shattering glass as metal crumples and exhaust fumes rise in thick black clouds.

Minutes pass. The echoes of the impact fade and the dust clouds settle. The police scanner crackles as the roaming frequencies locate Debbie's transmission:

"Sheriff? You disappeared on me again. Is everything all right?"

A wind picks up. The patrol car headlights dim. "Sheriff…? Sheriff…?"

No response.

The road is silent.

SIMON'S EMPTINESS:

"How are you feeling today, Simon?" Dr. Fredrick Grover asks of his patient as he enters his living quarters (room 28-C), located on the fourth floor of the mental ward inside Jessup County Hospital.

Simon is sitting at the edge of his neatly folded bed, a suitcase at his feet.

"I'm fine," he replies and his appearance suggests that this is the case. For the first time in weeks he is clean-shaven and wearing civilian clothes (donated to the Hospital by members of a local Protestant church).

Dr. Grover is pleased to see his patient looking sharp, but the sullen tone combined with his demure manner is somewhat unnerving. After this should be an exciting day for him.

The doctor grabs a metal folding chair that's been placed near the front door beside the chrome sink area and sets it directly across from the bed.

Simon tilts his head at an angle, intrigued by the folder Dr. Grover is carrying under his left arm. A thin label is printed in the corner: FIELDING, SIMON.

Under the name is a personal identification code used for filing purposes. Simon studies the numerical sequence then drops his gaze to the polished marble floor

The doctor senses his discomfort and briefly eyes the suitcase.

"All set to go I see…" He opens his folder and sifts through several pages of handwritten notes, most of which are simple observations made during weekly sessions with his favorite patient. There are other notes left by substituting psychologists who filled in while he was on vacation or sick leave, but these are rarely considered by the hospital staff who meet twice a month to examine their patients' progress and discuss further methods of treatment.

Dr. Grover is mainly concerning himself with the last six pages near the back section of the folder that are stapled to a Xeroxed copy of Mr. Fielding's discharge papers. These pages consist of notes from last week's session.

"You're quiet today, Simon," the doctor remarks, glancing up from his papers. "Are you sure everything is fine?"

Simon raises his head slowly, his expression shifting to one of dreariness. "I'm ready to leave this place."

The doctor nods his sympathies. "I'm sure you are."

A brief silence follows.

Simon's gaze returns to the floor. "I want to thank you for putting in your recommendation."

Dr. Grover leans back in his chair. "Well Simon, I have great confidence in you, as do many of the others on staff."

Simon's timid smile vanishes. He eyes the doctor suspiciously. "Your hands are shaking, Dr. Grover. Is something the matter?"

The doctor laughs, but there's an underlying nervousness that seems, on the surface, unwarranted. "I am a bit shaky, aren't I? I suppose I had a little too much caffeine this morning..."

Simon's glare darkens. "Did you?"

Dr. Grover clears his throat, ready for a change of subject. "Let's stay on track here, shall we? We have very little time this morning. I'm supposed to take you to the transitional housing center by noon and I want to finish our discussion from last week."

Simon frowns. "*You're* the one taking me to the halfway house?"

"Does that bother you?"

Simon shakes his head. "No. It's just...well you're a psychiatrist. Seems strange they would expect you to take the time."

"I volunteered," Grover says, a bit too quickly.

Simon turns to face the curtains over the sealed window above his bed. "I see..."

Grover retrieves a retractable pen from his sport coat and clicks the tip open. "Let's get on with the session shall we?"

Simon looks back from the curtains, unable to ignore the doctor's rising impatience. "I had the dream again last night," he says and the doctor immediate poses interest.

"You mean the one about the road?" he presses.

Simon shuts his eyes, nodding. "And the policeman...Keylee..."

Grover flips to an empty page, jotting brief notes. "The one whose death you feel responsible for?"

Simon's lids open, he stares blankly at a wall. "I *am* the one responsible."

Dr. Grover sighs. "Simon we've been over this. There are no officers in this county - in this state for that matter – with the last name 'Keylee'. Nor are there any records of any law enforcement officers dying in a car accident while on duty. Your dream is a symbolic reflection of your own suppressed guilt. The victim represents your unresolved issues. An inner self you can't remember."

Smile can't help but smile. "You say that so convincingly."

Ignoring the humor, Grover shakes his head. "I think we should continue with what we were discussing previously."

Simon cranes his neck, glancing toward the ceiling. "You mean, Shepherd's Pass?"

"Yes," Grover replies. Once again, his nervous energy betrays him.

Simon shifts his weight on the mattress. "Something's happened to you. Hasn't it, Dr. Grover?"

The doctor's lips part, but there's a subtle hesitation. The chance for denial passes as silence prevails and both men remain still.

"I'll tell you what, Dr. Grover" Simon finally begins. "How 'bout we make a deal? I'll tell you about Shepherd's Pass, if *you* tell *me* whatever it is you're hiding."

Again the room goes quiet. From behind the door, footsteps can be heard. A full minute passes. Then two. At last the doctor speaks.

"Very well, Simon..." The doctor places his pen back into his pocket and points a steady finger. "You go first."

Simon cocks an eyebrow. "So, we have a deal then, doctor?"

Grover nods curtly. "Yes. We have a deal."

"Okay," he says. "So where did we leave off?"

Dr. Grover sits up, instantly alert. "You were describing that first night."

"Right...I remember now."

Simon shuts his eyes, ready to begin.

MEMORIES OF THE FUTURE:

I wake up in a hospital room. I know it's a hospital room because I'm connected to an IV drip and a loudly beeping heart monitor. My head is firmly bandaged, although I do not sense injury. In fact, if anything, I feel a tremendous sense of elation. I sit up quickly and unhook the tubes in my skin. Next, I unravel the bandages and focus on the front door, left partially open to reveal the empty ward beyond.

As I rise from my position on the bed and drift slowly out of the room, I am amazed to discover that the entire floor of the hospital is utterly deserted. No nurses, no doctors, no other patients; I am completely alone.

Making my way along the narrow corridors of the building I locate an exit by way of a staircase and once I descend the three flights that lead the first floor I enter the lobby (also empty) and head for the automated doors, which direct me to a massive parking lot where there are no cars and the sky is pitch black and the moon is a bright crescent, partially concealed by dark looming clouds.

There are no stars out tonight and as I look down at my bare feet, I'm forced to wonder if I should locate a pair of shoes. I test the feel of the pavement beyond the edge of the hospital grounds. I discover a bleak path that eventually progresses into the rough terrain of an open field, expanding outward into a desolate stretch of highway. Somehow I walk onward without discomfort even as the asphalt joins with the barren earth. Somehow, I visualize myself being lifted. In the dream, I move upwards and with each step I take I'm miraculously guided above a fiercely blowing wind which carries my weightless body through the air.

The wind increases the higher I ascend. Finally, I achieve great distance from the field below me and I'm overtaken by an invisible force that wraps itself tightly around my chest. The sound of flapping wings echoes above my shoulders. Suddenly I hear a voice. It speaks to me in whispers. This is what is says: "Remember all that you see…and all you will be shown."

Though these words are unnerving, I remain unafraid. I do not cry out or demand to be released. Instead I embrace the hidden power and I allow myself to be flown through the clouds, until at last the wind changes and I'm gradually moving downward, returning to the landscape that is no longer an open field, but a path of white light: the intended destination.

"Where am I?" I ask, hoping that the voice will respond. And it does.

"This is the Road of Things to Come..." Then it repeats: "Remember all that you see...and all you will be shown."

Before I can ask what "things" I will see, the power around me dissipates and I fall to the earth like a discarded stone. Again, I'm alone, but the light beckons me onward.

With only slight hesitation caused by caution of the unknown, I take my first step down the brightly lit path. Silence becomes deafening - an eruption of space - as intense vibrations swarm all around me.

Somewhere the world is shaking.

Somewhere a void is preparing to open.

A figure emerges from the shallow end of whiteness; not a person exactly, but rather a translucent being, similar to myself, but without definition, save for a pair of illuminate pupils that shimmer as they stare at me. I cease all movement. Both arms are at my sides. The shifting form levitates and I am transfixed with fascination as I gaze longingly into its disappearing eyes.

Simon stops talking and studies the doctor's captivated expression. "You're believing every word of this, aren't you?"

Grover blinks and immediately shifts in his chair. "Why wouldn't I believe it?"

Simon shrugs casually. "Well, according to you and your staff I'm a diagnosed schizophrenic..."

Grover realizes the trap and quickly defends himself. "Schizophrenia is a fairly open ended diagnosis, Simon. When you were first brought here-"

Simon cuts him off, raising a dismissive hand. "When I was first brought here, you didn't believe a word I said. All this time you have never once considered anything I've told you to be anything other than paranoid delusion. Everything I'm telling you now, I've told you before, but until last week you've never really listened. Why is that, doctor? Why are you so suddenly interested?"

Grover crosses his legs, avoiding eye contact. "This is our last session together…I just want to make sure that we don't leave anything half dealt with."

Simon shakes his head. "Doctor Grover, please don't lie to me. Remember we have a deal."

Grover takes a breath, inhaling deeply as he considers something. The moment passes and he recovers. "I think we should get back to what we were discussing."

Simon nods with full agreement. "You're absolutely right. I wasn't finished yet. It's still my turn…"

GLEAMING VISIONS:

I stare at the glowing image for what seems an eternity and when the voice speaks again, a question is imposed: "Do you know why you've been brought here?"

Without moving my lips, I am able to respond. "You want to show me something…"

The shape moves closer. "That's right, Mr. Fielding. I want to show you the future. Do you wish to see it?"

Without hesitation: "Yes. I do."

"Then you must close your eyes."

"But how will I see?"

The image raises both hands. "Your own vision impairs you. There is only one way to examine the future…and that is through me."

I shut my eyes, my body trembling as cold fingertips caress my cheeks and gradually move up toward my eyes. Instinctively, I flinch. That's when it happens: the fingers seize my skull, thumbs sink deep into my sockets - an eruption of pain - and instantly I'm screaming.

A fantastic blue light bursts inside my head. Electric waves shoot down my spine. A magnetic force is pulling me. Draining my energy. The blue light intensifies then abruptly vanishes. I lose all sound. And everything is black.

-FLASH-

I'm in a car, the front passenger's seat. There's someone else with me and they're driving the car. For some strange reason, I can't see their face. A scene of a suburban morning surrounds us: a rising sun, a neighborhood of three storey houses, fresh cut lawns, children with backpacks walking to school.

Another -FLASH- the person driving disappears. I'm all alone now. The car is still in motion, racing to high speeds. Something is coming for me, a massive white shape, and I'm terrified. It's headed straight for me...

Impact. My world endlessly spins. Instantly, I am dizzy. My pain is constant. A part of me has broken. And I'm whirling upside down, the sky becoming pavement, the streets becoming clouds. In the distance I hear voices. Some of them are screaming. From across the street I see a man at a bus stop is clutching his cell phone, he's frantically dialing numbers, calling for an ambulance.

The roof of the car caves and I am trapped inside.

Next comes the blood, it's splattered against the windshield. The smell of smoke is choking me, but there's one last image to see. I remember it very clearly. It reminds me that I'm dreaming. It's the sight of golden apples, falling in reverse - from the blue sky below me to the paved road above – and there are hundreds of them, falling like rain, landing in piles that form all around me.

That's it, doctor.
That's my vision.
Golden apples.
Everywhere.

BETWEEN TWO DREAMS:

"That's it?" Grover demands. "Don't you see anything else?"
Simon sighs. "Dr. Grover, I've told you before..."

"I know you have, Simon," the doctor says irritably. "But I think you might be forgetting something."

"I'm not," he insists.

"You must be."

"I'm not. Why don't you believe me?"

"Because you have *amnesia* or at least you claim to. And I think you're deliberately blocking something."

"I remember what I'm supposed to," Simon argues quietly. "And that's more than I care to. And they've already locked me up for the things I've tried to explain…"

Grover shakes his head. "What did you expect, Simon? You were found wandering aimlessly on the Interstate. You told the police you could see the future. Of course they locked you up."

"I expected them to do exactly as they did," Simon says simply.

"So you knew no one would believe you?"

"Well, apparently *you* believe me."

Grover shifts again in his chair. "What I believe…is that you need to elaborate on what you saw. Stop holding back and tell me everything."

"What is it that you hope I'll explain, doctor? What is it you think I've seen that I'm not telling you?"

Grover leans forward. "I want to know what you saw…*about me.*"

"What?"

"You heard me."

"Why would I see anything about you?"

Grover drops his folder with the notes. "God damn it, you know something!"

"There's nothing else," Simon protests."

Grover's outburst surprises even himself. Confused, he picks up the folder and quietly says, "You're lying…I want to know what they showed you. Do hear me? I want to know what they showed you about *me.*"

Simon face is unreadable. "I have no reason to keep anything from you. The only one hiding something here is you. I know something's happened to you and until you tell me what that is, there's nothing more to say."

Dr. Grover bows his head in remorse. "I'm sorry," he says. "I shouldn't have raised my voice. There's no excuse for my actions. Please forgive me."

Simon calmly nods and rises from the bed. "You've been to Shepherd's Pass, haven't you?"

The doctor shuts his eyes, an admission forming. "I've been there…"

Simon's face dims. "When?"

"Three nights ago."

"You drove there?"

"Yes."

"Why?"

The doctor exhales quickly and reopens his eyes. "I don't know. Your case was up for review…I was intrigued by the story-"

Simon shifts his stance. "But do you *believe*?"

The doctor hesitates before answering. "I'm a psychiatrist…"

"And?"

"And I know that the mind is very powerful…"

"It is."

"It can make anything seem real. *Any*thing."

"Dr. Grover?"

"What?"

"Tell me what you saw."

THE DOCTOR'S VISION

I was on my way home from the hospital, exhausted from a full day of board meetings. I remember I accidentally took the wrong exit, heading North instead of South. When I crossed the county line, I had to take an alternate route going east to get back on the Interstate. That's when I noticed the sign.

The wooden board was old, the black lettering, scarcely legible, especially in the night. I had to squint to make out what it said.

Shepherd's Pass.

Underneath the words, there was a painted arrow pointing to my left, but when I looked in the designated direction I only saw the endless fields of wheat.

Then I looked more carefully.

About three yards from where the field began there was a partially paved road. I thought about you and the things we'd discussed, your fascination with the road, which I had always surmised was a way for you to detach from your real issues. But I never knew the road actually existed.

I slowed my car to a near halt, checked my rearview to see if any vehicles were approaching from behind. There weren't any so I turned and drove into the field which then became the relatively hidden Pass.

I went the entire six miles. The only sight of interest is a thin stretch of CAUTION tape wrapped around the branches of a dying tree.

At some point there must have been an accident out there. Other than that, the road was precisely what it appeared to be, desolate and forgotten.

When I arrived home that night I went directly to bed, but I had trouble sleeping. I found myself lying over my sheets, staring into the darkness and thinking about the road. There was something irregular about the way I'd come across it. I felt as if my getting lost on the freeway had not simply been an accident. Something had led me astray. I was beginning to feel as if I had been out there before. I shook the thought, disregarding it as nonsense.

Finally, I shut my eyes. I was monitoring my breathing (a technique I'd used many times during my heavy bouts of insomnia throughout my years at college). Within a few minutes, I was fast asleep and dreaming.

When my eyes reopened, I found myself in motion.

INSIDE THE VISION:

I'm walking to the main entrance of the "Disturbed" ward on the third floor of the hospital. I'm carrying a briefcase and approaching the Oakwood desk where a man in an olive green officer's uniform sits in rotating chair and quietly reads a newspaper. This bothers me because I don't see the computer console or the bullet proof panel that the hospital had recently put in for to increase its level of security. For some reason, I know better than to inquire about this with the officer whom I've never seen this man before, yet somehow I know his name.

"Evening, Avery."

"Evening, Dr. Grover. Working late, huh?"

I tell him I'm here to finish some paperwork and without hesitation, he buzzes me through the sliding doors and I walk through quickly. The adjoining corridor is exceedingly old fashioned in appearance. The layout of the ward is completely different than how it should be. There are no cameras monitoring the halls, the locks on the doors are manual and the hallway seems distinctly narrower. I recall then a picture I'd once seen: the hospital in its early days, back in the 1960's. The scene before me is identical to that picture.

"Have I traveled back in time?" I wonder as I halt in my steps and set my suitcase down on the checkered tile floor.

The thought vanishes and I'm crouching down now to open the lid of suitcase. Inside, I discover a small glass bottle filled with ether. Beside it: a white rag and a handgun, nothing more.

What am I doing? I ask myself. But somehow I already know.

I dump the ether onto the rag, grab hold of the gun and rise to a standing position. Cautiously, quietly, I walk back through the glass doors and sneak up behind Avery.

All at once, I'm attacking him. Gun in hand, I thrust the chrome butt down on the back of his skull and force the wet rag over his screaming mouth. There's no struggle whatsoever as Avery breathes in the fumes. In seconds he's unconscious.

I spread him out on the floor and remove his set of keys. Then I'm racing through the doors, making my way toward 28-C. Once inside I find the patient I'm looking for. He's sitting on the bed, alert in the dark. I know now that he's been expecting me.

"Are you ready?" I ask.

"Yes," he replies.

I reach for the light switch and immediately turn it on. The fluorescents above us flood the empty room. The patient rises from his bed and looks at me. Immediately I recognize him: It's you.

"Me?" Simon asks, stunned.

Grover nods his head. "Yes. *You.* I helped you escape. That's what the dream was showing me."

Simon looks away, thinking of his own visions. "Then it's true."

The doctor frowns. "What?"

"The escape," he explains. "I thought it was a rumor. But now we know. It really did happen."

"What are you saying?"

Simon looks back at him. "I'm saying I dreamed it too. Someone is trying to tell us something, doctor…"

Grover shakes his head. "You haven't let me finish. There's still a lot more…"

THE BOOK:

The next morning I woke up feeling the same way as you do now. I was certain what I had seen was real. Obviously, I did not believe that it was really I who had helped a patient escape, nor did I believe that you really were the one who had fled. I suspected that the dream had used our faces to fill in the blanks of a possible incident that had transpired long ago. My head was full of questions. Had there really been an escape? Had a doctor aided in the process? I was going to find out.

That day, after finishing my shift at the hospital, I went down to the Records Department and inquired with the woman who worked there being any reports of missing patients.

After completing a few searches, the woman explained that there was nothing on file. She added that she had been employed with the hospital for 20 years and had never heard of any "missing" or "escaped" patients during that time.

I informed her that the incident may have occurred even further back than 20 years. She said that if that was in fact the case then there wouldn't be any record of it in their system. The files on hand only went back two decades. She then advised me to check the county library for newspaper articles that might have run a story. I thanked her and left, thinking to myself that she was probably correct. Unless, of course, the hospital had covered it up. (I hadn't told her about the possibility of a doctor being involved.)

That same afternoon, I stopped off at the library and asked the man working there the exact questions I'd posed to the woman in Records. He gave similar replies, saying that he had lived in Jessup County for 52 years and had never heard of an escaped mental patient.

I asked him about the library's stock of old newspapers and he directed me to the section of computer terminals and old fashioned machines designed for reading microfilm. Then he showed me their selection.

On microfilm the possibilities were endless. There must have been thousands of articles, going back nearly a hundred years. It could take weeks before I found what I was looking for (assuming it was really there to begin with).

I decide to take a different approach. I asked the man if he knew of any articles concerning the history of Shepherd's Pass.

He said he had plenty and in less than five minutes, I was sitting at the microfilm machine, reading the countless articles. Most of them were simply the coverage of a raging debate that occurred over a month-long period in the Jessup County Hall of Justice in which the decision to permanently close the road was underway. City officials were claiming that the tax money spent on labor for maintenance wasn't merited. There were only a few farmers who used the road as means to transport their goods across the county and what the hell did their opinions matter anyway? There was also speculation that the local townspeople regarded the road in a highly superstitious manner, but the articles didn't go into any further detail.

Two hours passed as I searched futilely for a more thorough explanation of the road's ultimate closing and I was about to give up and abandon the entire project when suddenly I heard a familiar voice – that of an elderly woman - speaking to me from over my shoulder.

"You won't find anything helpful there."

I turned around. It was old Mrs. Clarkson. I knew her well. Everyone in Jessup County did. She was very active in the church, though that was not how I knew her.

Mrs. Clarkson had a severe case of arthritis and refused to take pain medications. I had seen her on the emergency ward of the hospital many times when I was on the floor counseling burn victims or people who had been in serious car accidents. I had heard her many times complaining to her church member friends (who had forced her to come to the ER) when the pain caused her joints to lock up and she was unable to move her fingers. She would shout loud enough for the entire staff to hear that medications were "of the devil" and that we were committing unholy deeds, forcing her to take injections to alleviate her suffering.

"If God wants to take away my pain He will," she had said to the doctors and nurses who continually persisted with offering her pills.

They had suggested that I attempt to console her, perhaps persuade her to see through her religious hysteria, but it was useless. She adamantly refused my services, claiming that psychiatry was most certainly "of the devil" and that I was unquestionably an equivalent of The Antichrist.

Only now here she was again, standing beside me, insisting that my search was useless.

"How do you know what I'm looking for?" I asked.

"I know," was all she said in response.

"Ok then," I said, deciding to humor her. "Where do you suggest I look?"

"In fiction. Where else? Come. I'll show you."

Confused yet somewhat intrigued, I followed Mrs. Clarkson to the other side of the library, passing several rows of bookshelves, the titles changing from non-fiction "How to" and "The Complete History of" into "Faust," "Canterbury Tales" and "Catcher in the Rye."

Mrs. Clarkson directed me all the way through "classic fiction," made a left turn and finally stopped near a laminated sign: Short Story Fiction, Collected Works.

"Here is where you'll find your answers," she said to me.

I smiled patiently. "I'm afraid you don't understand, Mrs. Clarkson. I'm looking for information about-"

"I know what you're looking for," she said, cutting me off. She took a step closer to me, staring deep into my eyes, wanting me to know how serious she was about whatever she would say next.

"Sometimes the truth hides in places where you wouldn't expect to find it," she explained. "Sometimes you must keep an open mind. Even a

man like you, a man who's strictly after logic can eventually grasp what I'm talking about. In fact, I know you will. Now, here...take this book..."

She reached out to the nearest shelf and selected a hardcover between two sizeable novels. Had she not pointed it out, I probably would have skimmed right past it (that is, if I were looking for a book of short stories) because of it's nondescript cover: plain white, no unique designs or formatting.

Mrs. Clarkson winced with a sudden pain. The effort from simply lifting the book had triggered her arthritis. I helped by taking the book with both hands.

"No, no, no," she said and snatched the book back from me, opening it to its middle pages. I kept one hand on the cover to help her support the weight.

That's when I noticed the book's title: The Other Stories.

I was curious, but more concerned about Mrs. Clarkson's pain. Whatever she was looking for I had doubts of its usefulness. Obviously her age was affecting her behavior. Perhaps she was even showing signs of-

"Here," she said, breaking my train of thought. "Story Two. Don't bother with the others. They're of no concern to you."

I gently took the book from her again and right away caught my attention: **THE ROAD OF THINGS TO COME**

My interest perked considerably as I scanned the first few paragraphs. Then - about halfway through the second page - my heart skipped a beat. There it was. Two simple words that forced me to shiver: Shepherd's Pass.

I looked up from the book and frowned at Mrs. Clarkson. "What is this? Who wrote this story? How'd you find it?"

Mrs. Clarkson stepped back. "Just read," she instructed. "But be careful...that book is of the devil."

"Then why are you showing it to me?" I asked.
She didn't answer.
She just turned and walked away.

QUESTIONS UNANSWERED:

"What else was in the book, doctor?" Simon asks desperately, still standing.

Grover rises from his chair and nervously paces the room. "There were two stories in one," he pauses to consider this. "It's difficult to explain."

Simon relaxes and takes his seat on the bed. "Please, Dr. Grover. I have to know."

Grover swallows hard. "The first one was about a psychiatrist who worked right *here* in County Hospital...back when it first opened in the early 1960's. He was secretly doing research with a patient that believed he could see into the future. And over the course of their time together, the doctor came to recognize that his patient's claims were true. He also believed that the road offered the key to a consciousness exchange, a kind of spiritual transference... "

"Go on," Simon says eagerly.

Grover stops pacing and position himself against the chrome sink. "One night the doctor is lying in bed and that's when he has a vision."

Simon nods expectantly. "And it's the same vision you had, isn't it Dr. Grover?"

The doctor hesitates, but finally concedes. "Yes. The exact same..."

"When did you have it?"

"Last night."

"Tell me."

Grover takes a deep breath and softens his tone. "I saw a man..."

THE FINAL VISION:

He was standing in a doorway, watching me. I was lying on a bed in a great deal of pain, unable to move. I didn't know where I was, I just knew that I was in danger.

The man in the doorway was dressed in a lab coat and wearing a surgeon's mask. He had something hidden behind his back and as he entered the room I begged for him to "stay away", but he only moved closer. When he reached the foot of the bed, he raised his hands and that's when I saw the syringe.

The man looked at me then glanced at my left arm. He placed the needle to my skin and prepared to make an injection. Suddenly I felt a terrible drain of energy. I fought hard to stay awake, but eventually the drowsiness took hold. The last thing I remember was the man removing his mask, but I never saw his face.

RESURFACING:

"Now do you see?" Grover asks. "There's something going on here that doesn't add up."

 Simon nods silently.

Grover continues. "In the next chapter, the doctor awakens from the dream and goes straight to the hospital. Then, just as I envisioned, he helps his patient escape. The scenes in the book are virtually identical to the scenarios in my mind: the doctor taking out the guard, stealing his keys, going to the patient's room, helping him escape..."

"And then what?" Simon cuts in. "How does it end, Dr. Grover?"

Grover tenses in his seat. "They drive out to the road and instantly disappear. The following morning a search team locates the car. The vehicle had been in some kind of accident. They found the car flipped upside down in a ditch. The doctor was still in the driver's seat...but the patient was nowhere to be found."

"Taken by the road," Simon adds wearily.

Grover nods. "That's what the book implies, yes."

Simon leans back, drifting into his own thoughts. When he speaks again, there's a strange sort of confidence to his words: "The book is a dictation of our dreams."

Grover agrees. "You see why I'm so desperate? I need to know everything that you know about the road...about everything."

"If there was more to my vision, Dr. Grover, I swear I don't remember it."

"But you believe the story is true?"

Simon searches Grover's face. "Don't you?"

The doctor shrugs, dejectedly. "I don't know what to think anymore. I tried to tell myself that this whole thing is symbolic, that it's simply about the struggle between two halves of the same mind; the doctor representing the rational side, the patient representing the irrational. The road is simply the line that separates the two."

"But you don't really believe that, do you?" Simon asks suspiciously.

"What's the alternative? That we're both crazy?"

Simon sits up, angry. "The alternative is that the story is *real*. Remember Doctor, I know what's out there on that road. I've been there."

"So have I!" Grover snaps. "There isn't anything!"

"Not for you. Or so you think. But if there's one thing I know, it's that the road is not a barrier...it's a gateway."

Grover eases forward. "A gateway to what?"

Simon's confidence fades and he draws back in defeat. "If I knew the answer to that I don't think I'd be in here..."

The doctor contemplates something. "Do you think if you went back there...you might be shown more?"

"Do you?" Simon replies.

Grover closes his file and stands from his chair. "I don't know...but I'm willing to find out."

Simon looks up at him. "What are you saying?"

"I'm saying our session's over."

The doctor places his chair back into the corner and opens the door to the room. He stands in the entrance and motions for Simon to join him.

"Let's get you out of here."

Simon rises to his feet, then pauses. "Something's still missing. There's a connection we haven't made."

Grover frowns. "And what's that?"

Simon turns away, his dreary expression darkening his eyes. "The golden apples..."

...OF THE DEVIL:

The discharging of patient "Fielding" takes less than hour. Many forms are signed, both by the doctor and by Simon. A 30-day supply of medications is quickly dispersed and personal belongings are then accounted for. When Simon finally exits the facility he is exhausted. He sets his suitcase on the pavement and quietly surveys the outside world.

The overwhelming display of activity beyond the parking lot is almost too much for him. There are several men and women conversing with one another as they exit their cars and head for the administration building near the back of the main clinic. Simon watches their hurried pace then switches his focus to a nearby construction site across the street where workers in orange vests take measurements of the broken asphalt and drink hot coffee in Styrofoam cups. Some of them work silently, others laugh and tell jokes.

Grover studies his patient, who turns to study a row of eucalyptus trees lining the foreground of a freshly cut lawn that acts as a perimeter within the secured lot.

Simon is recalling his supervised walks, the ones taken twice a week, guided by the hospital's security team who followed in him from a respectable distance as he'd wander the designated area of a gated courtyard. The trees planted in that recreation area never moved to a breeze, because a cement wall protected the yard from any and all wind.

But out here, amidst all this freedom, the branches of eucalyptuses sway peacefully, leaves flapping as the gusts continue to strengthen in force.

For Simon this is unquestionably the greatest sign that his stay in the ward has at last come to an end. It isn't long before tears start to swell and he is moved to stance of inward relief.

"Are you all right?" Grover asks, mildly concerned,

Simon slowly nods and picks up his suitcase. "Lead the way, Dr. Grover..."

Three minutes later, Simon is in the passenger's seat of Dr. Grover's silver Lexus GS Hybrid. The doctor is behind the wheel maneuvering out of the parking space. Once they exit the hospital grounds, Grover heads east down a stretch of avenue that allows them to travel a more scenic route of the neighborhood. He explains to Simon that they should make time for him to adjust to his new surroundings. Simon agrees and stares quietly out the window, watching the three-storey houses (freshly painted with beiges and bright yellows) that pass his line of sight.

"Everything looks so different…none of this was here before."

How long has it been? He can't seem to remember. And the more he tries to focus on the concept of time the more his ability to conceive it fades, until he is no longer capable of discerning ten years from ten minutes.

"You really want to us to go back?" Simon asks suddenly.

Dr. Grover makes a sharp left and speeds through an intersecting street. "Don't you?"

Simon draws a short breath then gradually exhales, evoking sadness that quickly envelopes his sense of relief. "I just want to be free of this."

The doctor nods. "Well, I can't think of a better way to get closure than to face what's been haunting you."

Simon gaze narrows. "You don't have to pretend like this is strictly for my benefit, Dr. Grover. We both know that this really about all the- Oh my god…"

Grover turns, concerned. "What's wrong?"

Simon is silent. Something out his window has absorbed his attention. And all at once, he starts to tremble.

"Simon, talk to me…"

Simon opens his mouth, struggling to formulate words. "That sign back there…"

The doctor glances at his rearview mirror, forehead creasing. "What sign? You mean the *street* sign?"

Simon smiles, he's speaking to himself now. "My God, how did I not see it coming?"

Grover is unnerved. "Simon, are you alright? Should I pull over?"

Simon ignores the question and continues talking. "I didn't know…I didn't make the connection…I just didn't *know*…"

"Know *what*?" the doctor shouts frantically. "Simon! Talk to me."

Simon cranes his neck, still smiling. "Would you like me to tell you what's happening, doctor?"

"Yes!"

Simon begins to laugh. "That story? The one you say you read? It isn't fiction."

Grover takes another turn. "What are talking about? Of course it is. I told I looked into it. There are no records of any missing patients…"

Simon raises a finger, a gesture of demonstration. "That's because the story didn't happen *here*."

There's a pause.

"You're not making sense, Simon."

Simon sighs. "You said it yourself. The book is two stories, intertwined. Remember?"

Grover says nothing. His eyes focus on the street in front of him. The Lexus has slowed to 20mph. Traffic is rushing by from both sides, the driver's staring angrily.

"Dr. Grover? Do you remember saying that?"

"I remember," he says at last, but his tone has changed, he seems coy, almost menacing.

"I think I know what's going on," Simon exclaims.

"Do you?" Again the doctor seems patronizing.

"Yes!" Simon hollers, excited, but afraid. "Doctor, don't you get it? *The second story*. This is it! We're in it right now! It's *here*! This place! It's all around us! The road is tricking us! It's got us locked inside an illusion. And the two stories intertwine to ensure that it never ends. Don't you see? *We're still on the road...*"

The Lexus roars to life as Grover hits the accelerator, chuckling maliciously. Something has changed in his expression. He seems stable, void of concern, like a man who's been playing a sick kind of game.

"Well, well, Simon. That's a *very* interesting theory."

Simon glares at him, aware of what's happening. (The game is moving.) "You should know. You read about it."

"On the contrary...you did...*Doctor*."

The word "Doctor" hangs in the air.

"What did you just call me?" Simon finally asks. The Lexus is moving faster. Suddenly there are horns.

"You heard me," he says, his face still grinning. "I was wondering what it was going to take for you to figure this whole thing out."

Simon stirs in his seat, ignoring the obscenities shouted by the drivers who pass them. "What is this? What are you doing?"

"Oh stop pretending," Grover snaps. "I think we're ready to take the masks off, aren't we?"

"What're saying? Are you trying to tell me that *I'm* Dr. Grover?"

"You said it yourself not two seconds ago. It's all switched around. Everything's reversed."

"I meant the *stories*!"

"Aw, but you *are* the story Simon...I mean...Dr. Grover." He laughs wickedly at himself. "You'll have to excuse me. Even I get a bit confused sometimes."

Simon looks down at his hands as a light blue static fills his palms. *Could it really be? Had he really been the doctor all along?*

A question emerges. Simon looks up. "If I'm the doctor…then who are you? And why are you doing this? Why did you pretend to be me?"

Dr. Grover shakes his head. His skin tone is grey and the change in his features becomes something ethereal, like a vapor, like a spirit. Like a ghost.

"Why are you asking questions you already know the answer to? You researched them yourself when you were studying to write the book. Mass delusion? Clairvoyance? Remember your studies, doctor. That's the best way to-"

"Stop calling me 'doctor'! *You're* the doctor! You're Dr. Grover! I'm Simon Fielding!"

"Oh please. There is no Simon Fielding. That's all in your head…along with everything else. Face it, my friend. You've snapped. Gone nuts. Too many nights on the disturbed ward, maybe. You've lost your grip on what's real."

"Stop it!" Simon screams. "Stop messing with my mind! What are trying to do?"

Suddenly, the spirit's eyes glow. The accelerator increases to 50mph. The laughing does not stop.

"I just want to help," the ghost says innocently.

Realizing his danger, Simon begs for him to stop. But the car only moves faster.

65mph

70mph

80mph

Simon's fear turns to rage. He points at the "being" accusingly. "You're the one that doesn't exist! *I'm* real! *I'm* Simon Fielding!"

The being casually shrugs. "Well doctor, if that's true then I'd say that puts you in quite a predicament."

Simon's heart skips a beat. "Why's that?"

"Well, if I don't exist," the being suggests, blue eyes gleaming. "Then tell me one thing: *Who's driving this car?*"

The blood drains from Simon's face. "Oh no…The dream…"

-FLASH-

The ghost vanishes, leaving the driver's seat empty. The Lexus swerves dramatically into the neighboring lane. Oncoming traffic emerges.

Simon screams, desperately reaching for the wheel - *but it's too late.* With the remaining seconds of his life, he gazes out the windshield, eye fixating on the massive produce truck and the panicking driver who slams his horn repeatedly and attempts to-

Rrrrrrrrrrrrrrrrrrrrrrrrrrrrrrrrrrrrrrrrrrreeeeeeeeeeeeeeeeeeeeeeeeeeeeee eeee...

ANOTHER POINT OF VIEW:

The man sitting at the bus stop hears the thunder of impact. His eyes dart quickly to the middle of the street - just in time to witness the explosion – as glass shatters and a collision of metal erupts in fumes of gray and black.

The Lexus is struck so hard on the passenger's side that car whips around half circle, flipping onto its back in the process; the roof caving as streaks of blood splatter the front windshield.

The truck veers left from the collision; the driver unconscious as a Victory Red Chevy engages from the panic of traffic and smashes directly into the truck's storage compartment.

The rear doors burst open. Over two dozen crates spill out of the truck's the storage unit and splinter into pieces as a white Audi S4 plows into both vehicles as well as the left over carts.

The man at the bus stop gasps as he watches the crates explode. A wave of gold apples rain down, filling the tragedy will a twinge of the surreal.

Golden apples.

Everywhere.

Suddenly a crowd of pedestrians come running from their houses. Several passing cars stop abruptly and the passengers quickly exit to race over and join the scene.

The man at the bus stop breaks from his trance. He reaches into his plaid sport coat and retrieves his iphone, frantically dialing 9-11. Within two seconds he's speaking to a dispatcher.

"Police! Yes. Look, there's been an accident! Oh God…It's awful. Please. Send an ambulance. I'm at…"

The man pauses, realizing he's unaware of his exact location. He steps out of the bus stop and speed-walks to the corner. At the sidewalks crossing he locates the intersecting street.

"I'm on...First and May...the corner of First and May...Please hurry! I don't think they're gonna make it..."

The man shuts off his phone and shifts his attention to the carnage in front of him, a single thought entering his mind: *I will not sleep tonight.*

THE ROAD'S END:

When the medics pull the sheriff from the front seat of the patrol car and out of the ditch, they realize immediately that he's still alive and partially conscious (his eyelids are fluttering and his chest is heaving). They decide to set him on the ground about five yards distance from the wreckage so they can examine him while a gurney is quickly fetched.

"Sheriff? Can you hear me?" one of the medics asks, a young man, maybe 20 with name "J. Lynnwood" stitched above the shirt pocket of his starched-white uniform.

Too weak to reply, the sheriff just lays there, squinting at the red and blue lights that penetrate the darkness.

Lynnwood places two fingers on the sheriff's throat. "I got a pulse!" he announces to three medics standing over him.

"Let's get him on that stretcher," one of them replies and a serious of movement commence as the gurney is finally brought over.

"Ready? Lift!"

The sheriff moans as he is gently placed on the plastic/metal stretcher and fastened in tightly by way of leather straps. Lynnwood continues to speak to him while shining a handheld flashlight into both of his shrinking pupils.

"Sheriff, can you hear me?" he repeats.

The sheriff blinks a signal of response and the flashlight moves away. Spots fill his vision, deleting the features of Lynnwood's face, previously illuminated by the two ambulances' headlights.

"Everything's gonna to be fine, Sheriff. You've been in an accident. We're gonna take you to the hospital. Now sheriff, if can, please tell me...do you where you are? Do you know your name?"

The sheriff strains to remain conscious, gasping for breath as he attempt to speak. The medics hear him wheezing and it's Lynnwood who leans in closer. "Sheriff, please try not to move your head. Just relax."

The sheriff's eyes narrow. "Am I...still dreaming?" .

The confusion escalates. A group of state troopers shout frantically to each other, ordering the area to be sealed off with CAUTION tape.

"I can't hear him," Lynnwood tells the others as they head toward the rear ambulance doors.

"I think he might've asked if he was dreaming."

"He's delusional," another replies.

"Probably in shock," Lynnwood agrees. "Let's get set for blood pressure. I need this man's vitals. A-sap!"

"I'm on it," a fourth medic shouts, opening the red, plastic kit he carries at his side.

The sheriff stares dazedly, looking to Lynnwood. "Am I out? Am I free?"

A commotion of voices rises.

"What's he saying now?"

"I don't know."

"It's probably a concussion. Ask him again to give us his name."

Lynnwood touches the sheriff's forehead as if testing for a fever. "Sheriff, please sir...can you tell us your name?"

The sheriff clears his throat. "My name...is Douglas Grover...I'm a doctor."

Pause.

The medics all look to each other.

"He's delusional alright," one of them says. "C'mon, let's get this guy in here and get a move. Now!"

The crew eases the gurney into the ambulance. Two medics climb inside, while Lynnwood and another man shut the vehicle doors and move around opposite sides of the vehicle (Lynnwood driving).

Within 30 seconds the ambulance is speeding away, sirens blaring. Dr. Grover lies motionless on the stretcher and quietly shuts his eyes.

I'm free.

I made it out.

He feels sorry for the man whose body he has taken, but there was simply no other way. A switch had to be made. He had figured out that much after reading the book. And even now, the story remains embedded in his mind.

After all, he was the one who had written it.

And now that the crossover has occurred, now that Simon is gone and the character of the sheriff has been taken, there are no other loose ends to worry about.

Or so he thinks.

THE ONE FORGOTTEN:

With the ambulance gone the rest of the officers examine the inside of the police cruiser, attempting to assess what had happened.

They already know that the dispatcher, Debbie had called Ralph Jenkins for back up (who in turn called the state police) after she repeatedly lost contact with the sheriff. She also mentioned that Keylee had taken a man into custody. But when the officers check the backseat no one is there. So they radio in for an APB and Debbie quickly provides them with a name and description of the assailant. The officers assume the man is fleeing on foot and is probably still wandering the Interstate. They're assumption becomes a certainty once a trail of footprints are discovered, leading away from the scene. After 45 minutes of searching, a helicopter is flown in, but ultimately this added effort proves futile.

Simon Fielding is nowhere to be found.

AWAKENING TO THE DREAM:

When Dr. Grover opens his eyes he discovers he's lying in a hospital bed of Intensive Care Unit on the fourth floor of County Hospital.

Alert and sensing movement, the doctor quickly looks to entrance of the room. The door is wide open and a man in a white lab coat and a surgeon's mask slowly proceeds to the bed. His hands are behind his back, he's concealing something.

"I know you," the doctor says to him. "I've seen you before..."

"Indeed you have," the surgeon remarks (his voice is hushed, but nevertheless familiar) revealing the syringe held carefully in his left hand. "Hiding in some else doesn't change who you are, Dr. Grover."

The doctor's eyes widen. He knows what's coming. He knows what happens next. The man in the mask leans forward, inserts the needle and slowly pushes down on the plunger.

The doctor gasps in horror as the poison races through his veins and the man at his bedside removes his surgical mask.

"But…you're dead," Grover says, bewildered.

The face of Simon smiles. "You didn't read carefully enough. You forgot the footsteps. In this story…I'm alive…"

Grover moans in agony. "No…please…stay away."

"Two halves of the same mind, doctor," Simon reminds him. "Those were your exact words. I read the stories too…" He leans in further to whisper: "Remember all that you see and all that will be shown."

"Please…don't do this…"

"Shhh…quiet, little sheep. You're going back where you belong…back to the road with *me…*"

THE FINAL SWITCH:

Your eyes open. You're in a strange room. You're lying in a bed, your head is bandaged and you're dressed in hospital clothes. You're also barefoot.

Slowly you get up and disconnect the IV tube that's stuck in your left arm. The hospital ward is empty as you venture through the corridors and take the three flights of stairs that lead you into the lobby where you head straight for the sliding glass that lead you out of the deserted hospital and into the wavy field. As you drift into the darkness, a crescent moon covered by clouds, guides you toward the Interstate. Your destination is clear. Remember what you are shown.

"Evenin' Simon. Where you off to tonight?"

The ghost has arrived in a flash – taking the appearance of a man in a sheriff's uniform, one who doesn't know he's dead. *And neither do you, Simon.* That's why you respond.

"The corner of First and May…"

Then the ghost makes a suggestion: "How 'bout I give ya a lift?"

A hand appears on your shoulder. All at once, the ghost is standing beside you, leading you toward a patrol car. It places you into the vehicle and gently shuts the door.

When you see the ghost again, it's climbing into the front seat. Next it puts the car in motion and grabs the radio transmitter. You listen for awhile as it converses with the one who resides in the static. Then you lose interest (you've heard their words before) and you shift your gaze to your reflection in the rearview mirror. You smile at yourself. Your reflection smiles back. The smirk expands as your image gradually darkness; then quietly fades away.

See you in The Dream, Mr. Fielding.

AUTHOR BIOGRAPHIES

COREY R. SCALES – Corey R. Scales, the son of a Baptist minister and a supervisor for the Social Security Administration, has been everything from a movie theater usher to a Tarot card reader at a psychic hotline. A native of Baltimore, MD., he formerly attended New York City's School of Visual Arts and began focusing on fiction writing as a break from submitting screenplays. His work has appeared on Soren Narnia's former dark fiction site, knifepointhorror, New Visions In Fiction, and Buried.Com. In addition to co-writing issue #1 of the indie comic, Immortal Kiss, Mr. Scales has recently finished his first novel, A Tendency to Start Fires, and a collection of short fiction, Begotten Sons.

JASMINE JUNE – Jasmine June Cabanaw is passionate about two things: writing and dancing. She merges her passions by writing dance history. Her articles can be found on GildedSerpent.com, where she is a regular columnist. She has worked as a journalist and for college magazines. She writes about her travel and dance adventures on her blog: Traveling Belly Dancer.

CHANDRU BHOJWANI – Born in Africa, Chandru grew up between Nigeria, India & the UK. With a Masters in International Business from the University of Westminster, he moved to New York where he worked as a Business Development Manager for three years before returning to Nigeria in 2002 to run a trading company. Chandru has been writing for Beyond Sindh (www.beyondsindh.com) since 2004 and his debut novel, The Journey of Om was published in India by Cedar Books in late 2009. For more on Chandru visit www.chandrubhojwani.com

ANNASTAYSIA SAVAGE – Annastaysia Savage is a writer and artist who lives and works in the middle of several hundred acres of river bottom forest in Pennsylvania. She is inspired by anything macabre. The motivation behind her art and writing comes from scratching at the back door, autumn, stormy nights, black cats, being afraid and gnarled old trees. She has currently completed a YA Fantasy novel in the works for publication, which she is illustrating as well. She also has several short horror stories published.

AVERY K. TINGLE - Avery K. Tingle was born and raised in San Francisco, California. Throughout his childhood, his mother encouraged him to write, which she continues to do today. Avery currently lives in mid-Missouri with his editor/girlfriend and their cat, Ben, and their dog, Tali.

CHRISTOPHER C. PAYNE – Christopher C. Payne was born in January 1967 and grew up in DeSoto, IL. He received his bachelor's degree in finance from Southern Illinois University at Carbondale, graduating in 1990. Currently, he lives in San Francisco, CA. In his spare time, he enjoys biking and snowboarding with his three daughters and his fiancée.

RHONDA E. KACHUR – Rhonda Kachur AKA Rhonny Reaper is a 20 year old horror fan from Cleveland Ohio who's been watching horror films since the age of 4. Her favorite film is "The Bride of Frankenstein", but she has a soft spot for killer doll films. She is the creator of the horror review blog Dollar Bin Horror (dollarbinhorror.blogspot.com) and the horror picto-blog Monster Beauty (monster-beauty.blogspot.com). She is currently working on a journalistic style zombie book for the Dead On Earth series, her own anthology, and short horror stories for various horror anthologies and magazines. You can check out her personal blog at RhonnyReaper.blogspot.com

MORELLA LA MUERTE – When Morella La Muerte isn't dredging up morbid tales from the dark side of her psyche, she works as a caretaker for the elderly. Her literary influences include such writers as Ambrose Bierce, H.P. Lovecraft, Stephen King, and of course, Edgar Allan Poe. She also cites the late Rod Serling (The Twilight Zone, Night Gallery) as a strong influence on her writing style. Morella lives in Colorado with her twenty year old son and her seven cats and two dachshunds. She considers the phrase 'Crazy Cat Lady' a compliment.

MICHAEL D. GRIFFITHS – Michael D. Griffiths is a man who likes to keep busy. He loves camping with his wife in the wilds of Arizona, playing poker, and debating such topics as mysticism, creativity, anarchy, and punk rock. In the past, his writing has been published in periodicals including: Abandoned Towers, C.H.A.O.S., Golden Visions, Innsmouth Free press, M-Brane, Necrology, Rope and Wire, Sonar 4, The Smoking Mirror, and Withersins. He was awarded first place in Withersin's 666 writer's contest. And won first place in the 2009 Golden Visions Online Fiction Contest. He has become the Marketing Manager for Abandoned Towers. He is on the staff of The Daily Discord, Innsmouth Free Press, and The Noise magazines. His Skinjumper Series has been chronicled in M-Brane magazine. Recently The Living Dead Press has published his novel, The Chronicles Of Jack Primus.

WILLIAM TODD ROSE – William Todd Rose is a speculative fiction author currently residing in Parkersburg, WV. His short fiction has appeared in a variety of magazines and anthologies, as well as having been featured on several podcasts. To date, his novels include the surreal and experimental *Shadow of the Woodpile*, the apocalyptic thriller *Cry Havoc*, and *The 7 Habits of Highly Infective People: A Novel of Contagion, Drugs, Time Travel, & the Living Dead.* In the Fall of 2010, Library of the Living Dead Press will release *The Dead & Dying,* which will soon be followed up with a grindhouse-inspired experiment in brutality entitled *Shut the Fuck Up and Die!* For more information on the author, or to download the free e-book *Sex in the Time of Zombies*, please visit him online at www.williamtoddrose.com

ELIZABETH REUTER – Elizabeth Reuter saw her first horror movie as a kid. It scared her so badly she had to sleep with her mother for a week, so God knows why she was dumb enough to watch *more* of the stupid things, but she did. Now she can't get enough of them, along with horror novels and comics, and she's got a few novels of her own in the works.

J. FRANKLIN EVANS – J Franklin Evans lives in Savannah, GA, where by day he works for an insurance company. By night he composes and records heavy metal music, and writes stories and screenplays.

WEDNESDAY LEE FRIDAY – Wednesday Lee Friday lives in Ann Arbor, Michigan with some carnivorous plants, a few cats, and her husband. She has a wide range of interests including (but not limited to) writing, cooking, Criminal Minds, preparing for the zombie apocalypse, trying to learn an instrument, more writing, The Simpsons, crafty things, and quality horror of all kinds. She is a published novelist and produces the audiobook horror podcast, "Take a Stab at This!" Check her out online at http://www.wednesdayleefriday.com

BENSON PHILLIP LOTT – Born in Alaska, Benson Lott now lives and works in San Rafael, California, where he has written short stories since age six. He recently completed two novels and a story collection. He is thirty years old.